W9-CEL-669

THE GOOD WIFE

THE GOOD WIFE

Jane A. Adams

severn
House

This first world edition published 2020
in Great Britain and the USA by
SEVERN HOUSE PUBLISHERS LTD of
Eardley House, 4 Uxbridge Street, London W8 7SY.
Trade paperback edition first published
in Great Britain and the USA 2020 by
SEVERN HOUSE PUBLISHERS LTD.

British Library Cataloguing in Publication Data
A CIP catalogue record for this title is available from the British Library.

ISBN-13: 978-0-7278-8962-1 (cased)
ISBN-13: 978-1-78029-676-0 (trade paper)
ISBN-13: 978-1-4483-0380-9 (e-book)

All Severn House titles are printed on acid-free paper.

Severn House Publishers support the Forest Stewardship Council™ [FSC™],
the leading international forest certification organisation.
All our titles that are printed on FSC certified paper carry the FSC logo.

Typeset by Palimpsest Book Production Ltd.,
Falkirk, Stirlingshire, Scotland.
Printed and bound in Great Britain by
TJ International, Padstow, Cornwall.

PROLOGUE

Southwell Races, Spring Bank Holiday, 1929

It wasn't the first time he had been summoned that day, but so far there had been nothing unexpected. A driver detained because he was suspected of having imbibed a little too much – Dr Mason had tested his responses and agreed with the constable. A jockey with a dislocated shoulder, already put back in place by his boss and a couple of colleagues. He had been treating the pain with heavy doses of brandy, but Mason had given him analgesic powders and told him to rest, conscious that the powders would be taken with yet more brandy and that it would be a waste of breath to advise to the contrary.

Other than this, race day had passed off pleasantly. He had spent most of it with his friends, Ephraim Phillips and his wife, Nora. Ephraim was also a medic and also on the list of police surgeons and the two had shared rooms at college and now practised in the same area. Mason's own wife, Martha, was friendly with Nora and all had seemed right with the world.

The constable that came and found Dr Mason informed him that a woman had been bashed over the head and her bag stolen. He thought she might be dead but he didn't know.

Serious, Mason thought. He left Ephraim at the bar, chatting to another group of friends, and he followed the constable away from the main stands, round the enclosure where horses and riders made ready for the next race, and to a quiet field at the back that had been designated for horseboxes and vehicles.

'What was a woman doing here?' Mason commented.

'I wouldn't like to say, sir. But it's been known for the toms to make use of the empty horseboxes . . .' He trailed off, not sure this was something to be saying to a respectable police surgeon.

Mason grinned. He should have thought of that. It was obvious when it was pointed out. 'Well, whoever the poor unfortunate is, she didn't deserve to be bashed over the head and have her property stolen.'

'No, sir, I think she did not.'

Two other officers stood beside a large horsebox. One a constable and one, from his stripes, a sergeant who introduced himself as Emory.

'Nasty business, sir. I'm afraid the young woman is deceased. One of the grooms found her, spotted that the door was open and came for a look-see and there she was.'

Mason nodded his thanks and swung the door aside.

And then he stopped dead. Shock seizing him, freezing him in place as for a moment or two he could not comprehend what he was seeing.

'Martha!'

'You know the young lady, sir?'

'My wife,' Mason managed to choke out before his legs gave way beneath him and he came crashing to the floor.

ONE

'**N**ora, you're certain she said nothing else?'

'No!' Nora was getting impatient with her husband now. 'I've told you. She was standing with us waiting for me to finish fussing over Beth. You've no idea how far that child can spread a chocolate bar—' She broke off, glancing over to where Clive sat, head in hands and shoulders slumped.

'Sorry,' she said. 'It's just so hard to remember exactly. I wasn't really paying attention. I expected her to go over and speak to her friend, whoever that was, and then come back to us. But we stood there waiting for a full fifteen minutes.'

'And you're certain she saw someone she recognized in the crowd?'

'Well, yes.' Nora nodded fierce confirmation. 'She just said something like, "Oh, I had no idea they'd be here. It's been an age since I last saw them." And then something like, "Won't be a tick", and then she was gone.'

'They,' her husband emphasized, 'not he or she?'

Nora looked baffled for a moment and then said, 'Oh, I see what you mean. No, I'm sure she said *they*. Then she just took off. You know how busy it was this afternoon. I lost sight of her in the crowd and it's not as if I could have followed her, not with the children in tow. We would have looked like a school crocodile, wouldn't we . . .'

Sergeant Emory tapped his pen on his notepad. He'd been content to see what the husband could ascertain. In Emory's view the wife was a flighty, scatty sort of woman who would need strong guidance if anything useful were to be got out of her. So he let the husband give it a try first.

Now however, he saw it would behove him to regain some semblance of control.

He had arranged for the adult witnesses (the children having been carted off by a housemaid) to be taken to the Crown Hotel and a small sitting room had been made available. The husband had barely moved or spoken since they had arrived; slumped forward in a winged chair, he had let his tea go cold and hardly seemed to be listening to the proceedings. The other doctor had been doing his best to find out what had happened, but he seemed to have exhausted his wife's knowledge.

An unobservant type, Emory decided.

'And how did she seem this afternoon? Not troubled about anything?' he asked.

'No.' Nora's tone was exasperated now. 'I've told you several times, Martha seemed very settled, very happy. We'd had a picnic and the children wanted to go on the fairground rides and that's where we were heading. I just noticed that Beth still had chocolate around her mouth, and in her ears if I'm honest, so I was doing my best to clean her up. The other two were planning what rides they were going to go on and Martha was just chatting to them about the carousel and . . . and that sort of thing. She's very good with the children considering she has none of her own.'

Nora lifted a hand to her mouth and her eyes grew wide as she suddenly realized what she said. 'Oh dear, I am making such a mess of this. Martha *was* very good with the children.' She took a small handkerchief from her bag and dabbed her eyes.

For the first time Clive, Dr Mason, lifted his head and looked at his friends as though noticing suddenly that they were in the room with him. He blinked rapidly and wiped his own eyes with the back of his hand.

'Sadly Martha and Clive were not blessed with children' – Nora leaned towards Emory confidentially, but did not bother to lower her voice – 'but she was wonderful with ours. In fact, she was wonderful with most people.' She dabbed her eyes again and then wailed, 'Who would be so cruel as to do this thing. Martha was just so . . .'

Nora's husband reached across and patted her hand. 'Here, have some more tea. That's right, plenty of sugar.' He cast what Emory interpreted as an apologetic look across at his friend and Emory wondered if the subject of children was more touchy than Nora realized.

'And the two of you, sirs. You were on duty as police surgeons. Is it usual that both of you are on call?'

'As you know, Sergeant, we are both on the register and as this is one of the busiest race meets of the year we knew it was in high likelihood that one or other would be called out. As you can see we are all friends, it seemed like a good plan to enjoy the day and to be available should we be required.'

'But it's rare for your duties to include murder,' Emory said quietly.

'Indeed so. We expected to be called to cases of drunkenness. Perhaps a fight that led to serious consequences, but that is all. All in all we hoped for an uneventful day.'

You couldn't get much more eventful than a murder, Emory thought. 'Inspector Milligan will no doubt want to speak to you,' he said. 'I hope it's satisfactory, sirs, but I've arranged rooms for you all here overnight. Just so it's convenient.'

'Convenient for whom?' Ephraim Phillips wanted to know. 'We have children to deal with, I have a practise to run and a locum to arrange for Clive.'

'I don't need a locum.' It was the first full sentence he had managed, Emory thought. 'I need to be back at work. I couldn't bear to be in that house alone. Brooding. What good has brooding ever done anyone?'

Dr Phillips looked about to argue and Nora Phillips looked shocked so Emory stepped in. 'No need to make any decisions tonight, sir. The rooms have been arranged. It might be more private for you all to stay the night, if you get my meaning. Our friends in the press will be interested in this story and you may well find them camped out on your doorsteps.'

'I see,' Dr Phillips said. 'Truthfully, I had not considered that. Very well then, we will remain here tonight.'

'And I'm sure you will be able to administer a sleeping draft for your friend. If you have need of anything, then a constable can be summoned to get it for you. My inspector will want to speak to you all either later today or first thing tomorrow, but chances are he'll be calling in a murder detective to handle this.'

'A murder detective?' Nora asked.

'That's right, Mrs Phillips. Come up from London, they will. They've got experience, you see, the capital being what it is. We don't get so many murders up this way, or not so many mystery murders at any rate.'

'Mystery murders?' Nora again.

'I think the sergeant means as opposed to one man thumping another too hard in a pub brawl or a man coming home in a drunken rage and attacking his wife.' Dr Phillips looked embarrassed at the mention of dead wives.

Emory nodded. 'Those type of incidents are easily solved,' he said. 'But this is a different kettle of fish. This will need the experts. That's not to say my inspector isn't capable,' he added, though something in his tone cast doubt on the assertion, 'but it makes sense in an important case like this to get the best in to help.'

'I'm sure it does,' Phillips agreed. He glanced at his watch. 'We should arrange for some food to be brought in,' he said. 'I don't think any of us wants to brave the dining room.'

Emory, deciding that he was being dismissed, and also that there really was nothing more he could usefully do, told Phillips that he'd have a word with the staff on his way out.

This he did, and also stopped off in the manager's office to call his inspector.

'It's a funny business,' he said. 'The husband is either a fine actor or he's genuinely distressed. The couple they were with, Dr and Mrs Phillips – the wife's a bit of a flibbertigibbet if you ask me, and I imagine a full day of her could be a trial. It occurs to me the dead woman might have invented this friend in the crowd, just to give herself a bit of a break. But on the other hand, if she did see someone, it's possible that someone is who killed her.'

It was agreed, the doctors being respectable men and, after all, both on the list of police surgeons, that reinforcements should be called and the inspector duly sent his request to the Central Office – otherwise known as the Murder Room

– of the Metropolitan Police. He was told to expect officers to arrive the next day in the shape of Detective Chief Inspector Henry Johnstone and his sergeant, Michael – Mickey – Hitchens. They would be on the first available train.

TWO

Sergeant Emory was waiting for the detectives to arrive. Standing on the station platform he had a police car and driver on standby but suspected that they would not be required immediately. The station for Southwell, at Rolleston Junction, was on a curve of the line that ran at an oblique angle to the racecourse. The crime scene was within walking distance.

It not being a race day few passengers alighted at the small station and Emory had no trouble identifying the detectives. It helped that the shorter, squarer one, that Emory immediately guessed was the detective sergeant, carried the now famous murder bag along with his own valise. The taller man must be the inspector. He brought to mind a thoroughbred horse, Emory thought. Lean and strong and somewhat aloof. As he came close Emory caught sight of the intelligence in the grey eyes – and a hardness too that did nothing to belie his thoroughbred analogy. Racehorses could be mean buggers, Emory thought. He too carried a valise and Emory was suddenly glad he had laid on a car and driver. They could be usefully employed in transporting luggage to the hotel.

'Sergeant Emory,' he said, holding out a hand.

Mickey Hitchens dumped his bag on the ground and shook his hand with enthusiasm. 'Sergeant Mickey Hitchens. It's good-looking country round here, isn't it?'

Emory smiled broadly. 'It is indeed. And you, sir, must be Chief Inspector Johnstone.'

Henry inclined his head and shook the sergeant by the hand but Emory could see that his mind was elsewhere, the keen gaze taking in the lie of the land. Emory sensed that he was just impatient to get on.

'There's a car and driver outside,' he said. 'He will transport your bags to the hotel. The crime scene is only a walk away.'

He could see from the grin on Mickey's face that he had

guessed right. His boss was not a man who liked to hang around. Minutes later their luggage had been deposited in the police car, the driver given instructions for meeting them in a couple of hours' time and Emory was leading the way on to the racecourse.

On non-race days it was possible to view the course unobstructed by the bustle of crowds and of the punters cheering on their bets. Emory noticed that while Mickey Hitchens seemed content to chat, his inspector was more inclined to look, pausing every now and then to take in the view and, presumably, draw some conclusion from his scrutiny. Sergeant Hitchens never paused to wait for his boss – something that surprised Emory at first – but DCI Johnstone's long stride soon brought him back alongside. Twice he asked questions, briefly interrupting Mickey's flow.

'How far from the station to the paddock where the woman was found?'

Emory was glad he had already anticipated that one and told him in both fractions of a mile and in yards.

'And on race days, what would be the most direct route?'

Emory had thought of that one too. 'There's a choice of possibilities,' he said. 'If you cut round the back of the stands you'd come out on to Crew Lane and through the space where the wagons and most of the horseboxes are parked up. Take that route and you'd be at the station in about twenty-five minutes even on a race day. If our boyo wanted to lose himself in the crowd then chances are he'd have taken a more direct, but in real terms a slower, route. I'll indicate when we get there, but you can get out of the paddock by a side gate, cut back through where the fairground was set up – it's take-down day so most of the showmen are still around. My men have told them you might well have questions.

'The crowd would slow him up that way, but unless he was bloodied up, no one would take much notice. He'd have been lost in the mass within minutes, back at the station within the half hour, I reckon.'

'And would he have been bloodied?' Mickey asked.

'The woman was hit from behind. If the blood spattered then chummy might have picked up some drops and spatter.

Chances are, nothing that would have been noticed if you looked at him casual. One blow killed her, so the police surgeon reckoned.'

'And this police surgeon is a friend of the dead woman's husband?'

'Dr Ephraim Phillips. Friend and colleague, yes. Mrs Mason was with the doctor's wife, Mrs Nora Phillips, for most of the day. Both doctors are on the list of local police surgeons. They thought they'd combine business with a chance at pleasure.'

'Didn't quite go to plan, did it,' Mickey observed.

'No, indeed it did not.' Emory pointed. They had reached the paddock now and he paused to indicate the horsebox, still where it had been – though it had taken some threats and persuasion on Emory's part to keep it so.

'Across there is the side gate I mentioned. You can see the showmen's wagons.'

Mickey nodded. Men were dismantling the rides, women and children assisting with the packing. Henry glanced in the direction Emory indicated and then crossed to the horsebox and looked inside.

Mickey stayed put and instinctively Emory remained at his side. 'He'll want to speak to the travellers,' Mickey said. 'I'll get on and photograph the scene, dust for fingerprints, which I'm sure you'll tell me is a futile effort. I don't for a minute think the scene of a grizzly murder has gone untouched for all this time.'

'I had a constable here,' Emory told him, 'but he was also patrolling the perimeter so . . .' He shrugged.

'You take the guvnor over to talk to the fairground people,' Mickey said as Henry stepped away from the horsebox. 'And mind, he can be a bit sharp,' Mickey added with a grin.

'I imagine he can,' Emory said. 'I'll be sure to be ready with the oil to pour on any choppy waters.'

'That would be wise,' Mickey agreed.

Mickey worked methodically, focusing his initial interest on the horsebox. He photographed the interior and took contextual shots, remarking the location within the fenced-off area. Then he used the fingerprint camera, an instrument set up for a particular focal length, so that the print was somewhat enlarged and of a particular and standardized aspect, and so easily compared to those on record. As he'd suspected, there were many prints on the doors, both partial and smeared and varied, but there were a few nice, clear examples and one never knew, Mickey thought, they might strike lucky.

Faint indications remained in the grass where other vehicles had been parked and it was possible to discern, from the crushed turf, where temporary pathways had been created between the vehicles.

Mickey photographed what he could and then set about making a sketch map of these features, roping into service two of the stable boys who had come to watch the strange antics of this stocky stranger, with his camera and measuring tape.

With help from the two boys, and then from their boss who turned up, wondering where they'd gone off to and found himself caught up in the action, Mickey completed his task quickly. Mickey was never one to turn down a helping hand when one was offered or could be persuaded or coerced.

After an hour of this he stood beside the horsebox and studied the maps that he had constructed, the boys and their boss peering over his shoulders.

'Looks to me like that line is off,' Jenks, the ostler, proposed, pointing to the position of a vehicle Mickey had sketched out. 'You look from here and now the way the shadows are falling on it, I reckon there was something parked up at the back of it.'

Mickey was inclined to agree and that being the case, he noted, there would have been a natural hideaway made between three vehicles and only a few paces from the horsebox where the body had been found. Significant, he thought.

'Let me walk across there,' Mickey said, 'see if there's anything to be seen and then we'll get the marks put back in right, if you two lads can give me a hand. We'll have Mr Jenks stay put to direct operations.'

Jenks and the boys agreed. He was creating a welcome diversion, Mickey thought, the investigation preventing this

group and their last horse from leaving until the final box had
been released. Mickey guessed that the owners would have
left the previous day and most of their entourage with them.
Jenks and the boys had suddenly found themselves with free
time.

He took a slow walk to the spot and looked back to Jenks
who gave him the thumbs up. I'll bet my boots she wasn't killed
inside the box, Mickey thought. There'd been no cast-off, no
splatter and something would have been expected even if the
woman had been felled with a single blow. The other thing that
militated against the horsebox being the murder scene was
that there was little space to make ready to deliver such a blow
as would kill instantly. No, she had been killed outside and then
the body dumped.

He crouched down and surveyed the ground. The grass was
crushed and flattened by vehicle wheels. It was short here in
the paddock which meant marks were not as obvious, but they
could still be discerned, as could the indentations of feet. So,
Mickey thought, people walked here, then something was
parked, then it went away and people walked here again. He
nodded, satisfied that he had it right. 'Now what's that there?'
Mickey said aloud.

Small spots of something dark, staining the clover. Mickey
took a small envelope from his pocket and pulled the clump
from the ground. It looked like blood to him.

There being nothing more that he could see, he summoned
the boys across with the measuring tape and added this latest
vehicle to the plan, drawing it in a dotted line to indicate what
Mickey felt certain was a transient event.

Had it been the killer's vehicle? Had he therefore driven
away from the scene?

That, Mickey thought, would be very convenient if anyone
happened to have noticed the make of vehicle and perhaps the
registration number.

He asked the boys and Mr Jenks. 'It may have been a
small green van,' Jenks said. One of the boys thought an
Austin car.

'It was a busy afternoon,' Jenks stated with a shrug.
'Comings and goings and the lads and I were over near the

start line for most of it and in the winners' enclosure too, fetching the horses back.' He sounded proud of that and Mickey spent the next ten minutes listening as Jenks recounted the successes of his stable. Mickey was content to listen and to provide the occasional question by way of lubrication. He was well practised in the art of listening to one thing and thinking about something else and he did so now, running through the plan they had drawn in his mind and plotting possible routes and scenarios.

'So there'd not be much reason for anyone to be here,' he asked finally, having established that the horses were taken from the winners' enclosure, back to their designated areas, rubbed down and unsaddled, cooled slowly and carefully so as not to get the colic. The non-winners were met at the finish line and similarly dealt with.

Jenks rubbed his nose thoughtfully, a habit Mickey had had plenty of opportunity to observe that afternoon. 'Well, no, see. Everything parked up here would be transport or equipment no one was likely to need in any kind of rush. Anything anybody might need you'd have sense to keep close to hand, wouldn't you? Like you keep your bag handy.'

Mickey couldn't argue with that.

'So a good place for a clandestine meeting,' he commented.

Jenks put his head to one side, rubbed his nose again and considered. 'I can't think of none better,' he agreed. 'And you got the noise too, from the fairground. Music and steam engines and all the people yelling and shouting.'

'So if anyone did happen to hear a scream they'd assume it came from the fairground,' Mickey agreed. 'So whoever came here most likely knew all of those things. Ticked them off on his own personal list and enticed the woman here with clear intent to do harm.'

Jenks looked uncomfortable. The boys had taken themselves off and were nosing about in Mickey's murder bag. He shouted at them to 'get their mucky little fingers out of where they don't belong' and then turned back to Jenks, fairly certain he knew what the man was hesitating about. 'When the doctor was called over, the constable assumed the victim might have been a working girl.'

Jenks looked relieved and then nodded. 'I ain't saying it's commonplace,' he insisted, 'but the girls sometimes get up to no good here. The boys too, I suppose,' he added. 'If you take my meaning.'

Mickey had at first thought he meant male clients, but maybe did not. 'Ay, well, I think we'll have difficulty tracking down those particular potential witnesses,' he said. 'Look,' he added, 'if you've got the time, how about walking me from here to the winners' enclosure and then to where your horses were kept, just so I get a feel for the distances.'

Jenks agreed with an alacrity that told Mickey he was happy to leave so sensitive a subject behind. It still surprised him what folk got in a dither about. Discussion of a nasty murder was acceptable even at the politest of dinner tables, but a hint of sex in the conversation and you'd soon be persona non grata in most circles.

Jenks called the boys, Mickey retrieved his gear and Jenks led them out through the side gate, through which Henry had earlier passed with Sergeant Emory.

Emory had soon realized that the chief inspector was a man of few words and little casual conversation – not that this bothered him in the least. He had the feeling that this tall man, straight as a length of pump water, was more inclined to thinking and doing than to chatting about it. Bearing Mickey Hitchens' warning in mind, that the inspector could be sharp, he decided to get his ameliorating in first – after all, the inspector would leave once the murder had been solved; Emory would be remaining and the fairground folk, in Emory's experience, remembered bad treatment long after the perpetrator had forgotten even having dealings with them.

'If you will allow me to make introductions, Inspector? I know most of these people and who you might need to speak to first. If the head man don't cooperate—'

'I know that, Sergeant,' Henry said. 'So, yes, the correct introductions should be made.'

His tone was cold. Emory glanced sidelong at him. Chief Inspector Johnstone was still looking about him, taking it all in, and the sergeant decided that there was nothing personally meant in his frigidity. Still, I'll bet you take some handling, he thought.

Henry nodded to where three men stood in conversation beside a newly dismantled helter-skelter. 'The middle one of those three, I'm guessing, is the headman. The one to the right being his lieutenant.'

Emory chuckled softly. 'Edgar Reece,' he agreed. 'Third generation to be running the show. The lieutenant as you call him is his brother-in-law. One Gavin Cafferty and an incomer, in truth. Irish traveller, when you maybe know it's not common for the two to mix, but the sister fell for him, and he's proved his worth, so it's said. Started as a booth fighter. You can probably tell that from his broken nose and well . . . his general demeanour, shall we say.'

The three men had noticed them now and paused their conversation. Waiting. 'And the third?'

'A cousin. Another Reece. Head of another part of the family. Only time they bring both shows together is here and, I believe, Chepstow. Otherwise they travel separate. Strong family bonds though.'

'Of course there are,' Henry agreed.

'So what's this, Sergeant?' Reece Senior asked. 'Come with more questions, is it?'

'This is Inspector Henry Johnstone,' Emory said. 'A murder detective from London, come to investigate the death of that poor woman.'

Reece's eyes narrowed and Emory was immediately put on guard.

'I know of you,' Reece said. 'I 'eard of you from dealings down in Kent.'

Henry nodded. 'No doubt word spreads,' he said. Last winter they'd been searching for a killer who had links to another group of travelling folk – though they'd long ago sought to turn their backs on him. Henry recalled that there'd been showmen present at the stopping place when he had investigated. Henry did not believe that he had left a bad impression among them; he found he was hoping that they felt the same.

'First any of us knew about it were when the police came walking across with that doctor.'

'When they were going to the murder scene,' Henry suggested.

Reece shook his head. 'No, we spotted them going over, figured it for a drunk, then minutes later he's coming back across with two constables, looking like he's seen a ghost. Must have been one hell of a shock.'

'You have men posted around the perimeter,' Henry said. It wasn't a question.

'In case of trouble, yes, we do.'

'Was anyone posted near that far gate, going into that area where the vehicles were parked?'

'There were. If that woman had gone that way, and a man with her, my men would have noticed it.'

Henry nodded, accepting that. That was useful to know. The dead woman's friend had been heading towards the fairground when Martha Morgan had left her and gone haring off into the crowd in search of this acquaintance she had supposedly spotted. It would make sense for her to avoid cutting through the fairground, had she met up with this *friend* in case she ran into Nora Phillips and the children.

'So the doctor was escorted away from the scene. Presumably other officers came after that?'

Emory opened his mouth to answer that and then closed it again. Henry's attention was on Reece and Emory sensed that he would not welcome the interruption. The big man nodded. 'Them two constables came back, with another doctor. Hurrying like. Well, we had word of what was up by then, that a woman had been found with their head bashed in. We knew it weren't one of ours, so we carried on with business.'

'You had no vehicles parked in that enclosure?'

'You know better than that. We keep our people close and property close. Ain't no need for us to have been parked in there.'

Henry nodded; he had expected this answer. 'The men you have on watch, would they have noticed anything being taken from that area?'

'They might.' Reece glanced about and then whistled and

beckoned someone over. A young man strolled up, jacketless, sleeves rolled up to the elbows, coiling a heavy rope between his hands. He nodded to Emory, clearly recognizing him and then scrutinized Henry.

'Man wants to know if you saw any vehicles coming and going,' Reece told him.

'What, from over in the paddock there?' He thought about it for a moment or two and then nodded. 'Small green van came in, round about midday, drove in through the main gates and parked up behind a big wagon. Wagon belongs to the Macavees, so I kept an eye for any pilfering. That left after an hour, maybe two. Small blue car came in later, parked up in more or less the same place. There weren't much choice to be honest, not much free space in there. The marshals pack them in tight.'

'And the blue car, did you notice when it left?'

Another moment's thought. 'Must have been after four. Just on four I nipped home for a brew. Charlie took over for an hour so he might've seen it go.'

'And did you see the driver?'

'Glimpsed someone get out, then they went back the way they'd driven in, closed the gate and off they went. I can tell you it was a man, but not much else. Just a man in a blue suit moving between the wagons. Dark hair maybe. Not wearing a hat.'

Henry nodded. 'I would like to speak to Charlie.'

Reece nodded assent and Charlie was summoned. He proved to be a boy in his mid-teens looking nervously at the adults. He hadn't particularly noticed the car, but was aware that a vehicle had left just after he'd taken up his post. Not as skilled or as practised at keeping tabs on everything that was going on, Charlie seemed embarrassed that he might have missed something but Reece ruffled his hair and sent him on his way without asking Henry's permission.

So the timeframe was about right, Henry thought. The body had been discovered around four and by half past Dr Mason had been brought across and had identified the woman as his dead wife. So the blue car and the man in the suit were useful leads.

Judging that the inspector was ready to leave, Emory thanked Reece and the two of them walked away. 'I had men asking if they'd seen anything unusual,' Emory sounded thoroughly annoyed. 'They said not.'

'A vehicle driving in, parking up and then leaving is hardly unusual,' Henry commented.

'True enough. You think that's our man, the one driving the blue car?'

'I think I do not like coincidence,' Henry said. 'In my experience coincidences take far too much organizing for them to be mere chance.'

Emory laughed shortly and then wondered if the man would take offence. So far no oil on water had been required but that seemed to be because Inspector Henry Johnstone was known, or known of. Emory was curious about this. 'So you've had dealings with the travelling folk before?'

'I have.'

'And what do you make of them? They can be devious buggers, not the easiest to deal with. But Reece seemed to be honest enough with you.'

'Honest enough,' Henry agreed, 'because nothing of what he said impugned or threatened his own people. Our Mr Reece had no one to protect and therefore could speak the truth.'

Emory nodded, recognizing the reality of that fact and also, oddly, suspecting that Inspector Johnstone rather admired that level of loyalty. 'Where to now, sir?' he asked.

'I imagine my sergeant will be walking the course, getting a feel for the place and the lie of the land,' Henry said. 'So if you could suggest a vantage point where we might see him?'

Emory nodded and led Henry up into the stands, from where the seats on the top level could see right across the racecourse. They soon spied Mickey Hitchens; he seemed to be in company with a man and two boys. 'Looks like he's found himself some assistance,' Emory said.

Henry sat back in the seat and folded his hands together across his chest. 'Sergeant Hitchens is good at that,' he said. 'I, on the other hand, am good at being an awkward, cussed son of a bastard,' Henry said without rancour. 'Or so I am frequently told.'

Emory considered his response for a moment, and then said, 'So you make a good team then.'

And then, that most unusual of sounds: Henry Johnstone laughed.

THREE

I t had been assumed that Martha Mason's bag had been stolen when she'd been attacked, but when Sergeant Emory, Mickey and Henry re-joined the police driver, he informed them that the bag had been handed in as lost property. A fact that had not come to light until early that afternoon.

'All the lost property was brought to the station and gone through,' he explained. 'It wasn't realized at first this bag belonged to the dead lady, only when it was opened up and the contents examined.'

The intent had been to go and interview the victim's husband and the friends that she had been with, but Henry now decided that they should go immediately to look at the handbag and so they were driven to the police station on Burgage Lane.

Martha Mason's handbag was of good quality, Henry thought. Black leather, lined with purple silk and closed with a gilt clasp shaped like a butterfly. He looked for a label but was unable to find one so he asked Mickey to take a photograph of it, not so much for purposes of evidence but because he suspected this might be more expensive than most doctor's wives would possess. His sister Cynthia would know.

Inside was a blue, leather frame purse which also closed with a gilt clasp, though this one much simpler. 'Do we know how much money she had on her?' he asked.

Emory consulted his notes. 'The husband thinks she would have had loose change, probably a ten-shilling note and perhaps a five-pound note tucked into the lining of her bag. She was apparently in the habit of keeping that for emergencies.'

'In the lining?' Henry looked. There was no obvious pocket in the interior of the bag so he decided that this was meant literally, though obviously in some way that could be accessed without tearing anything. The base of the bag was reinforced and stiffened and the inner reinforcement was held in place by four small brass rivets; Henry supposed that something could be concealed beneath. At the base of the bag on the outside were four tiny little feet, to protect the leather from wear, should it be placed on the floor. Henry experimentally twisted these and discovered that they did in fact unscrew, releasing the lining reinforcement which, when lifted free, revealed not one but two five-pound notes, neatly folded together with a small key.

'Interesting,' Mickey observed.

The bag also contained a handkerchief, a powder compact – dark-green, faux snakeskin, which seem to Henry to be at odds with the rest of the contents – a key ring with two keys on it.

'House keys?' Henry suggested. 'Show them to the husband.'

A lipstick. 'Do you think this was the shade she was wearing?' Henry asked.

Emory shrugged. 'Both are red. I'm afraid I'm not much of an expert in women's mysteries.'

'Mysteries indeed,' Henry agreed. There was a small address book, with an attached pencil, and Henry flicked through this then handed it to Emory. 'I wish every contact to be followed up,' he said. 'On the face of it nothing seemed obviously to be missing, but the husband might know.'

'More likely the friend, Mrs Nora Phillips, would be aware of what was usually in Mrs Mason's bag,' Mickey suggested.

'But we will ask both, and see what answers we get.' Henry surveyed the small collection of items laid out on the table and then looked again at the bag. It wasn't an oversized bag but it comfortably held the purse, the compact and the other things. 'Would you say there was anything missing?' he asked, not directing the question at anybody in particular.

'I'm not so familiar with women's bags,' Emory protested mildly. 'Not being a married man I miss out on that sort of thing. But I reckon my sisters usually have more in the nature of general detritus, if you get my meaning. Bus tickets and the like. But if this is not her regular everyday bag—'

'My lady wife likes to be prepared,' Mickey agreed. 'I know she carries a small sewing kit, safety pins and the like. But then she does travel a good deal.' He picked up the little bag and examined it thoughtfully. 'The bag is nice quality,' he said, 'and it looks quite new, there is no fading to the lining, no wear on those little feet, no chafing on the handle. Perhaps it is a best bag, a going-out bag. Again the husband or the friend would know.' He glanced up at his boss. 'You think that despite appearances something might have been taken?'

Henry was reading the report about where the bag had been found – by a young couple who had noticed it kicked under a bush and assumed that it had been stolen from somebody. They had picked it up and given it to one of the stewards who had eventually put it in lost property and thence it had come to the police station.

'So how far from where the body was found was the bag discovered?'

'Quite a way,' Emory said. 'Closer to where she left her friend than to where she was found.'

'So, that suggests that the bag was taken from her and then cast aside and the woman was either taken or went voluntarily to the paddock where the vehicles were parked. Taken through a crowded place, perhaps reluctantly. Someone would have seen. Many people would have seen.'

'All of whom probably went home yesterday,' Mickey observed. 'Tracking them down now would be impossible, though an appeal for witnesses should still be made. It's possible someone saw the lady with her killer.'

'And most will probably have assumed anything they'd seen was a lover's quarrel or just *not* seen because they were focusing on the race, or on the betting, or on being determined to have a good day out no matter what,' Emory added.

Henry conceded all of that with a nod. 'There has been an appeal for witnesses already put out?'

'There has, both locally and in the national papers. That will be in today so we might get results if we're lucky,' Emory told him. 'And we now know about the blue car and the man in the suit without the hat and that he probably left by that far gate. There'd be less people around to see him coming in that way and my guess is the couple entered by that far gate too.'

'So we need to think about likely routes,' Henry agreed.

'He would have wanted to avoid crowds. The thing is, she appears to have gone to him willingly – assuming that the friend she saw in the crowds was this man.'

'Nora Phillips said *they*,' Emory emphasized. 'I remember it particularly because her husband questioned her about it. He asked if she was certain it was "they" and not he or she, but definitely "they" and she said that Mrs Mason definitely said "they". "I didn't know *they* would be here and I haven't seen *them* in an age" – which is suggestive.'

'Suggestive but not definitive. If the dead woman wanted to conceal who she was meeting, if the meeting had been prearranged, then perhaps she might have prevaricated.'

Emory frowned. 'Everyone reckons Mrs Mason to have been a good woman, a good wife, a solid figure in the community. You will not find anyone say anything against her.'

'And yet she is a woman who kept secrets,' Henry stated. 'Her husband knew that she might have one five-pound note concealed, and that would have been sufficient for any emergency, but to have two plus this little key, whatever this little key fits, that suggests more.'

'To me it just suggests that she is an average woman,' Mickey argued. 'Women's handbags are always a mystery to their men. And women like to feel secure; having a little money put aside is what makes them feel secure most of the time. Both your sister and my wife would tell you that.'

Henry frowned. Mickey certainly had a point. When he and Cynthia had been growing up and had been desperately poor, his sister had been in the habit of concealing small amounts of money in various places 'just in case', and as far as he knew she still did this, even though she had married well and her future was secure. Perhaps he had a point. Five extra pounds was useful money but not so much that it might be suspicious.

'So,' he said, 'we will think on this. We'll go now and interview the husband and the friends.'

'And then we'll have usefully achieved all we can for today,' Mickey said pointedly. Neither of them had eaten since leaving London, apart from sandwiches that Mickey had brought with him and shared with his friend and governor. 'My stomach thinks my throat's been cut and so will yours when it gets time to consider it.'

Emory watched the interchange with interest noting how close these two men seemed. 'You'll find the food good at the hotel,' he promised. He went out and called the driver.

Although Dr Phillips had his practice in Newark-on-Trent, both he and Dr Mason lived in Southwell, close enough to the racecourse that they could have walked on race day. A few members of the press had, as Emory had anticipated, tried to photograph or interview the families involved in the murder. Emory had constables posted to scoot them away from the Phillips' door and told them, firmly, that they'd be better served waiting out events on Burgage Green. At least they'd then be able to decamp to the nearest pub, the Last Whistle, at lunchtime and in the evening.

Both Henry and Mickey had been photographed entering and leaving the police station and Henry knew that it would not be long before the newshounds had established precisely who they were. No doubt, until they could report progress on this case, there would be a reprise of other cases on which he and Mickey worked, appearing in the local papers the following day and in the national press on the day after.

Dr Phillips had opened his surgery that morning but had, as promised, arrived home for mid-afternoon and he had left a young assistant in charge of dispensing or general queries. Dr Mason, though he had wanted to go into work, had finally been persuaded that he'd be no use to anyone and was better off staying at home.

'I understand that he wanted to bury himself in the work,' Dr Phillips told Henry, 'but the man can hardly string two sentences together. This has been a desperate shock to us all, and you can imagine what it must have been like for Clive to suddenly recognize his wife under such circumstances.'

'It *must* have been a terrible shock,' Henry agreed. 'And Dr Mason was with you when the constable came for him, I understand.'

'We'd been together for most of the afternoon, most of the day, in fact. We all had a picnic lunch, ourselves and the wives and the children and then Mason and I repaired to the bar, where we'd arranged to meet colleagues and friends. Truth be told, we'd all had a jolly afternoon. Mason had been called out twice. He was duty surgeon for the day and I was just there as backup should things go . . . Anyway, Clive had gone to attend to a drunk who had fallen and cut his head and to a jockey who I believe had dislocated his shoulder. Both minor incidences and neither of which in the end required police intervention. The drunk was taken home by his friends and reports that the jockey had been in a fight were apparently exaggerated.'

'And Dr Mason was in good spirits, Mrs Mason also?'

'Martha is always in good spirits. Was. One of the most cheerful women you would ever meet. Busy too, always on some committee or another. Frankly I don't know what Clive would have done without her and I don't know what he'll do without her now. He could never have built the practice without her help. She did all the secretarial and reception in those first years, learnt basic dispensing, served as his assistant, even delivered his messages and his medications until he could afford to get a young man in. In fact, we now share an assistant – Gerald does two and a half days with each of us and I don't mind telling you, Inspector, the first years of setting up in practice are tough. But we finally both have things on an even keel, with a good patient list and, largely due to Martha's intervention, I have to say, we both donate a few hours free time every week at the workhouse, or the asylum, or the soup kitchens. And, of course, we are both on the register of police surgeons. You can imagine, our lives are busy and not always predictable. A man needs a good wife to hold the fort when there are so many demands on his time and Martha was a very level-headed sort – and, as I say, cheerful.'

Henry glanced across at his sergeant. He wondered if Dr Phillips was inferring that his own wife was perhaps lacking in some of these departments. Mickey's twitch of a smile told him that his sergeant was thinking the same thing.

'You both moved here at the same time, I believe.'

'Indeed, we did. We went through medical school together and when a practice came up for sale in this area, we decided we would share responsibility for a time. That was a decade ago. Clive, and of course my wife's family, helped me to set up my own practice and he continued with the original one. We have been at risk of sounding sentimental, Inspector, more like brothers than friends. Neither of us had much in the way of family and it has been a real blessing to have such a stead-fast influence. I hope Clive will think the same of me.'

'And you presumably married after you moved here?' Henry queried. He was well aware of how poverty-stricken most young doctors were until they became established, unless they were lucky enough to raise the capital of a hundred pounds or more to buy into an existing practice.

'I met Nora after I'd been here for about a year. Her father is in trade, owns two local grocery shops and Nora's brothers have followed into the family business. In fact, it is through one of her brothers that I met Nora. He was a patient of the practice that we took over, he came along to check that we were still suitable, we got into conversation and over time we became friends. I received an invitation to dine and I met my future wife.' Ephraim Phillips smiled and Henry gained the impression that he was in fact very fond of his wife, even if she was, as Sergeant Emory had turned it, somewhat flighty. It was interesting, Henry mused for a moment, had his sister used the term flighty she would have meant unreliable and somewhat wild; Emory simply meant that the woman was a little feather-brained.

'And Dr Mason? Did he meet his wife here?'

For the first time Ephraim Phillips seemed uncertain, even a little uncomfortable. 'No, he had occasion to make a trip to the south coast, and he met her there. They courted by letter for a time, and then she was persuaded to come and see if she could settle in this rather more rural environment than she was used to. In fact, she stayed with us for a few days and she and Nora became fast friends. Clive seemed even more smitten than he had been before and within months they were married.'

'Did you find that strange?' Henry asked.

Dr Phillips considered carefully before replying. 'At first I was worried that my friend was plunging too fast and too deep. We knew nothing of this young woman, only that she and Clive had got into conversation on a promenade, of all places. This had led to them going to have tea in a Lyons tearoom – all very respectable. But Clive had fallen hard and of course we were worried. As it turned out, Martha was everything Clive had ever needed and indeed more. She has proved to be the perfect wife for a country doctor, and I have to say, a steadying influence on Nora. Nora can be a little excitable at times, but Martha has encouraged her to take on work with committees and to spread her wings socially. Nora will miss her terribly.'

At that moment came a light tap on the door which then opened, and Nora herself stepped through. She was a pretty woman, Henry thought. A mass of fair hair piled up in a loose bun, blue eyes and full lips which were now turned down with anxiety when really they seemed designed only for smiling. Henry and Mickey were introduced and Nora took a seat at her husband's side. Henry was rather gratified to see that he took Nora's hand, patting it gently.

'Just tell the inspector everything that happened. Just try to keep to the point,' her husband instructed.

'I'll do my best,' she said as she smiled at her husband, and Henry realized that she had taken no offence at his words, just recognized perhaps that she often didn't keep to the point.

'You all had lunch together, a picnic lunch.' Henry decided to begin with certainties before moving forward.

She nodded. 'Martha and I had packed a picnic, and we all ate together in that little area beyond where the fairground had set up. It's less busy there and the children could run around and not interfere with anyone. Occasionally the grooms bring the horses in to brush them down but it's more of a cut through than anything else and the holiday crowd like to be closer to the racetrack.'

Henry could see that Nora's husband was about to tell her to keep to the point but actually this was useful information. He asked Mickey for the sketch map they had drawn and asked her to point out where this was. He could see Dr Phillips itching to do this himself but Henry's glance halted the impulse. Nora looked carefully at the map, asking Henry and then Mickey questions about it and then pointed. 'It would be here,'

she said, pointing to a small enclosure at the back of the
stadium. 'Just there is where the fairground was set up. Beyond
that is the paddock where poor Martha was found, isn't it?'

Henry nodded.

'Over there is where most of the horses are kept and in this
area here, people cut through from one side to the other but
it's in the shade at that time of the day, at noon time, and it's
also away from the racetrack. The only people who picnic
there really are families and there were a few families, perhaps
a half-dozen. Some of them we knew and the children played
together.'

'If you could compile a list of names,' Mickey said, 'that
would be useful to us. The more eyes on this, the better.'

'And Martha seemed content, happy?' prompted Henry gently.

'She seemed very happy. The children love her. *Loved* her.
We were all laughing and talking, and she even took a glass
of wine, which is unusual for Martha. We had packed lemonade
for the children, and usually Martha would have drunk the
lemonade as well. But that day she did have a glass of wine.'

Her husband looked slightly surprised, but then nodded. 'I
hadn't thought about it,' he said. 'But I think you are correct.
You may not know, but Newark-on-Trent is quite a centre
for the temperance movement and although none of us has
signed the pledge, we *are* in favour of *temperance,* particularly
among the working men. Clive and I have both seen first-hand
the damage that can be done to communities and to marriages
due to inebriation. Martha in fact rarely indulged.'

Unlike yourself and Clive Mason, Henry thought. The pair
of you having spent the afternoon in the bar. But he did not
say this out loud and congratulated himself on his tact. Mickey
would be proud, he thought wryly.

'And then after lunch?'

'Well, our husbands went away to speak to friends they had
spotted earlier, and arranged to meet with after lunch, so
Martha and I packed away and then we sat for a time watching
the children play. Then we took the picnic basket to the left
luggage office – they have a service on race days where it is
possible to leave baggage as so many people come up by train.
And then we walked for a time, looking at the crowds and the

horses and watching the tic-tac men. Martha knew quite a lot about them,' she said with a smile. 'She had great fun interpreting their signals for me.'

'Really?' her husband enquired. 'And how did she know that? Are you sure she wasn't pretending?'

'And why would she do that?'

Interesting, Henry thought.

'And then?'

'The children wanted to go on the fairground. We had made them wait for a time after they had lunch so they weren't sick, but at around two o'clock we began to wend our way back. It's not a quick process with three children in tow, as you can imagine. I was so grateful for Martha being there. And then she saw someone in the crowd.'

'She did not say who?'

'No, I've thought about this so much. Worrying in case I'd missed something. But I'm sure I haven't. Martha said, as close as I can remember it: "Oh, I had no idea they would be here. It's been such a long time. Won't be a tick." And then off she went and disappeared into the crowd.' She looked mournfully at Henry and he could see that her grief was genuine. 'And that was the last time I saw her.'

A maid in a starched white apron had opened the door to them at the Phillips' house, one of two dailies who came in to help, Dr Phillips had told them. The Phillips' house was a three-storey, semi-detached affair, with a small front garden and – a glimpse out of the back window told Henry – quite a substantial rear one. Initially it reminded him of the house where he had grown up, Henry's father having also been a doctor. Although, the moment he had stepped through the front door, he had realized that this was different. His father's house had been a cold and austere place where children were meant to be invisible, whereas here Henry and Mickey had been greeted at once by three little ones running into the hall to see who the visitors were. They had been shooed away by the maid who had smiled at Henry and told him that she would bring tea and would the gentlemen like to wait in the parlour. It was clearly an informal household.

However, at this second house it was Dr Clive Mason who opened his own front door to them and the contrast between the noise and bustle of the Phillips' household and the intense quiet in this one could not have been greater. This was also a semi-detached house but here the front room had been given over to the doctor's surgery and chairs were lined up in what was quite a broad, tiled hall from which stairs rose steeply. A second room, behind the surgery, seemed to have been designated for paperwork and dispensing and Henry glimpsed a kitchen at the end of the hall.

'We live upstairs,' Dr Mason told them, and led the way up the steep flight.

The layout of the upstairs was very similar, what was the surgery below was a living room on the first floor, with a small dining room next to it and above the kitchen, a bathroom. A second flight of stairs rose to what were presumably bedrooms. It was not a grand house but it was warm and friendly, the walls hung with pictures and inexpensive but pretty ornaments sat beside a marble clock on the mantelpiece. Books occupied most of the shelf space with photographs and other ornaments set in front of them. The furniture was not new, but it was comfortable and bright with throws and cushions. The curtains that hung in the bay window looked surprisingly expensive compared to the rest of the furnishings; old but heavy velvet. Clive Mason noticed him looking. 'They were here when we moved in,' he said. 'Martha took them down, brushed and mended them, and they certainly do keep out the drafts in the winter.'

It seemed, Henry thought, that Dr Phillips was in a generally better financial position that his friend. Was that down to his marriage, Henry wondered, or to the quality of patients the doctors had on their lists?

Clive Mason sat down, and then stood up again, his hand to his head. 'Forgive me, can I offer you—'

'We need nothing, thank you,' Mickey told him. 'Please sit down, Dr Mason. We will try not to keep you for too long.'

Clive Mason took a seat. He looked lost, Mickey thought. Absolutely knocked sideways by events. 'We have just been to see your friend and colleague Dr Phillips and spoken to him and to his wife. They told us that Mrs Mason seemed in good spirits. That she saw a friend in the crowd and went after them, after which they know nothing.'

Clive Mason blinked. 'I was with Ephraim in the bar. We had all picnicked together and then he and I had gone to meet friends. It had been such a happy day. Martha loved being around the children. We have not been blessed and that had been something to regret, but I'm glad of it now.' He took a deep breath. 'The constable came for me at just after four o'clock. We walked across to where they had found . . . on the way he told me they had found a body. He speculated that it was a woman who had been entertaining a man. Of course, he did not know who it really was, and it was a reasonable speculation, given the location. When I got there, I found other constables and the owner of the horsebox and I think one of his assistants standing around. The door was open, I looked inside. At first, I thought I recognized the shoes. One shoe had come off and was lying on the straw and I thought it looked like Martha's. But I never . . . never imagined. And then I got closer. She was lying with her face down in the straw but I knew immediately it was her. There was a most terrible wound to the back of her head. I knew at once that she was dead.'

'It must have been a terrible, terrible shock,' Mickey sympathized. 'Dr Mason, everyone has spoken very warmly of your wife, but did she have any enemies, anyone she had upset? Anyone who might have wished her harm?'

Dr Mason looked puzzled and confused. 'I thought it was a robbery,' he said. 'Her bag was missing, someone had stolen her bag and hit her over the head.'

Of course, Mickey thought, he didn't know that the bag had been found. How could he? He watched the doctor carefully as he said, 'It seems the bag had been handed in, it turned up at the police station amongst a batch of other lost property today. We've seen it; there does not appear to be anything missing. A purse, her money and her other possessions seem still to have been inside.'

He watched as the confusion deepened on Dr Mason's face. As the realization came that this was not some random violent robbery. 'You are telling me that somebody killed my wife deliberately. That it was not a robbery that met with misadventure. You are telling me that she was deliberately murdered.'

'As of now, we are keeping an open mind. It could still be that someone attacked her for her bag, kicked the bag into the bushes where it was found, intending to return for it later but realizing that they had hit this lady far too hard, sought then to hide the body.' Even as Mickey said it, he realized how convoluted it sounded, nevertheless that was still a possibility.

Dr Mason was staring at him, his disbelief evident. 'They would have taken the bag and run, emptied it, cast it aside, not given any care to hiding a body. Where was the bag found?'

Mickey once more took out the map and showed him, glad now that he had produced it.

'No, no, you have it all wrong. On race day that area would be packed solid with people. You have never been here on race day, you have no idea how the crowd ebbs and flows, but in that area and at the time they suspect she was killed, this would be full of people waiting to place bets. There is no way an assailant would have killed her there, not without being seen. No one could have delivered a blow like that in such a crowded and busy place.'

Mickey nodded, interested. This accorded with what they had already been told and what they had already seen. 'Which leads us to a question, Dr Mason. The place where your wife was found is away from crowds, a quiet and less-travelled area. We suspect that this is where your wife was in fact killed, probably not in the horsebox itself but nearby. Traces of blood have been found. To go to such a place, your wife must have trusted the person she was with. Or it is possible she was taken under duress, which begs the question why did she not cry out for help given that she must have passed through many crowded spots in order to get to that particular place.'

'The motive may still have been robbery,' Mason argued. 'She may have gone there with someone she considered to be a friend or acquaintance. Nora said she spotted someone in the crowd and went chasing after them. Though I have to say it's not like Martha to be so impulsive. But perhaps they then turned on her, hit her, took her bag.'

Mickey was shaking his head. 'According to the young couple who found the bag, they spotted it at around three in the afternoon. At first they thought it might simply have been dropped, because when the wife checked inside she could see that the contents were still there. She took it to a steward who then took it to the lost property office and eventually it came to the police station. Your wife left her friend at around two fifteen. By three o'clock the bag is missing and has just been found. By four o'clock the constable has come to fetch you. So we know that your wife lost her bag, was taken or went under duress, or even willingly, to the place where she was found and there she was killed. This is a problematic timeline, Dr Mason.'

Clive Mason was staring at him as though unable to really comprehend what he was saying. 'You are telling me that Martha saw someone she knew, she met with them and they took her away and killed her. And she made no protest going with them? I don't see how that is possible.'

Neither did Mickey but that was what the facts supported just now. 'On the face of it, no, it seems unlikely. There are gaps in our timeline and in our understanding of what was going on in your wife's mind. Mrs Phillips seems to think she was merely excited at the prospect of seeing an old friend, or possibly friends. She gave no explanation when she left Mrs Phillips, but does not seem to have been distressed or anxious. Surely had she been anxious to avoid these people she would simply have turned the other way. And we have large gaps in our timeline which must be filled.'

Dr Mason stared at him for a moment, obviously trying to put it all together in his mind. 'I cannot understand who would want to harm Martha. A random thief who hit someone too hard, that I can comprehend, but you were telling me that she was deliberately murdered and perhaps by somebody who knew her or whom she thought of as a friend. I find that so hard to understand.'

'Your wife was not a local woman,' Henry said.

'No, no we met on the south coast. I was in Brighton on

business. I was not yet fully employed up here, and an old acquaintance required a locum for two weeks. Frankly, I needed the money. It takes time to become established as a general practitioner. Ephraim had settled more quickly – he had managed to buy a practice from a doctor who had been on the verge of retirement. He allowed me to share space there, but of course it was his practice and not mine. I was grateful for the work, of course, and of him accommodating me, and I was slowly building a list of my own. Ephraim had married Nora, you see, and it pleased Nora's father to have a doctor in the family, so he helped with the finance and he directed many of his own customers that way, in addition to those left from the previous practice – though it has to be said, Dr Fitzgerald had let things run down somewhat in the final years before he retired. He was an old man and not as capable as he had once been.'

This was an interestingly different account to the one they had received from Dr Phillips, Henry thought. 'And then you met your wife, while you were down in Brighton.'

For the first time during the interview, Clive Mason smiled. 'I met her, and it was as though my life began. Yes, I know how that sounds, but Martha made all the difference both to my personal world and to my medical practice. Suddenly I wasn't alone. She worked beside me as hard and as long as ever I did and four years ago we managed to afford this place and I started up on my own. I could not have done this without her help.'

'Your wife's family, are they still down in Brighton?'

He shook his head. 'Like me, Martha was without family. Her parents had died in the Spanish flu epidemic and the aunt that had brought her up had passed away the year before we met. Martha was sharing a flat with two other girls and working as a typist. But she was clearly far more intelligent than her job demanded. For some time we simply corresponded and then I asked her if she could come and visit. I thought we needed to know one way or another and Ephraim and Nora were kind enough to give her accommodation. After that, I knew. I needed her, I wanted her to be my wife and I'm happy to say that she agreed. We had a very simple wedding with

Nora and Ephraim as witnesses and Nora arranged a wedding breakfast for us. I would love to have given Martha a proper church wedding, but she said it didn't matter to her and I believed her.'

He crossed the mantelpiece and picked up a photograph and passed it to Henry. 'This is our wedding photograph,' he said.

In it, Clive Mason looked deliriously happy and his bride seem to be smiling at him in amusement. She was small and slight, with dark hair. She wore a pretty dress and carried flowers, but yes it was a simple affair and Henry doubted the photograph was taken by a professional. It was simply rather a good snap.

He showed the photograph to Mickey before handing it back to Dr Mason. 'She looks kind,' Mickey said.

'Oh, she was. And patient. Which is as well, because I am a very impatient man.'

He sat staring at the photograph and the look on his face was one of despair.

'We will do all we can to get to the bottom of this,' Mickey told him.

Clive Mason turned weary eyes on to Sergeant Hitchens as though he didn't really believe that anything could be done. He nodded slowly but his look was bleak. 'I don't know what I'm going to do now,' he said. 'I just don't know how I can carry on.'

They had asked other questions: was this Martha's usual handbag? No, it was one used on special occasions.

Would he notice, did he think, if any of the usual contents of her bag were missing?

Probably not.

As a matter of routine they had asked to see Martha's usual bag, and any other possessions which were exclusively hers. Letters, perhaps a writing desk? Perhaps a box where she kept personal items?

Clive Mason nodded. 'I use the second bedroom as my study, and occasionally sleep there if I'm kept out late and don't want to disturb her on my return. We don't often have guests. Martha has a bureau in the bedroom.' He rose as if about to show them where and then sat back down.

Without asking, Mickey crossed to the sideboard and poured the man a brandy. 'You stay there – I'm sure we can find whatever we need. We'll be careful not to make a muddle.'

Dr Mason took the brandy glass automatically, and then sat staring into it. Henry and Mickey left him to his grief and went up the final flight of stairs and into the master bedroom. Like the living room it overlooked the street, and the bedroom also had quite a large side window that looked down into part of the garden. Unexpectedly sizeable, Henry thought. A hedge divided this garden from the neighbour's, a mix of privet and other shrubs and Henry thought he could discern the first of the wild roses coming into bloom. They were early this year, he thought, but then the weather had been unusually warm.

He turned back from the window and surveyed the room. Mickey was still standing by the door, waiting for Henry to finish his observations. The room was neat and clean and simply furnished. The mix of furnishings indicated that they had been bought piecemeal and probably as and when the young couple could afford. Bed, two wardrobes, tallboy and the bureau. A small dressing table had been improvised from an old-fashioned washstand with a mirror set upon it along Martha's brushes, pots of cream and bottles of rose and lavender water.

Judging that Henry had finished his ruminations, Mickey crossed to the dressing table and examined the bottles and pots. 'Cold cream, a glass jar of cotton wool and a near-empty bottle of Shalimar perfume,' he observed. 'Doesn't Cynthia wear that? A little expensive for a doctor's wife, but the label is worn and she may have had it for some time.' The hairbrush and the clothes brush were silver-backed, but they too looked old and similar to those which Mickey's wife owned and which they had picked up in a second-hand shop for very little money. He poked his fingers into a small, moulded, brass bowl that contained hairpins and removed the lid from another which contained two brooches and a couple of rings. 'Paste and silver, I'm guessing.' He picked up a brooch that looked like an amethyst and held it up to the light, unsure if it was glass or the real thing. It was in a gold-coloured setting and the stone was about as large as Mickey's thumbnail. He set it down again thoughtfully.

Henry had moved to the bureau and Mickey opened the first of the wardrobes. This was a man's wardrobe: suits, shirts, overcoat. Drawers and a foldaway mirror and a place for brushes. He opened the drawers, rifled through, finding only handkerchiefs and ties and underwear. He moved to the second wardrobe, glancing across at Henry who was examining the bureau with attention and focus. 'Anything?'

'Household bills, receipts, a postcard from Bournemouth and a bundle of letters which look as though they were written from her husband. No doubt when they were courting.' He set them aside, wondering if they would reveal anything useful about this young woman, before she had been married and moved to become a doctor's wife. 'An address book and an appointment diary.' He flicked through both and then slipped them into his pocket and after a moment added the letters too.

Mickey frowned, slightly ill at ease with that last act, but accepting that they knew very little about Martha Mason – though it seemed unlikely to Mickey that the cause of her death could have been something that happened eight or nine years ago, before she moved here. However, one never knew.

He opened the second wardrobe. Dresses, a winter coat, knitwear packed away in linen bags and laid on the floor of the wardrobe. Shoes and then: 'This must be her ordinary handbag,' Mickey said. He brought it over to the bed and tipped it out. 'Shopping lists, bus tickets, receipts for groceries. A little purse containing change, a comb and mirror and another address book.'

'Hold on to the address book, then we can compare.'

Mickey nodded, put the rest of the contents back into the bag and stowed the bag back in the wardrobe. He bent down to examine two of the shoeboxes, wondering why she didn't keep her shoes in them, but when he touched them he realized that the weight was wrong for shoes. He opened them up and then brought both back to the bed.

The first contained photographs, Christmas cards, little

mementos such as theatre tickets. The shoebox itself had been covered with flowered cretonne and decorated with a blue bow. A quick survey revealed that these were things that Martha must have collected since her marriage and included small tokens of affection and snapshots of days out with friends. He turned to the second box, this one feeling heavier, and when he opened it Mickey was quite surprised to see silk scarves. He moved these aside and discovered that one was wrapped around something unexpected.

'Well, well. That is not something I thought to find.'

Henry looked over and then crossed to where Mickey was standing, staring at the gun, a Beretta and clip containing five rounds of ammunition which had been neatly wrapped in a red silk scarf and placed at the bottom of the box. 'Now what would a respectable doctor's wife be doing with one of these?'

FOUR

D r Mason had been shocked. He had never seen that before, he told Henry and Mickey. 'Inspector, I have no idea where that came from. It couldn't possibly be Martha's. What on earth would she need a gun for?'

'You are aware of the box?'

'Yes, of course. There are two shoeboxes, she covered them with that fancy fabric and used them to keep postcards and photographs and keepsakes. Martha was like most women – she had a tendency towards sentiment. Not that I have any argument with that, women are emotional creatures. Keeping these remembrances gave her pleasure.'

'I do not think this is a remembrance.' Mickey pointed at the gun.

Dr Mason stared at it. 'I served as a medic in the war, it has left me with a dislike and discomfort with all weaponry. I saw enough of the hurt that arms could inflict back then. That Martha could have such a thing is beyond belief. It must have come from somewhere else . . . why would she have a gun? Why would she bring a gun into our house, knowing how I felt about such things?'

To that there was no immediate answer.

'Dr Mason, we have made a cursory search but now it seems a more thorough search might be necessary. Your wife possessing such a thing suggests that—'

'Suggests what? Martha was a good woman – anyone will tell you that. There has to be a reasonable explanation for this. There has to be a reasonable explanation for—'

'Someone having killed her?' Henry suggested. 'I doubt any explanation could be reasonable when it comes to murder.'

Dr Mason was either genuinely deeply shocked or very good at dissembling, Mickey thought. He took Henry aside and suggested that they send for Dr Phillips and ask him to take his friend home for a few days and Henry agreed, noting this would make it easier to carry out an efficient search if the owner of the house was not present. It wasn't quite what had led to Mickey's suggestion but he didn't bother trying to explain that to his boss. Henry was in full investigative mode now, and in that mood he steamrollered everybody and everything and had little concern for people's feelings.

Dr Phillips was summoned and the situation explained to him. He appeared equally shocked that his friend's wife should own any kind of weapon. The idea of Martha owning a gun he seemed to find almost laughable until it was shown to him, nestling in among the scarves and gloves and handkerchiefs in the box, a box her husband would never be likely to explore, being full of women's things and nothing to do with him.

Dr Mason, supervised by Mickey, packed a suitcase and then surrendered the house keys to Henry and went on his way. He looked white and shocked and even more defeated.

'Right.' Henry stood in the centre of the bedroom and looked around. 'So we begin again, and we treat this like a crime scene.'

'Agreed,' Mickey told him. 'But we begin again tomorrow, with fresh minds and a little more energy. It is now past seven in the evening, and I told you that my stomach thought my throat had been cut perhaps three hours ago. So now we go and we eat, and then we rest and we start tomorrow with clear heads.'

For a moment it looked as though Henry would argue, him being the senior officer, but he and Mickey had worked as a team for far too long for rank to matter and Henry had learned the sense of listening to his sergeant by now. So they locked the house and were driven to the hotel.

'So,' Mickey looked across at his boss and made sure that he had actually tackled most of his meal before raising the subject of the investigation, 'what do we make of this so far?'

Henry Johnstone took a sip of his beer, then to Mickey's satisfaction speared a piece of pie from his plate. 'That this young woman perhaps took advantage of a doctor's affection in order to reinvent herself. Maybe too great a conclusion to reach on the evidence so far, but I wonder how much anyone knew about her life before she arrived. Before she agreed to marry.'

'She seems to have made a success of her reinvention,' Mickey observed. 'The majority verdict is she was respectable, helpful, devoted and in general a good wife. But what else was she before she arrived here, and does this have a bearing on whoever killed her? Or is it some random act – we cannot rule that out.'

Henry nodded, chewing thoughtfully. 'So we need to find out who Martha Mason was before she became Martha Mason. I have the letters with me and will read through them tonight, and if you can compare the two address books and see who can be identified . . . The diary seems to contain little: appointments to meet with friends, notes to remind her husband of events such as business meetings and committees of various charities with which they seem both to have been involved. She seems still to have acted as his secretary. I will give you the diary, and you can compare the names to those in the address book and contact them. We should begin with those she has seen most recently.'

'And then tomorrow begin a systematic search,' Mickey agreed. 'She seemed confident, concealing the gun in that box, that a husband would not be curious. My guess is that he is a man intent on his own work and also perhaps lacking in imagination where women are concerned; it would not occur to him she would conceal or dissemble or have such skill that he might not know what she was doing. For a woman to keep a gun implies that she feels her life is threatened. But for a woman not to keep that weapon with her, perhaps implies that she thinks the threat is no longer immediate.'

'But she was wrong about that,' Henry responded. 'Her husband mentioned that she was working as a typist. He must be asked where and if she had any particular friends that she continues to be in touch with. I think he did mention that there was somebody.'

Mickey nodded, having a similar memory of the conversation. 'I would also like to look into Dr Mason's background. He and Phillips seem to have gone through medical school together; both claim to have no family and make the same claim also of Martha. The only person in this to have any familial ties is the Phillips wife, Nora. Everyone else seems oddly cut loose and I have to ask myself if it's too much of a coincidence, that three people without anchor of family and friends should fetch up together in the same place and form such a close alliance.'

'That could be the reason for such a close alliance,' Henry posited. 'Like calls to like. I have always found it hard to understand those families who seem to be happy in one another's company and to imagine what that must be like. I feel alienated from it as you well know.'

'And yet your sister has set up a very happy home, you've seen first-hand that it can be done.'

'And as you also well know, I tend to view anything my sister does as unique and not necessarily replicable by other people.' Henry allowed himself a slight smile, knowing that this was a weakness on his part.

Mickey merely acknowledged this with a nod. Had he been pushed to it he would probably have made a similar comment about his wife. Both men valued the women in their lives very highly.

'So tomorrow, we see what has emerged from our appeal for witnesses, a photograph of Mrs Mason has been widely circulated now both in the local and the national press. It's to be hoped that people get in touch and to be further hoped that someone has seen her with this presumed friend she met in the crowd. Added to that we have the van, the blue Austin car and the man in the dark blue suit without the hat and we should appeal for witnesses to this combination. It could be that he is totally innocent and has missed the appeal for information and has yet to come forward.'

'And we have in our favour the fact this is a woman well known in her community and highly thought of in that community, so the public will no doubt want to help. Of course that will lead to many false leads, but it is easier to gain information about a respectable woman than it is about one of the more unfortunate kind.'

Mickey acknowledge the truth of that with a wry smile. It was something that made neither man happy but it was nonetheless a fact. 'Somehow,' he said, 'I doubt now that the full answers are here, in this place. My guess is that whatever history this murder has, the story began down south with whoever this woman was back then.'

FIVE

The post-mortem was to be held the following morning at the workhouse infirmary, and the driver arrived just as they were finishing breakfast.

They collected their gear and settled in the back of the Wolseley Seven. Henry watched the passing scenery through the car window. It was only a short drive from the Saracen's Head to the site of the workhouse which, Henry was saddened to learn, was still in use though it was now termed a Public Assistance Institution.

He doubted the change of terminology improved the situation for those resident there.

Emory had told him that there was also a fever hospital on the same site and also an infirmary, which is why the post-mortem was to be performed there.

It had rained during the night, but the morning was clean and clear and the air in this predominantly rural area was fresh and scented by cow parsley and hawthorn. Henry had always loved the scent of hawthorn, though he knew this was considered strange. In the village where he had grown up hawthorn was never brought into the house because, the old people said, it carried the scent of death and was suitable only for funerals. He could remember his mother arranging cow parsley in among the June roses on the kitchen table. She would never have taken such flowers into the rest of the house, but their father rarely came into the kitchen and therefore this was a safer place. Henry reflected that his mother had made little impression on the rest of the house; everything else was arranged and organized to his father's taste and there was no room for compromise.

He wondered again how on earth she had come to be married to such a man. It came to him that had Cynthia made a similar mistake he would probably have committed murder rather than subject Cynthia's children to the kind of childhood they had shared. Then he reminded himself that his sister had far more sense and strength, hard-won but rock solid.

An orderly lead them into a cold, tiled space. Martha Mason's body had already been laid out and the surgeon had already made his preliminary notes.

'Apologies for the early start, gentlemen, but I have a full day of operating on the living.'

Henry was silent but Mickey thanked the surgeon for fitting this investigation into his schedule.

'I think there can be little doubt about what killed her,' the medic said, turning the woman's head for their inspection. The blood had been washed away and the deep wound was now visible, a single impacted fracture that had sent bone into brain and split the skull wide.

'That was a heavy blow,' Mickey observed. 'And single too. No hesitation, no smaller blows to put her down first. Just this one.'

'And as you say, delivered with considerable force and definite malice. This was no accident; I doubt it was a question of someone knocking her down in order to rob her.'

Mickey would not normally encourage such speculation, but he nodded; he had no doubt this was the correct assessment.

Henry was examining the woman's hands and wrists. Bruises had developed post-mortem and fingermarks could now clearly be seen on her left arm.

'Someone held her hard. Could the blow be struck while she was being held?' he mused. He stepped back, raising an arm and extending his hand as though holding somebody, swinging a practice blow. The other two watched him and Henry nodded. 'It could be done, but I think it would seem awkward. I wonder if he released her and then she began to run so he struck hard to stop her from running. Any speculation as to the weapon?'

'Until I open the skull I can only speculate, but see here . . .' The surgeon inserted a finger into the wound. The finger disappeared almost to the second knuckle.

'Not a simple hammer, then,' Mickey said thoughtfully. 'Something with more of a point? A brick hammer, perhaps. Is there a curve that you can feel or is the line straight?'

'I can say more when I section the brain, but from touch alone the hole feels straight but somewhat tapered. A point, a poleaxe perhaps would be my guess, such as the slaughterman might use. Something that would easily pass through even the skull of a great beast such as a bull or a horse.'

'Would such a tool be available on the racecourse?' Henry asked.

'Unlikely. If a horse is injured such that it needs to be put down, then the vet usually deals with it by shooting.'

'And there would seem to be no defensive wounds,' Henry noted, looking again at the woman's hands and arms.

'Overall, she seems to have been in generally good health. Will you stay for the remainder of the post-mortem? Or should I send a message to you of anything significant I might find? The cause of death seems obvious – it would be a waste of your time, gentlemen, to remain for the formalities.'

Henry agreed with him and he and Mickey left soon after.

'If he's right,' Mickey commented, 'then it does not seem to have been a random sort of weapon. Not one that was picked up on the spur of the moment.'

'No one commented on there being signage on the van that was seen. Had it been from a butcher's shop or something similar I would have expected observation of that, particularly from our travelling friends. Local butchers no doubt dispatch their own animals, but I doubt many carry the tools of their trade around with them in their delivery vans.'

They sat in silence in the back seat of the police car, each puzzling it out on the short drive back to Dr Mason's house. All was locked up tight and extra checks had been made during the night. A beat constable was hovering by the gate as they arrived. 'I'm glad to have caught you, sirs,' he said. 'The house is secure, but the neighbours reported a disturbance in the early hours of the morning. Someone prowling in the back garden. They let the dogs out and they made barking enough to drive the devil away and the neighbour then took a torch and went to inspect the rear garden. There are footprints near the French window, and the neighbour tells me that the latch is faulty and could easily be forced. I have checked it and it seems to be in order, but I thought you might wish to know this. I would have got word to you earlier,' he added, 'but the neighbour, Mr Morris, and his wife, having had their sleep disturbed decided that to summon a constable in the middle of the night seemed a little . . . superfluous, once the dogs had seen off any would-be intruders. They left the dogs to roam in the yard to raise the alarm and went back to bed.'

Interesting, Henry thought.

Mickey thanked the constable and said that he would go and speak to these neighbours forthwith. Mr Morris had already left for work, the constable told him. But Mrs Morris and the live-in maid, Elsie, were expecting them.

Mickey followed the constable into the next door front garden and rang the bell, the constable being eager to make introductions and, Henry thought, to be in on the excitement of this being a murder case. Henry let himself into Dr Mason's house and stood in the hallway, listening to the sound the house made now that it was unoccupied. It had been quiet when they had called yesterday, but now it was deathly so. Hushed and stilled and already taking on that lonely abandoned air that homes adopt when their families are absent for long. Not, Henry thought, that this ever presented as a family home. It was a place of business where Dr Mason and his wife lived above the shop. The gardens were well attended and designed to give a good impression, but they were formal and strictly ordered and somehow Henry could not imagine children playing there, not even in the long garden at the back.

He let himself out through the kitchen door. The kitchen jutted from the rear of the premises, making an L shape with the wall of what would have been the dining room, had it not been used as Dr Mason's study and dispensary. There were indeed footprints in the flower bed beside the French windows and the catch, even from the outside, looked flimsy. Henry guessed that rather than force the latch the would-be intruder would simply have broken one of the small panes of glass and reached in to open it. The breaking glass might have made a little noise but as Henry looked more closely, he decided that even that would be unnecessary. The windows in the door were small panes fastened into rather delicate-looking transoms. The putty that held them in place was old and brittle, and it would have been merely the work of a few minutes only for a single pane to have been silently extracted and a hand slipped through to raise the catch on the inside. The neighbours, Henry thought, must either have been very light sleepers or must have been anxious enough about events to have been listening out for something untoward. Perhaps, he thought, as he heard barking from across the wall, the dogs had heard something and raised the alarm. If so then he was grateful to the mutts. He heard Mickey's voice and that of a woman, no doubt Mrs Morris telling Mickey all about the night's events.

Henry retreated to the kitchen door, noting that beyond the kitchen the house extended into a single storey that encompassed outside lavatory and coal shed and small lock-up used for tools. He inspected these briefly. Beyond this the garden was very long though quite narrow. He glimpsed fruit trees and what looked like another shed at the bottom. Henry wandered down the garden and discovered that this was in fact a summerhouse. It was painted a dark blue and like the rest of the garden was well tended. He opened the door and revealed a very pleasant space inside with two old armchairs, a small table and a bright red rug on the floor. A low oak bookshelf was set against one wall and glancing at the titles Henry decided that these were books that belonged to Mrs Mason and not the doctor. There were a few cheap romances, some books of fairy tales and history and also bundles of dress patterns. When he had opened the door he had not noticed the treadle sewing machine, which the door obscured as he stepped into the summerhouse. This was very evidently Martha Mason's spot. She might have purposefully occupied a part of the bedroom, *her* desk and *her* wardrobe, *her* drawers in the chest of drawers, but this spoke of a place where a woman might be peaceful and calm and quiet and away from everything and in which there were no compromises, there was no accommodation of a husband and his sense of what was required.

Henry sat down in one of the chairs, noting the little paraffin stove in the corner and that there were curtains at the windows, heavier and thicker than you'd normally expect to find in a summerhouse. She must, he thought, have spent a good deal of time here.

Having decided that was the case, Henry began his search in the summerhouse instead of the residence she had shared with her husband. He went through the books from the book-case, opened the dress patterns and unfolded them enough to satisfy himself that nothing was hidden inside. He inspected the sewing machine, and even the stove. He checked for loose floorboards and ran a hand down the backs of the cushions on the chairs, upended them and studied the upholstery beneath. He stood precariously on the bentwood chair that she used when seated at the treadle and inspected the roof joists and then went outside and continued his perusal.

By the time Mickey joined him about an hour later Henry had collected a number of small items and laid them out on the round occasional table that had been set between the armchairs.

'Nice dogs,' Mickey commented. 'One is the size of a wolf and the other is some kind of terrier and I'll tell you which makes the most noise.'

'I expect it's the terrier,' Henry told him. 'In my experience they usually have ideas far above their size and station.'

'Find anything interesting?'

Henry gestured towards the table. 'I'm not certain,' he said. 'This is evidently a space where she felt comfortable, but interestingly she didn't deem it safe enough to keep the gun hidden here and besides she probably wanted that to be in the house. There are enough small items that puzzle me, though, and make me think she has not left her old life behind entirely.'

Mickey looked interested. He plonked himself down in one of the easy chairs and pulled the table closer. Henry sat on the other chair and watched as Mickey inspected the little collection.

'Postcard from Brighton, signed Felicity. A business card, for a solicitor. And another, now that is interesting, for a private detective agency. What's this, a little bunch of pressed violets? The sort of thing a lover might give to a woman and she might keep but not necessarily want her husband to know about. Where did you find it?'

Henry reached into the bookcase and withdrew a book that had seemed out of place. 'It is a history of the French

Revolution,' he said, handing it to Mickey. 'And it has a dedication on the flyleaf, though I'd not really thought it might be important as it seems to be much older.'

Mickey flicked open the book. '"To my dearest George, Christmas 1892". Martha Mason would not even have been born in Christmas 1892. But there could be a family connection perhaps. It's a pity there is no last name and no address and no bookplate. Nothing that may guide us, in fact.'

'And apart from your liking for their dogs, did you gain anything from the neighbours?'

'Nothing that the constable hadn't already told us. No description to speak of, they thought it was a man of about average height, and on hearing the dogs he ran down the garden and leapt over the wall at the bottom. It's high but not impossible and there are trees and a bench which make it easier to climb.'

Henry nodded. Very easy, he thought. He took a manila envelope from his pocket, unfolded it and slipped the objects he had found inside. And then they walked back together to the house. Henry wished he had more bodies to help with the search but knew also that there were few he would trust to do it properly, especially here where he did not know the local constabulary. But Sergeant Emory would be helpful, he thought. And there was a telephone in the house, from which he could call the station and summon Emory and anyone else that he thought appropriate. He suggested this to Mickey who agreed.

'Emory strikes me as a solid man,' he agreed. 'And it is a big house for two people to go through.'

Mr Otis Freeland had observed the comings and goings of the murder detectives with great interest. His colleagues in the press were unknown to him – mostly they were local or from major Midland publications and he was as yet the only novelty, come up from London.

That novelty had brought him a number of questions the previous evening, lubricated by offers of liquid refreshment that he had happily taken up.

Yes, he had been able to tell the curious, he knew the

identities of the two murder detectives and yes, he had observed their work at close quarters. Both had enviable reputations, Otis revealed, and he had spent a companionable evening recounting to various members of the Fourth Estate tales of previous Henry Johnstone exploits. He had observed the frantic, scribbled notetaking of some and wondered how his tales would pan out once they made it into print. He was only too aware that he may be providing copy for more than one of the local dailies, there being little to report about this current crime.

He in turn had asked about the Masons and the Phillipses and about the history of the little market town in which they all found themselves billeted.

And, of course, everyone and his dog had a pet theory.

'Mark my works it'll be one of them gyppos.'

'Reece and his folk are showmen, not gyppos. And he keeps a tight rein on his people. He makes too much good money here to risk it on trouble.'

'Well, it won't be a local. When was the last time we had a murder round here?'

'Ay, but like as not it's someone come up by train.'

'Robbery gone wrong . . .'

'But what was the woman doing up in the paddock? Up to no good, if you ask me.'

'Well, no one did! Mrs Mason was a good soul. A respectable sort—'

Otis listened to it all. He knew about Reece, had in fact met the man on occasion and travelled for a short while with cousins of his, and occasionally used these contacts to carry messages, but he didn't mention that here. Among this company, Otis was just another hack trying to scrape a living. Eyebrows, both sympathetic and derisory, had been raised when he announced himself to be a free agent, selling his stories where he liked or where he could.

This morning he had been up early, walking and watching as the small town awakened. He had seen Henry and Mickey collected in the police car and taken to the infirmary. Had seen the more bleary-eyed of his colleagues assembling after breakfast and then, guessing at the inspector's next destination, had found himself a nice spot from which to observe the Mason house and by purest chance overheard a conversation between neighbours about the attempted breaking and entering of the night before.

Interesting, Otis thought. And now at least he was aware that there were dogs. Aware too that there was a faulty lock on one of the rear windows.

Seeing the detectives arrive and ensconce themselves for the duration, Otis took himself for a walk. Earlier he had wandered around the workhouse grounds, taking in the layout and the exit points and deciding on his best play. He had slipped inside the infirmary building, assessed the easiest route to the mortuary and left with a green canvas jacket that he had noted was used by the few orderlies already working.

The jacket was concealed beneath a hedge at the perimeter of the site. He headed back there now, strolling contentedly in the early summer sunshine with his camera stowed in a larger bag and nothing to suggest that he was not a local man of the middling sort on perfectly legitimate business.

Sergeant Emory arrived about half an hour after Mickey had summoned him, bringing with him a young constable who looked very daunted to be in the presence of superior officers. Emory introduced him as Constable Potter and suggested that while Henry and Mickey make up one team, he and Potter should make up a secondary one and he could teach the young man the ropes while they were about it. Mickey agreed in principle but suggested that Potter accompany him while he photographed and also dusted for fingerprints where the intruder had tried to gain access the night before.

Emory also had news. The surgeon had called the police station just before he had left with a message for Chief Inspector Johnstone and his sergeant. There had been no surprises in stomach contents, rate of digestions and so on and Mrs Mason was in good health but there was one thing that deepened the sadness of the situation. Martha had been pregnant, perhaps no more than ten weeks' duration and it was even possible that she was not yet aware of this. Certainly no one had mentioned it, and Henry thought it would have been a very natural thing for somebody to mention. He doubted very much that the woman had been unaware; in his, admittedly, very limited experience, women knew there was something not right very much sooner, and most suspected pregnancy much more quickly than the doctors could confirm.

So why wait? Was she concerned that her husband might disapprove? He had heard of a friend of his sisters who, after three miscarriages, had told no one about the subsequent pregnancy until it was halfway through – though many had presumably guessed by then. She didn't want to jinx it, Cynthia had told him. Thankfully this one was delivered safe.

He remembered what Nora had said about Martha being good with children, and his sense then that this had been a delicate subject and one which she regretted having raised.

He put the puzzle aside and told Emory that he wished for another look at the master bedroom before moving on elsewhere. Emory obediently followed him up the stairs.

'It's a nice place this. I remember it was just tenanted before, and quite rundown it was getting. I think we were all glad when someone decent moved into the place and more pleased still when we found out that it was a doctor and his wife. Someone respectable. It doesn't take much for an area to go downhill, but I'm sure I don't need to tell you that.'

Henry nodded but didn't trouble to reply, and noted that Emory seemed unfazed by his lack of response. 'I wish to go through the contents of the desk again,' he told Emory. 'I would like you to inspect the husband's wardrobe. Our examination was somewhat cursory the first time, though I doubt we'll need to spend long on this room.'

'Anything particular you'd like to keep an eye open for?'

'Letters, bills, business cards – anything of that sort. Just lay them out on the bed and anything not relevant we can put back.'

They worked in silence for a time, or at least almost silence. Emory hummed contentedly to himself, which amused Henry, but he noted that the man was doing a very thorough job, turning out pockets, looking beneath drawers and beneath the newspapers that had been used to line the base of the wardrobe. Henry turned more careful attention to the woman's desk, laying out separate piles from each drawer and cubbyhole on the bed and then checking for secret compartments. Satisfied that the desk was thoroughly solid and had no secrets in and of itself, he pulled up a chair at the side of the bed and used it like a table to lay out what he'd found so far. After a time, Emory joined him, though his haul was not so great. A few receipts, a piece of paper torn from an envelope with an address scribbled on it, a cinema ticket for a film, *Piccadilly*, that Emory remembered being on in Newark a few weeks before. 'About a dancing couple, if I recall correctly.'

Henry discovered that Martha Mason had liked fancy stationery – nothing expensive but pretty notecards. There was a household account book in which everything was itemised and Henry put that aside. He was surprised to find that the bank statements were also on her desk rather than in her husband's keeping, as was the cheque book for her husband's account. But there seemed to be nothing else that was unexpected that would give Henry any further clues.

He replaced the items from the desk and told Emory to do the same, retaining only from this stash the envelope with the address scribbled on it. He assigned Emory to look through Martha's wardrobe while he inspected the chest of drawers.

'Pay particular attention to the pockets of coats and dresses,' he said remembering that his own investigation had pretty much come to a stop when Mickey had discovered the contents of the shoeboxes. Once again, anything that might be of interest was placed upon the bed.

The chest of drawers seemed to contain only clothes, but Henry was interested to find that the newspapers lining these were not local. He removed the pages, interested to know that they too came from a Brighton newspaper, so that south coast connection seemed to be maintained. The newspaper in question was only six months old.

'Nothing much to report,' Emory said, 'but I did find this.' He held a slip of paper. 'And it's not a local telephone number. It was pushed into the corner of this evening bag.' He paused and held the bag up for Henry's inspection. It was white metal mesh, with a small chain. Looking closely at it Henry doubted it was silver though it was lined with a nice purple silk.

Examining it closer, Henry came to the conclusion that Martha had probably lined the bag herself. The stitches were neat but he thought it unlikely that they had been professionally done and besides, these chainmail bags were usually unlined.

He looked at the telephone number. 'Definitely not a local number?'

'It doesn't look like the local exchange. No, my guess is it would be a trunk call to make this.'

'Have it checked,' he instructed.

Carefully Henry ran his fingers along the lining of the little bag and he frowned. He found his pocketknife and used it to cut through the stitching where the lining was attached to the mesh. Emory watched with interest. The lining turned out to be doubled and created room for a pocket in which, laid out flat, were a quantity of notes. Emory laid out eight, large, white, five-pound notes, at Henry's instruction being careful to handle the money by the corners just in case prints could be found.

Interesting, Henry thought.

'It's almost as though she wanted to be ready in case she had to run away, if that's not being too fanciful,' Emory proffered.

'I do not think you are being fanciful at all,' Henry told him. 'I suspect that is exactly why she hid this money. We know that she had charge over the household accounts, but five pounds is a quantity that would be noticed, and she would have had to repeat the embezzlement on several occasions to have accumulated this much in cash. A few shillings here and there, a few pounds over a period of time, but—'

'So if it did not come from her husband, where did she get it? Do you think she had it before she married him?'

'It is possible. Yet another mystery to solve. Sergeant Emory, I think it is time for me to go and pay a visit to Dr Mason.'

Otis had walked straight into the infirmary and turned towards the mortuary. He wore the green canvas jacket over his own clothes and felt somewhat hot and restricted by the tightly woven and heavy cloth. One glance at his trousers and shoes would reveal he was not an orderly but Otis knew from experience that people take little notice of individuals who seem to be about legitimate business and so he was not gravely concerned by this.

The mortuary was down in the basement and the white-tiled rooms were quiet and empty. He had little trouble in finding the body of Martha Mason.

He turned on the lights, hoping not to need to use the camera flash bulbs, but in the end, after taking several pictures without, he risked the flash for one final shot, focusing on the wound that had killed her so efficiently. The searing brightness worried him. He hurried away before anyone could investigate the sudden brilliant light showing through the basement windows, high up in the white-tiled walls.

He paused only to kick the remnants of the flash bulb – still too hot to touch – beneath a convenient cabinet and then he switched off the lights and he left.

He removed the jacket as soon as he left the basement, dropping it on a convenient chair, the scant disguise being no use to him now. He heard voices drifting from an adjoining corridor but saw no one and moments later was out in the daylight and walking back towards the road, camera stowed away once more in the capacious bag.

Henry went alone to the Phillips' house. If Mickey had been surprised that his boss should leave him behind to continue the search with these two local officers, he didn't give any indication. Henry knew that Mickey usually mitigated what was often referred to as Chief Inspector Johnstone's sharpness and lack of tact but, Henry thought, sometimes sharpness was exactly what was required to get answers.

The maid at Dr Phillips' house announced him to Nora, who told him that her husband wasn't present, but if he'd come to see Dr Mason, well Clive was sitting in the garden reading a book.

Henry told Nora he could find his own way but was aware that she stood watching him as he headed out of the French windows and into the garden. In some ways this house was just a larger version of that occupied by the Masons; it was as though a mirror image had been attached to the side of the Mason house and a duplicate built twice the size for the Phillipses.

He found Dr Mason sitting beneath the shade of a tree in a folding canvas chair, not reading the book that he had laid on his lap. He looked up expectantly when he saw Henry. 'You have news for me?'

'Nothing that can tell you who killed your wife. I'm sorry, but we are no further with that yet. However, there are two items I wish to discuss with you. You know that your wife was in possession of one of these chainmail-type evening bags?'

Dr Mason looked puzzled but nodded. 'Yes, she rarely uses it because she complained that the links caught on her clothes. I suspect it was not the best quality. She bought it before we were married.'

Henry frowned, suddenly diverted by a thought. 'And you bought the bag that she had on the day at the races? The one with the butterfly clasp.'

'I purchased that for her. It was a Christmas present, this last Christmas. I felt that she had gone without nice things for so long, while we were trying to build our business together, that she deserved something nice. Nora helped with the purchase. Why do you ask?'

Henry didn't answer directly, and instead said, 'Are you aware that your wife liked to conceal money? I realize that this perhaps stems from some insecurity, and that you may be fully aware of this, but—'

'Conceal money? I don't think I know what you mean. I told you that she might have a five-pound note hidden in a handbag, just in case of emergencies, but—'

'In fact, she had two concealed beneath the stiffening at the base of the bag. But we found a considerably greater amount in this little mesh bag. She had made a pocket in the lining – did she sew the lining of this herself?'

Mason just looked confused now. 'I believe so. Inspector, what is all this about? What money? My wife had no money of her own, and while I ensured that she had sufficient house-keeping and pin money, of course, she showed me the accounts weekly. I tallied them with my bank statement then gave these into her keeping. There is no way that she could have hidden something from me.' He shook his head. 'It is possible, of course, that she kept a little back from the housekeeping or that she kept a little back from her allowance, but it will only have been a little. We are less frugal than we have been, but we still must be careful if we are to pay all our bills. I have not been supported by others as has Ephraim. With the help of Nora's family, he was able to buy a practice that mostly served wealthy elderly ladies and their various ailments, imagined or not. Ephraim's main purchases for his pharmacy are the makings for sugar pills and nerve tonic. As for my own patients, many are working people who must save to see a doctor and do so only in extremis.'

'And are you jealous of his good fortune?'

Clive Mason looked shocked. 'Of course not, he's my friend. He and Nora have been good to us and he frequently directs patients my way – his practice becoming a little unwieldy, he rarely adds to his list these days.'

'But no doubt, the less well-off patients,' Henry observed.

'Chief Inspector, what are you saying to me? My wife is dead, you should be getting to the bottom of that, not impugning a friend.'

Abruptly, Henry changed tack. 'Why did you not tell me that your wife was pregnant?'

The colour completely drained from Clive Mason's face. He stood up suddenly and then as suddenly sat down again and for a moment Henry thought that he was going to faint. This was not quite the reaction that Henry had expected.

'She can't have been pregnant.'

'You mean you didn't know? I thought doctors would have noted this sort of thing.'

'No, she can't have been. I don't understand this. There must be a mistake. A cyst perhaps, though she had not complained of anything.' He seemed genuinely at a loss.

'The surgeon who examined her is perfectly competent. Your wife was pregnant. The duration of the pregnancy was between ten and twelve weeks, he believes, and yet you tell me that you did not know. Perhaps she confided in Mrs Phillips?'

Clive Mason seemed to have difficulty in getting his breath. He was shaking his head in the most agitated fashion.

'You don't understand,' he said. 'Martha and I, we did not have that kind of marriage. We rarely even shared a bed, I usually slept in the study. I love my wife, deeply and dearly, but she knew from the very beginning that my inclination . . . my inclinations did not . . .'

'Are you celibate? Or are you simply not interested in the fairer sex? Dr Mason, I will not be shocked by this – revelations of this kind are hardly new to me. I have met such perversions many times and I do not *entirely* disapprove of them. I have come to understand that some men are simply made that way.'

Mason looked even more shocked but finally he nodded in acknowledgement. 'I loved Martha, I love her still. I would do anything, give anything, to have her back beside me. But I had no idea that she was seeing someone else and certainly no idea that she was with child.'

'And if she had told you?'

'I suppose I would have been devastated. I'd like to think I would also have accommodated the fact. If she felt such need for a child, then . . . Inspector, I am aware that I may have been deeply unfair to this young woman who became my wife and who had all of the normal needs of her sex.'

'And yet you still married her.'

'I needed a wife. She needed to *be* a wife. I suppose at its simplest, Chief Inspector, we both needed the respectability of the marriage. And it worked for us – or at least I thought it did.'

A small movement caught Henry's eye and he realized that Nora was standing in the doorway and looking out at them. She was too far away to have heard their conversation, but she was looking concerned and a moment later she stepped aside and the maid came out with a tea tray and Nora followed with another chair.

'I thought you might like some refreshments,' Nora said brightly. She looked from one man to the other, realizing that something was going on that she didn't know about and that it was serious. 'Have you brought news, Inspector?'

'Nothing that can improve the situation,' Henry said. 'Forgive me, Mrs Phillips, but I would prefer to speak to Dr Mason alone.'

'The subject matter is not really for a woman's delicate ears,' Clive Mason said. He sounded hesitant and even to Henry didn't sound as though he meant it, but Nora merely nodded and Henry decided that she was probably used to being excluded from male conversation.

'Well, I'll leave you to it then,' she said.

Henry sat down in the second chair. A little colour had returned to Clive Mason's face and it was clear that Nora's interruption had given him time to gather himself.

'And did you have relations outside of your marriage?' he asked bluntly.

Clive Mason closed his eyes. 'If this gets out it will ruin me,' he said.

'I'm aware of that, Dr Mason. I have no wish to ruin anyone. You will not find me as virulent as many in my profession. Human frailty concerns me only when it harms others and just now I wish only to find out who killed your wife. If your proclivities have no bearing on that issue then no one will hear about them from me, or from my sergeant. If, however . . .'

'I've had no relations outside my marriage, or at least not here. Occasionally I go down to London, or even to the south coast. I . . . indulge myself a little. I have friends of long-standing, who share my tendencies.'

'And it was on one of these trips that you met your wife. How is it that she married you, understanding what you were? Or did you only tell her after you were safely married?'

'I told her, but I don't think she fully believed it. I think like many people she believed that the love of a good woman could cure me and in the first months of our marriage we both did try this . . . cure. I wanted to love her completely as a wife is entitled to be loved. In the end we realized that we must be content to be friends, married in every other way. Inspector, if she sought love elsewhere then I feel I have pushed her to it.'

Henry nodded. 'Most assuredly, I would think. Would she have believed that you might have accepted the child?'

Clive Mason looked shocked and then shook his head. 'I have no idea, though I suppose in order to avoid a scandal I might have done. That would hardly have been a good foundation for a happy home, would it.'

'Like the foundations you have already laid,' Henry said coldly. 'Does Dr Phillips know your—'

'No. I thought once that he might suspect, but it has never been discussed between us and I doubt he would allow me to stay in his house if he thought this were true. In his eyes, I might corrupt the innocent simply by my presence.'

'And yet you are friends.'

'And yet we are friends. I do not expect pity, Inspector, but we all must survive as best we can and most of us have things to hide.'

'It seems you and your wife both did,' Henry agreed. He stood. 'I found two business cards in your wife's effects. One for a solicitor and one for a private detective. What would she be doing with those?'

The pallor returned to Clive Mason's face and he shook his head violently. 'I have no idea.'

'It seems you have little idea about your wife at all. She had a gun, she concealed money from you, the source of which cannot be validated, she perhaps also sought the services of a solicitor and a private investigator. She was undoubtedly engaged in a romantic and sexual liaison. It seems to me, Dr Mason, that you knew almost nothing about your wife.'

He paused, his hand resting lightly on the back of the chair, aware that Nora was watching from the window and that no doubt she would report back to her husband that Henry had upset their guest. Questions would be asked; he hoped Dr Mason was up to evading them. As he had assured the doctor, he had no desire for anyone's ruination – provided they had not done harm to another, though he was aware that his views were out of kilter among those he worked with and that had another detective been called, Dr Mason would no doubt be about to face prosecution. Evidence would have been found, even if his affairs had been undertaken well away from home.

'Your wife was a busy woman, with her committees and her good works, so it is most likely that whoever fathered the child is among your friends and acquaintances or among those with whom she served on these committees. Make me a list please, Dr Mason, of anyone, man or woman, with whom she was close or indeed that she chose to avoid.'

Dr Mason looked puzzled. 'Avoid?'

'It is my experience that people often overcompensate when they are trying to hide an affair. They publicly avoid or even demean the other person in order to put others off the scent. Your wife was a clever woman from all accounts – it is quite possible that this is the course she took in order to conceal her affair. You can tell your hosts that I came only to inform you that your wife was pregnant – that will account for your obvious shock and devastation. Unless they were aware of the affair, they will have no reason to suspect that it is not your child she carried, and even if they suspect, they are hardly likely to tax you with their suspicions at this time. Add that I also sought a list of friends and acquaintances. Ask them to make the same so that we can crosscheck. It may be that Mrs Phillips is aware of friendships that you are not. In my experience, women often are and also in my experience women are often very conscious of when another strays.'

Henry saw the look of gratitude in Dr Mason's eyes and felt that Mickey would approve of his handling of this interview. The thought amused him. Henry had it within his gift to completely ruin the doctor but what good would that do? Henry had seen enough good men ruined and it was in his mind that Dr Mason was not a bad man, simply somewhat misguided.

He took his leave then, pausing to tell Nora Phillips that the doctor had received more bad news and to ask her if she would make a list of friends and acquaintances and request that her husband should do the same as this would help with the investigation. Nora Phillips, eyes wide, nodded. 'Martha was a popular woman,' she said. 'Everybody loved her.'

Something in her tone caused Henry to pause, and he said, 'Mrs Phillips, if there are any, what you might deem, inappropriate relations, you understand that you must still tell me about these. Sometimes even happily married women can be led into temptation. No one is immune to foolishness.'

She looked shocked. 'That is a ghastly thing to suggest,' she said. 'But Martha was a very beautiful woman and sometimes . . . sometimes people try their luck, I suppose you might say.'

'And did someone try their luck with Martha?'

Nora was retreating quickly from even this vague statement. She blushed and was relieved when one of the children came running into the hallway to find her. 'I will give it thought, Inspector,' she said as she took the child's hand and allowed herself to be led away. The maid saw Henry to the door, eyes downcast, and Henry wondered what she had overheard. 'And are you in agreement that everyone loved Mrs Mason?' he asked bluntly.

The girl coloured violently. 'Sir, I'm sure I have no opinion on that.'

'Of course you do,' Henry told her. 'My sergeant and I are staying at the Saracen's Head, should you wish to give that opinion air.'

She would not look at him as he moved past her to the door. He could see that she was genuinely shocked that he should even speak to her like that. She stared at the floor, her body rigid, her demeanour radiating something that Henry thought might be disgust.

He wondered if she would tell her mistress.

Henry was driven back to Dr Mason's house, where the search continued. He noted that it was past two in the afternoon and that no doubt Mickey would be telling him that it was time they all took a break. He decided that he and Mickey should go back to the hotel and have a late lunch there and also discuss what Henry had discovered. They had yet to talk about the letters that Henry had read the night before, the contacts from the address books and the appointment diary.

This murder, Henry thought, was never going to be simple, happening as it did in a place where witnesses were not likely to come forward, the population on race day being by its very nature a transient one. The one thing in their favour was that the victim of this murder happened to a woman that everyone accepted was a good wife, and model citizen, and that might well bring witnesses forward. Henry decided that they could cultivate the local press, allow them to create a mood of outrage and anxiety that would serve to encourage 'decent' people to come forward, one of their own having been brutally killed, there being a hierarchy to victimhood as there was in every other aspect of society.

Personally Henry doubted there was any such thing as a model citizen or anyone without something to hide – he agreed with Dr Mason on that – but in this particular case it also seemed there were more possibilities for the perpetrator of this murder and more reasons for it than had first appeared.

SIX

Mickey had left Sergeant Emory and his constable to continue with the search that he was increasingly thinking would now be fruitless. They had found the things that were important and Mickey had obtained fingerprints – two very clear prints, in fact, just where he expected them to be, on the handle of the French windows. They would have to obtain elimination fingerprints from Dr Mason, and from the daily maid who worked for the household, and also from Mrs Mason's body, but Mickey was willing to bet that these were from whoever had tried to break into the house.

'Of course, that's no help to us unless they have a record,' Mickey said.

They had returned to the hotel and had sandwiches and coffee sent to Henry's room, this being the larger of the two bedrooms, and Henry had explained to Mickey all that he had learnt from Dr Mason and almost learnt from Nora.

Mickey shook his head. 'It's a bad business,' he said, 'no matter how you look at it, and I do pity men like Dr Mason. The acting profession of course gives shelter to many and Belle has introduced me to a number, over the years, of perfectly decent men who have sadly been born with this problem. And I do believe people are born with it, there is nothing can be done to change their minds or to change their inclinations.'

Mickey's wife, Belle, was a successful actress who travelled frequently with her company. Henry nodded. 'And I'm inclined to believe here that it may well have been a cause of problems in their marriage, but not of the murder. Unless you take it that the man with whom she was having the affair is the murderer and that she would not have *had* the affair had her husband been otherwise more attentive in the marriage bed. But even in marriages where this is not a complication, husbands and wives go astray and for a variety of reasons. I think you would have been proud of me, Mickey, I offered my commiseration and I do not believe I was too harsh in the questioning of the man. I don't suspect him, at this stage, in being in any way engaged in the death of his wife. The look on the man's face, Mickey, even I could read that amount of grief.'

Mickey laughed out loud, then nodded sympathetically at his boss. 'And the letters written between Martha and her husband? In light of what you now know, do they read any differently?'

Henry picked them up and studied them thoughtfully. He opened one and handed it to Mickey. 'It occurred to me last night they could be letters simply between close friends. At the time I assumed that perhaps Dr Mason wished to maintain proprieties. After all Martha Edgerton as she was then was a younger woman and one he had not courted for long. The whole business from meeting to marriage was a mere eight months and while we know that people do marry hastily, considering this was a long-distance relationship I would almost have expected it to take more time to reach the conclusion of marriage.'

Mickey peered sceptically at him. 'You do have some strange ideas,' he said. He skimmed the letter, which was from Dr Mason to his intended and was written some three months before their wedding. 'Does he always sign off with "fondest regards"?' he asked.

'I believe so, as does she. She opens her letters more often than not with "my dearest love", or simply "dearest", and as you can see the letters are open and affectionate and talk of everyday events.'

Mickey read a few lines out loud: '"Last night we visited the theatre and I have to say that it was not the best performance I have seen. The leading man stomped around the stage and waved his arms in what he no doubt believed was an eloquent manner, but which did look as though he was scaring birds. I would have employed him as a scarecrow but as a romantic lead in an Ibsen play, oh for goodness' sake, no."'

He read on for a little and then said, 'If this is typical, then I would agree that they do seem to have been close friends.

As for affection shown between a man and a woman, you could no doubt look at letters between myself and my wife and see them also as letters simply between friends. We've been together long enough for our affections to be known and understood without flowery language. Belle knows well enough she is my right arm, a sounder woman you would never be likely to meet. I'm more interested in what this doctor's wife would be doing with a solicitor and a private investigator. What would she need a detective for? Why all the secrecy? Hiding money, the gun and now we know having an affair. Though I suppose I've answered my question, perhaps she meant to run away with this fella that she was seeing. As for Nora Phillips, d'you think she knew about it? D'you think she knew about the baby?'

'I get the impression she knows about something, but she's either not certain or not ready to tell. I think we need to get Nora Phillips on her own for her to confess what she knows.'

'Well, I doubt she knew that her husband's friend was a pansy,' he said, grabbing a ham sandwich from the thick pile Henry had placed on the chest of drawers. 'You want more coffee?'

Henry held out his cup. 'Both business cards, that for M. Giles, Esq., the solicitor and that for Conway, the private detective, look old and worn. And the addresses are both down south. One in London, one in Brighton, so these cards are likely from her life before. If that is the case, why did she need their services back then and why keep them for all this time? Mickey, does Belle sign her full name when she writes letters to you?'

'You mean does she sign Mrs Isabella Hitchens – no, I can't say she does,' he chuckled. 'Thinking about it, she usually just signs *B*, with a kiss.' There were no such kisses on the doctor's letters or on Martha's, he observed, but did that actually mean anything? And Martha Edgerton simply signed herself as *M*, but was that relevant either?

'The big question for me,' Mickey said, 'is if the killer knew that she was pregnant. If he did that makes it ten times worse in my book. Whoever the bastard was, he felled her like a cow sent for slaughter, no hesitation. One blow' – he mimed the action – 'smashed through the skull and into the brain. Poor woman never stood a chance.'

'Did she go willingly to what turned out to be her death, expecting something else?' Henry wondered. 'So what possibilities do we have?' He ticked them off on his fingers. 'The first is that this was a random act, by some equally random thief.'

'An option we can all but ignore,' Mickey argued. 'Nothing was stolen so far as we know. Unless she had something on her person that he wanted, of course. Which would still beg the question: how did her bag end up under a bush a good five minutes' walk from where she was found?' He took another bite of his sandwich and chewed thoughtfully.

'The second,' Henry continued, 'is that the husband found out about the affair and had her killed. I think that's unlikely. I believe that man is grieving and whatever the foundations for their marriage, I believe he cared for her. Besides, if we are simply looking at the evidentiary possibilities, he's a doctor and I have no doubt that he could find ways of disposing of an unwanted and unfaithful wife.'

'Doctors always come under suspicion if there is the possibility of poison being administered,' Mickey pointed out. 'No, but I agree the husband is less likely. I put it towards the bottom of my list. You would have to be a very cold beggar indeed or a much better actor than the one she described in the Ibsen play. So we'll put him to one side for the moment. Friends likewise, I don't see that either of the Phillipses would be involved in this, so let's put those in the same box as the husband and focus on the more likely.'

'The father of her child.' Henry sat down on the bed, adjusted the pillows and lent back against them, coffee cup in hand. Mickey could almost see the cogs whirring in his boss's brain. 'I have requested that the husband and the friends give me a list of other acquaintances and associates. It will be interesting to see how they compare. Speaking of which, have you compiled a list from the address books and the appointment diary?'

'I have indeed,' Mickey said, 'and given it to Emory. The locals will contact each name on the list, with instructions to ask when was the last time they saw Mrs Mason and also where they were on the day of her death.'

Henry nodded. Good enough. This was something that could easily be handed over to the local constabulary and then followed up later when they had the information from the doctors and from Mrs Phillips.

'The lover I would put at the top of the list,' Mickey said. 'What's the betting he is a married man not likely to want to be saddled with an illegitimate child? Whatever Dr Mason says, I can't see anyone willingly raising the child of another. And that's the other thing, she must have known that once he found out she was pregnant all of this would come out. She could hardly fool her husband into thinking that it might be his, if they never had relations. I've no doubt that a lot of men unknowingly raise such a child as their own, but this is hardly your typical case, is it?'

'Which brings us to the third option. Or possibly even fourth . . . But the third option is that something has followed her from her past life, into this one. Some misdeed or something she was running from. Dr Mason said something curious, he said that he *needed* to be married and so did she. They both sought the respectability the married state offered. His need I can understand, but now I think about it, why particularly did she need it?'

Mickey shook his head. 'There doesn't need to be a *particularly* about it. Life is tough for women unless they have a husband. Not so many can make it on their own, there are still none of the well-paid jobs open to them that a single man could go for. I don't suppose it is so bad when you're young, but as you get a little older and can foresee your middle years and your old age, the future can look very bleak indeed if you're a woman alone. I suspect a lot of women marry a lot less comfortably than this Martha, just for the assurance of keeping body and soul together. How many unfortunates do we meet up with, day-to-day, who have fallen into such a state because the marriage has broken or the parents have died and there are no family members to care for them and they have failed for whatever reason to make shift for themselves in any respectable way.'

'And yet many women do manage it,' Henry argued. 'Look at Malina Cooper as an example of this.' He was thinking about the girl who was now his sister's private secretary but who, very much like his sister, had fended for herself from her teenage years.

'And she is the exception that proves the rule,' Mickey said stoutly. 'For the doctor and his wife to have got together, worked as a team in the way they have, shows each capable of affection and consideration for the other. The obvious friendship. She must've valued that and yet she still goes off and finds somebody else. Something doesn't make sense here.' He shrugged. 'But then there is not one of us that can't be impulsive – except perhaps you. And I've known you to be so on occasions.'

'So, something from her past,' Henry reiterated. 'Something for which perhaps a solicitor and a private investigator were required. Question is do we go down south immediately to look into these two men, or do we trust local colleagues to do it for us?'

'I think we should remain here for a day or two,' Mickey said. 'We can send a telegram to Central Office and ask for investigation to be made, a background search to be done and all papers to be forwarded to us here. We need to talk to friends who are in the here and now, not in the past, eliminate those from our enquiries first. At least that's my feeling. At least shake this lover loose, see what he has to say for himself. Once we've eliminated the easy answers, we can, if it proves necessary, go searching for the more complicated possibilities.'

Henry agreed that this sounded sensible.

'You said you thought there was a fourth possibility?' Mickey questioned.

'That she saw something on the day of her death which led directly to it, and which had nothing to do with the lover, the baby, the marriage or the past. You and I both know what goes on during race days. Criminal gangs are everywhere, and Mrs Phillips mentioned that Mrs Mason understood or at least claimed to have understood the signals of the tic-tac men. It is possible she had knowledge of something or someone in the criminal fraternity and that she recognized them or they recognized her or that she saw something untoward.'

Mickey considered. 'All things are possible,' he said. 'But we should shake down this lover first and if we discover that he is a butcher with his own killing yard behind the shop, and that there is blood that is not from cattle on his poleaxe, then I will go home a happy man.'

SEVEN

Sergeant Emory joined them for breakfast the following morning. He had with him the list of contacts, collected from the Phillips residence, and also the preliminary reports from the enquiries that had been made by the local offices the previous day, establishing when Martha Mason's friends and acquaintances had last had contact with her, and where they had been on the day she had died.

'I'm not sure what you said to Mrs Phillips, but she is in a right mood with you,' Emory reported. 'She said something about you questioning her servants without her being present.'

Henry shrugged. 'I asked a simple question as I was leaving,' he said. 'I received no response that was worth the candle, so I see no harm done. Besides, she does not own her maids.'

'No, but she does own their discretion,' Mickey observed. 'You did put the poor girl in a difficult position with her employer. Do you think she knew anything?'

'Of course she did. You know as well as I do that people say things in front of those in service that they would never say to what they consider their equals. Those who serve them become invisible and unconsidered and even the best employer forgets that they have ears and eyes.'

'Well, Mrs Phillips is in a right tekkin' and that's no mistake,' Emory told him. He seemed amused at the prospect. 'Fortunately she don't seem to blame the young woman for you asking questions of her. There's some employers can take even the asking of questions the wrong way and answering would certainly have been a sacking offence.'

Henry thought about that and then nodded. 'I should have been more discreet,' he acknowledged. 'But there was something in the girl's demeanour that told me she was aware of what was going on and could have useful information.'

'Well,' Emory said, 'I know the family, and I'll have a word with her mum. If there's anything to be got out of her, her mother will do it and will do it discreetly enough. She won't want the girl to lose her place.'

Mickey was scanning the list that Emory had brought with him. Sergeant Emory had helped himself, as instructed, and now set about his bacon and eggs and sausage with great gusto. Henry poured him some coffee. He took the lists from Mickey and examined them himself.

'To save time, we should divide the list into three. First it needs cross-referencing and then we need some local advice, Sergeant. I propose that as a well-known officer, you choose from the list any names of individuals that are personally familiar to you and you and your constable attend to those interviews. I will draw up a list of questions. Mickey and I will divide the rest between us – and I promise not to question any of those in service without their employers being present.'

'Did anything interesting arise from the preliminary enquiries?' Mickey asked, helping himself to another piece of black pudding, cutting a section and then dipping it into the satisfactorily runny yolk of his egg.

'There were of course many expressions of concern and horror, as you'd expect, those marked have seen the young woman in the last week and I have put an M for those she met at the charity meetings she attended, and an S for those she met socially or casually. There's three without alibis for the time of her death, as you see one is a vicar, one is Lord Elliston who cannot remember if he was still at the races at that time and will confer with his wife. He confesses to being three sheets to the wind and that his valet brought him back to his car and his chauffeur drove him home. Not a usual state, it has to be said, for Lord Elliston, but we can probably dismiss him as a man both too easily recognized and also too easily drunk.'

'And the third?'

'That the third is more interesting, gentlemen. Mr Harry Benson, known to the Masons and the Phillipses and a member of at least two of the committees on which Mrs Mason served. He is a trustee at the workhouse and he is also on the medical board that oversees the local hospital. He is a man of some status and a private income, left to him by his father and also his uncle. He also has a reputation for being fond of the ladies with a particular liking for the married ones.'

'Interesting,' Mickey said. 'And he has no alibi for the time of Mrs Mason's death.'

'He claims to have been at the racecourse with friends all day and then home alone in the evening. It was his house-keeper's day off, it being a bank holiday and Mr Benson it seems being a model employer. His housekeeper was at the racecourse with her sister and she told me that when she returned home around six her master was nowhere to be seen, so she assumed he had gone out to dine somewhere. She apparently suggested that he could have been asleep in his room – apparently she didn't check. He'd already told her he needed nothing preparing for the evening so she accepted an invitation to go to her sister's house. She did not return till after ten, by which time Mr Benson was back home again and *definitely* in his room. She heard him snoring when she went to her own.'

'And you suspect him of being Martha Mason's lover because of his reputation alone?'

'And also because Mrs Nora Phillips made certain that I noted the name. She pointed out some special friends of Mrs Mason's, not saying the names aloud because her husband was present. The other three were female. So I'm not saying . . . But it is indicative, perhaps.'

'I think my sergeant and I need to attend to that one together,' Henry said. 'Was there anything else of note?'

'Two people volunteered that Mrs Mason seemed out of sorts in the past week, not quite her lively self. Mrs Stevens, who also serves on the hospital committee, mentioned that she actually arrived late for a board meeting, which was most unlike her. She is normally the first to get there and help serve the tea and the coffee and liked to spend a few moments in conversation with all of the other committee members before they begin. Mrs Stevens hinted that perhaps she had been very unsettled in this last few weeks and had twice felt sick. Of course Mrs Stevens and the other ladies of the committee discussed the matter and speculated . . .'

'That she might have been pregnant,' Henry finished.

'Indeed. It's my experience that women are often aware of these things almost before the mother-to-be,' Emory chuckled. 'And as Mrs Stevens observed, the Masons had been married for some years and there had been no sign.'

'You said two people commented that she had been unlike herself,' Mickey observed.

Emory poured himself some more tea and nodded thought-fully. 'The second subject worthy of a visit is an elderly lady, Miss Georgia Styles, something of a *grand dame* around here. I believe in her youth she was even presented to the king and had her season in London. Anyway, she rattles around in that great barn of a place called Magpie Lodge just beyond the workhouse, on the way out to Upton, and she told my constable that Mrs Mason called on her last week rather unexpectedly, making some excuse about the arrangements for a charity ball which were going to be discussed anyway at the meeting later in the week. She considered that Martha Mason was on the verge of explaining something to her, and those are the words that, according to my constable, she used. "Explaining something to her", which seems an odd choice of words, does it not.'

'And she did not elucidate?' Mickey asked. 'Would you say she was a precise old lady, which is say that she has all the marbles still?'

'Oh yes, sharp as a tack,' Emory assured him. 'Though she's got to be ninety. Has a live-in housekeeper that's not much younger.'

'So, Martha Mason seems to have had something on her mind – no surprise considering the child she carried. I have to wonder how she planned to get out of this. Emory, if this Mr Benson happens to be the father of her child, in your opinion, would he be likely to have stood by her?'

Emory paused before answering. He looked suddenly anxious, Mickey thought, and then, as though suddenly making up his mind, he shook his head. 'There are rumours about the man,' he said. 'That this would not be the first time he got some girl in the family way. I suppose this is why he prefers to involve himself with married women; less consequences should the worst happen. At least they have husbands to take the blame for their condition.'

'So he could not have known about Mrs Mason's predicament,' Henry mused.

Again, Emory seemed hesitant but then he agreed. 'If the rumour mill is in any way correct, he's the sort of man who would take advantage of such knowledge,' he said.

'You mean blackmail?'

'I can't say for certain and I don't reckon to listen too close to gossip, but—'

'Gossip is the meat and drink of the detective,' Mickey told him comfortably. 'Speaking of which, may I bag that last sausage?'

He didn't, Henry noted, give time for an objection before it was speared and sliced. 'So . . . blackmail? That would be a risk for any woman coming into his clutches.'

'I never said he was a pleasant man, only a rich and, to his own class, a charming one. The woman who keeps house for him is a widow. A no-nonsense type of woman, and I doubt very much he's tried his luck there. He employed a young maidservant who disappeared rather unexpected, like. Came back to town some months after but never settled. Too many gossiping tongues. And another who went away for good. He now has the housekeeper and daily woman who comes and helps but I heard tell the housekeeper threatened to pack her bags if he should try and employ another young'un. So like as not he only plays away now. It was after that the wagging tongues have it that he moved on to those that were married and there's talk about three or four – not Mrs Mason, though. There's also talk about him having the connections to solve such situations, should they occur again.'

'You mean he procures an abortion,' Mickey asked, low-voiced.

'It's just talk,' Emory said carefully. 'There's a woman on Church Street in Newark, used to be a midwife. We've raided her place a time or two but can prove nothing. Then there's a doctor out at Burton Joyce rumoured to be willing to assist in such situations but he's a man of influence and it's also rumoured that he's done the deed for some very high-born types and so considers himself well protected. We're fortunate, I suppose,' Emory continued wryly, 'that both of these alleged procurers of abortion have some degree of skill and knowledge. I pounded the beat in Nottingham for close on nine years and saw the results of such butchery as I'm sure so have you gentlemen.'

'Indeed,' Mickey agreed.

'About Dr Mason,' Emory began, a little hesitantly, Mickey thought. 'What you know about him—'

'Need go no further. The man no doubt lives in fear of discovery. I don't regard him as a suspect in his wife's murder, not at present, anyway. He is well alibied and if he falsified his grief when I spoke to him – well, *I* should be looking for another profession. If the evidence does turn his way, then I will consider again, but for now, even though I could arrest him for his proclivities alone, I've no evidence that he's acted upon them and don't have the time to spare to discover it, should the evidence exist.'

Emory nodded wisely. He looked, Mickey thought, somewhat reassured.

'So, Chief Inspector, if you should give me my list of names, I'll get on with my work,' he said.

The next five minutes had been spent in dividing the list. Henry was content to make use of Emory's local knowledge for this task and, saving only that Benson and the elderly Miss Georgia Styles be kept as their own task, allowed Emory to guide the division of labour.

Once he had gone, Mickey and Henry readied themselves for the work of the day. Benson would be visited just after lunch when, Emory suggested, he was most likely to be at home and Miss Styles would be left until later in the afternoon because 'she visits in the morning, likes to take a little nap in the early afternoon but always takes afternoon tea at four'.

Mickey, in the meantime, would take car and driver and visit those houses and businesses in Newark and outlying villages and Henry would concentrate his efforts on Southwell – the town being small enough to walk around without effort.

Henry and Mickey Hitchens reconvened just after one and made their way to the house of Mr Harry Benson, the man they suspected had been the father of Martha's child. Somewhat surprisingly he opened the door to them himself, accompanied by two dizzy, enthusiastic spaniels who sniffed their shoes eagerly.

'Gentlemen, it must be the police. Yes, I've been expecting you, come on inside. Coll, Spence, away with the pair of you.' He pointed a finger at the dogs who obediently scurried off down the corridor. 'They need their exercise,' Benson said. 'As do I, gentlemen, so I hope this won't take too long.'

He led them into a well-furnished room at the front of the house. A deep bay window was occupied by a window seat and this is where Benson sat. There were books around the walls, but they looked old and a little dusty and Henry doubted that Benson read any of them. A gun cabinet filled the wall next to the fireplace and photographs of Harry Benson posing alongside the corpses of various kills adorned the walls. He saw Henry looking and came over, jabbing one of the photographs with a stiff forefinger. 'Bangalore,' he said, 'and this—'

Henry cut him off. 'How well did you know Mrs Mason? We understand that your relationship with her was more than casual.'

Benson looked momentarily taken aback then he gathered himself and said bluntly, 'Of course it was, my dear chap, served on committees together, didn't we? I'm one of the hospital trustees. She was an excellent fundraiser and will be much missed for that.'

'Just for that?'

'No, of course not. Thoroughly decent woman. I like that husband of hers as well. Thoroughly decent chap, undertakes a great deal too much charity work if you ask me. I know it's good for the soul and all that, but not so good for the pocketbook.' He leaned in confidentially towards Henry. 'Money always a bit tight for them, if you know what I mean. Not that it's good form to discuss things like that, of course.'

'Were you having an affair with Mrs Mason?'

Harry Benson's mouth opened and closed several times as he stared at Henry. 'I say, I say, not the sort of thing to ask a chap at all. I understand you're a policeman, but common decency, you know.'

'A woman is dead, Mr Benson. The niceties tend to be

dispensed with during the murder investigation. The only thing that matters is to get to the truth of who the killer is and how we might best catch them. So uncomfortable questions have to be asked and so I ask you again: were you having an affair with Mrs Mason?'

Benson sat down beside a small table on which was set a decanter and several glasses. He poured himself a stiff drink and swallowed it. He seemed to be giving himself some thinking time. Mickey paced the room, examining the book-cases and the photographs and even the gun cabinet. Henry stood very still, waiting for Benson to respond.

'We were friends, certainly. I would not wish to impugn a lady's honour.'

'The lady is dead. I doubt she cares. And I care only to find who caused her death. You need not worry for your reputation, Mr Benson, it is already well established that you are a woman-izer and it is rumoured that you have fathered children. Your relationship with Mrs Mason will be kept quiet if at all possible, but only to protect her husband and her friends. Those worthy of our protection. But I ask you again, were you having an affair with Martha Mason?'

Henry could see that Mickey was quietly examining the contents of an open roll-top desk that stood on the other side of the room. He shifted position, sitting down without invita-tion in the winged armchair opposite Harry Benson. Steadily, he held the man's gaze and it was Benson who looked away quickly and his face flushed with embarrassment and anger. 'It was a brief thing,' he said. 'A very attractive young woman, and I didn't think her husband was paying sufficient attention to her. She seemed lonely and we were much thrown together when organizing a charity ball last year, or some such thing . . . Truthfully, I hardly remember.'

'I think your affair lasted longer than that,' Henry said quietly. 'Did she wish to break it off, and you did not? Was she blackmailing you perhaps?'

Benson was on his feet now, the glass falling from his hand and crashing to the floor. It was quality crystal, heavy and solid, Henry noted, and it did not break on the thick hearth rug but merely bounced and rolled away.

'I say, that's a dreadful thing, a dreadful thing to—'

'You knew that she was pregnant.'

'I heard rumours that she was pregnant, certainly, and so, and so . . .'

'But she is unlikely to have been blackmailing you about that,' Henry said. 'She is the last person to have wanted that to be revealed, that the child might be yours and not her husband's. But I suspect she was in some way threatening your equanimity.'

'All right, our affair did continue intermittently. Until just a few weeks ago when she decided she wanted to break it off, and I agreed. I was getting bored anyway. And then she told me it was because of the child, and that she must attend to her husband's needs, and that of their new family. I told her I understood. I gave her a little money, a trifle, not blackmailing you understand but just to help . . . I know this must've been a difficult time, an expensive time for anyone who is expecting a child. A gift, no more.'

'Where were you on the day she died? You were not at the races, I understand.'

Harry Benson laughed. 'Everyone who was anyone was at the races along with quite a few who weren't anyone,' he said. 'Of course I was there, in company for most of the day. I had a flutter or two, and broke even in the end, so a good day, a good day.'

'You told the constable that you were home alone.'

'No, he must have been mistaken. I was at the racecourse, with a number of friends. I told you, we had a fine old time.'

'Not so fine for the woman you had been intimate with. Where were you between three and five in the afternoon?'

Benson was incandescent now. His face red, his arms flailing. He reminded Henry of the actor described in Dr Mason's letter.

'Please sit down, Mr Benson,' Henry said sternly, and to his surprise Benson obeyed.

Mickey had moved away from the desk now and was studying a large display case fixed to the wall. Henry glanced briefly at it but did not want to draw Harry Benson's attention away. It seemed to contain various weaponry including one that Henry briefly noted was an assegai.

'So, do you have an alibi for that time?'

'Of course I do. Not that I should need one. Absurd to think.'

'So who were you with?'

'Hardly remember. But ask among my friends and cronies, someone will know. We were all a little cut by then. My chauffeur got me into my car and brought me home somewhere around six, I would think. There had been brief mention of meeting for dinner somewhere, but the truth is I fell asleep in my chair and that was it. When I woke up it was past midnight and I took myself off to bed. I didn't hear about this dreadful business until the following day.'

'So in essence, you have no one to vouch for you during that time.'

'I need no one to vouch for me. You come here asking these questions. It was someone who sought to steal from her, that was all. Tragic and all that, but a random act. To suspect someone like me—'

'A fine collection of weaponry,' Mickey said from across the room. 'Something would appear to be missing though.'

'Missing? What on earth do you mean?'

Henry looked curiously at his sergeant, surprised at the interruption to the interrogation. He followed Benson, who was now scurrying across the room to see what Mickey had meant. The case was large, floor-to-ceiling of the kind found in museums with a green baize backing and small handwritten labels affixed against each exhibit. It was quickly evident there were two or three gaps where something had been removed. Harry Benson blinked several times and then took off towards the door of this study, planted himself in the hall and yelled for his housekeeper.

'The sun has faded the green,' Mickey pointed out. 'There would appear to be three things missing. A curved weapon that looks something like a sickle. From the shadow I would say there was a Katar, an Indian push dagger, and that last looks to me like a medieval halberd.'

Henry nodded thoughtfully. It did indeed. An axehead pointing in the one direction with a tapering spike on the other, the spike at right angles to the axe.

A woman came bustling into the hall, the spaniels now twining around her legs. 'Whatever is the matter, sir?'

Benson marched back into the study and the woman followed. 'The meaning of this, Mrs Richardson?' He pointed theatrically at the display case and at the missing items.

Mrs Richardson looked completely puzzled. 'The meaning of what, sir?'

'Someone has been in here and removed items from this case. Someone has stolen from me.'

Mrs Richardson, a tall, stout, robust-looking lady turned on her employer. 'And how might I notice that, sir,' she said with some asperity. 'Since I'm not allowed even to come in here to dust.'

Mrs Richardson turned on her heel and marched out, much to Mickey's amusement.

Benson, thoroughly embarrassed, began to bluster. 'Been with me since . . . She was my nanny, if you must know. Seems to think she still is.'

'Mickey . . .' Henry indicated for his sergeant to follow the redoubtable Mrs Richardson. For a moment Benson looked as though he might object but then he thought better of it and sat down. He was not the most intelligent of men but he was bright enough to realize that this did not look good for him and said so to Henry.

'When did you last check this case? And is anything else missing? It looks to my eye as though there are three items gone, would you agree? And where is the key?'

'The key is generally in the lock. I have a tendency to lose these things, so I just turned it and left it there. As to how long ago these items went missing, I have no idea. I come in here of an evening to take a drink and to smoke a cigar. As you can see the gun cabinet is kept locked and no I did not leave the key in *that* lock. Those keys are in Mrs Richardson's care,' he admitted shamefacedly. 'She locks up at night also. Occasionally I have a little too much . . . too much to drink of an evening.'

'And so anyone could have got into this room, got into that cabinet, extracted your exhibits and made use of one of them to kill Martha Mason.'

He watched as Harry Benson's face changed from crimson to blue white and back again as the implications suddenly dawned. 'You think she was killed with something from my room.'

'The profile of the weapon used would fit something like the halberd that you had on display.'

'Halberd. Yes, I had one of those. Yes, that is missing. But I never . . . I never even handled the damn thing. This was my father's collection. Give me a gun and I'm a happy man, but as for the other stuff, well . . .'

'How many people knew about your collection?'

'Anyone could have known who has visited this house. I consider it my private space, even Mrs Richardson is not allowed into dust and clean, she moves and tidies and while I don't mind her doing that in the rest of the house, in here I consider it my sacred space. But the door is not locked. Anyone could have come in here.'

'But there is a key to the door?' Henry asked.

'Of course, I expect Mrs Richardson has that too, in the key cabinet in the old butler's pantry. There's no woman of the house, so we don't entertain very much, and Mrs Richardson tends to most of my needs. Then I have the chauffeur. I share him with Bertie Adams, over at the Lodge – it doesn't make any sense for us both to have a chauffeur when one will do. It is rare we both need the car at the same time and if we do, well, we come to an accommodation.'

'And was this Bertie Adams with you at the racecourse that day?'

'Some of the day, certainly.' He rubbed his eyes and said, 'To be truthful, Chief Inspector, the day is something of a blur.'

'Convenient,' Henry returned. 'Now, you will go to Mrs Richardson and you will ask her for the key and any other keys she might have to this room. This room is to be locked and the key given to my sergeant who will return later and will examine the room for fingerprints and any other evidence. I hope for your sake, Mr Benson, that he finds other prints here.'

'Are you going to arrest me? I will inform my lawyer, nothing will stick.'

'The key, Mr Benson.' Henry's tone was chill.

They left shortly thereafter. Mickey had spoken briefly to the housekeeper and the room was now being secured.

'You think he did it?' Mickey asked.

'Do you? No – had the woman been shot then he would have been an immediate suspect. I think our man likes to view his prey from the distance that a bullet will fly. I'm not certain that I see him clubbing a woman to death with a medieval weapon. That seems theatrical, unnecessarily so. As you said before a butcher's poleaxe would make a kind of sense, but this? And what also troubles me is that two other weapons were taken. This is a rural area, shotguns would be easy to obtain. If he wished someone dead then opportunity surely would arise to shoot them and have done with it. But no, Martha Mason was lured away from her friend and killed with a most unusual weapon – that is if our assumptions are correct and the halberd was the weapon used. It could be just more misdirection. But if it was, then something troubles me even more. The other two weapons that were taken, were they a mere distraction or are there two more intended victims?'

'Distraction, I would hope,' Mickey said.

The next appointment was with Miss Georgia Styles. She was indeed a very elderly lady, but spry and bright and with very clear grey eyes. Mickey took to her immediately.

'I usually take tea at four,' she told them, 'but I'm quite content to take tea twice in an afternoon. Company is always welcome.'

A grey-haired woman opened the door and wheeled in a chrome and glass trolley on which was set tea, cakes and small sandwiches. The rather modern piece seemed at odds with the heavy Victorian furniture in the small salon.

'Thank you, Ellie, dear,' Miss Styles said. She leaned confidentially towards Mickey as the elderly retainer departed. 'Ellie and I usually take tea together in the afternoon. I know it's a little unconventional, but the truth is she has become more of a companion over the years than a housekeeper. We read to one another of an evening and listen to the radio.' She clasped her hands delightedly at the thought. 'Oh, I do enjoy my radio.'

'So do I,' Mickey agreed.

'You told the constable that Mrs Mason came to visit you last week and she seemed about ready to tell you something, but then never did.'

'Oh dear, that poor girl.' Miss Styles dabbed at her eyes with the corner of her napkin. 'Chief Inspector, may I ask you to pour the tea? Arthritis in my hands makes it painful. Now, Martha. No doubt you have discovered by now that she was having a relationship with a man that she should really have ignored and avoided.'

Mickey and Henry exchanged a glance.

'I may be old, my dear, but I still have all my faculties, and I have the experience to know when a marriage is not all it seems. Now, Martha and her doctor, they were very much in love but there was something not quite right about that relationship, and sometime in the middle of last year I became aware that she was restless. Eventually she did confess this to me and the consequences of it. Like many young women, I don't think she was prepared for the strictures of marriage, or for the realities of marrying a country doctor still so early in his years of practice. They were not well off, you know, but Clive Mason really is a lovely man. He won't turn anyone from his door if they are in need of help and he encourages them just to pay what they can afford. It's very admirable but of no help when you're trying to run a household. I knew there were some months when Martha struggled to pay the rent on time. So when this rich man comes along and pays attention to her, well it's enough to turn anybody's head and we've all been young and foolish.'

'You're talking about Mr Harry Benson,' Mickey asked. He would not usually have revealed how much he knew, but he felt that this elderly lady deserved to have him be straight with her.

Miss Styles stared at him in horror and then laughed out loud. 'Oh, goodness, is that what you think? She didn't succumb to Harry's blandishments, did she? Oh dear Lord. I suppose the man can be charming and fun when the fit takes him. I did warn her about him and she told me not to worry. That her involvement was with someone else entirely.'

Mickey and Henry exchanged another glance. 'So who are you talking about?' Mickey asked.

Henry placed the tea on a little table. She thanked him and then leaned forward to add small sandwiches and tiny cakes to a china plate decorated with blue forget-me-nots. 'Please help yourself, gentlemen. No, you surprised me about Benson. So the minx was encouraging more than one gentleman. That was unwise, don't you think? I did like her, though, she had such spirit, and she worked so hard.'

'You can't have approved . . .' Mickey commented.

'My dear, when you have reached such a great age as I have, approval and disapproval seem such insignificant emotions. Whether I approve or disapprove of anything in the world will make no difference whatsoever. Whereas the pleasure of good conversation and a lively mind, such as Martha Mason had, will make a great difference to the quality of one's life. I hoped she could confide in me and she often did, although it seems not about everything.' She pursed her lips somewhat sadly and then sipped her tea, deep in thought.

'And you have no idea what it was she wanted to' – Mickey consulted his notebook – 'explain to you, was I think the phrase used.'

'Unfortunately she chose an afternoon when we were interrupted twice. Once was a trivial matter, some travelling salesmen or other trying to sell me stockings. Then the unexpected arrival of Anne Finch, that's the vicar's wife, who when she saw that Martha was here, settled herself in for a long and meaningful talk about the flower rota or some such. There is a stupid woman. So no, Martha didn't tell me what it was she had come to explain. And I only wish she had because it seems to me that it was important to her and may have had some bearing on this dreadful mess. I had the feeling, at the time, that she wanted to tell me about her . . . affair of the heart but she didn't get the chance. Who would want to kill Martha? This is what I cannot understand.'

'And you didn't see her at the racecourse?'

'Oh no, my dear, I have a nice little spot, high up in the stands. Ellie and I made our way up there with our picnic and we watched the proceedings from that eyrie. We're both of us too infirm to go traipsing around the place, but we do enjoy watching the horses and the liveliness of the atmosphere and friends know they can come and visit us in our little spot, and we had the most wonderful day. I'm just so sorry about Martha. No, I am beyond sorry that Martha is gone. I will miss her deeply.'

They talked for a little longer and Miss Styles promised that if she had any further thoughts she would not hesitate to contact them. Mickey then collected the murder bag, with all of his forensic equipment, and returned to the home of Mr Harry Benson to collect whatever fingerprints were available. Henry set off to consult with Emory and then to return to the hotel. There was, he thought, much to think about now and much of it was totally unexpected. This murder case was becoming more complex by the hour.

EIGHT

Henry arrived at the Saracen's Head to find a telegram had been sent from London. Enquiries had been made at the place Dr Mason had told them his wife had worked as a typist in Brighton before they had married.

Henry read the telegram twice and them borrowed the telephone at the reception desk and made a trunk call to Scotland Yard, eventually being put through to the sergeant who had sent him the telegram.

'I spoke to their personnel department and to two of their managers,' Henry was assured. 'They checked their records twice for me, and then spoke to an ex member of staff who'd run the department when your woman would have been there and also looked at all their records, just in case she'd not been a typist but worked in some other department. No one called Martha Edgerton ever worked for them, not in any department. They only have a couple of general office girls at any time and *part* of their job is as typists. Most of their staff is male and most are in the accounts departments or in dealing directly with the imports and exports licences and they share private secretaries, but she's not among them either. Crick & Son specialize in managing all the administration for smaller companies that want to import goods or export them. They even telephoned companies they had dealings with eight to ten years ago to see if this Miss Edgerton worked for them, but no joy.'

Henry spotted Mickey just entering the small reception area. He asked a few further questions and then thanked his colleague. He hung up and beckoned his sergeant over.

'More mystery,' he said. 'Martha Edgerton did not work as a typist for Crick & Sons in Brighton. No one there knows of her. So either Mason is lying to us or she contrived a major lie to him.'

'Another one,' Mickey said.

*   *   *

Nora Phillips was not pleased to see them. She glared at Henry but held her tongue and, dismissing the maid, took them through to her husband's study where Dr Mason was catching up with his correspondence.

'Everyone has been very kind,' he said, indicating the pile of letters that he was endeavouring to answer. 'But I have to admit, it's a bit of a struggle finding something to say in return.'

'I'm sure it is.' Mickey nodded.

Henry was not interested in conciliation. 'Why did you lie to us, Dr Mason?'

'Lie to you? I can't think what you mean.'

'Your wife did not work for Crick & Son before you married. Nor did she work for any of their associates. There is no trace even of a Martha Edgerton on the electoral register and certainly not at the address you informed us she lived at with friends. The address in question is a florist shop with a flat above, occupied for the past ten years by the florist's parents.'

Dr Mason stared at Henry but there was nothing in his face of the honest, grief-stricken reaction that Henry had observed the last time he had come with news. Mason had known all this. 'You think we wouldn't check, Dr Mason?'

'Truthfully, I never thought of it at all,' he said slowly.

'You'd better explain yourself.'

Dr Mason set his letters aside, took off his reading glasses and rubbed his eyes wearily. 'I told you what Martha told me when we first met,' he said. 'I never questioned it. Then one day I had an unexpected reason to be in Brighton. The colleague I had covered for previously had once again fallen ill and had called upon me. I had taken an early train and was not expected at the surgery until that evening and it occurred to me that I'd have time to meet Martha beforehand. Perhaps meet her from work. So I went to Cricks and I asked for her. No one had heard of her or recognized the description I gave.

'So I went to what she'd told me was her home address. The address I sent letters to and which she claimed to have sent her letters from. As you say, it is simply a flower shop. I was quite angry by then and the woman who owned the shop was, I think, somewhat alarmed. She told me that Martha had her mail sent there and collected it once or twice a week. This was a business arrangement and one this flower seller had with several people, mostly travelling and commercial salesmen who called in to collect instructions from their companies. But also a few private individuals who for one reason or another could not or didn't wish to have letters sent to their homes. She was paid a small fee for acting as an effective post restante and so I don't think she asked too many questions. She had a family to support, frail parents and a brother who had come back from the war suffering from shell-shock and was not much use for anything after. He helped out in the shop and did deliveries for her but was in this way also dependent.'

'And did you confront your fiancée?'

'Well, there was nothing I could do. I had no means of finding her. I have to say, Inspector, that I was terribly hurt and determined to break it off, and so I wrote this to her in a letter. She wrote back to me, very contrite and anxious that I should think so badly of her.'

'And did she have an explanation?'

Dr Mason nodded. 'She was working for a firm of solicitors and she gave me a telephone number so that I could confirm this. She was working as a general office assistant and had a small room, a bed-sitting room, which was in the same building. She believed that I would have judged the job not quite respectable.'

'And why was that?'

'Because the firm specialized almost exclusively in divorce cases. You can imagine . . . Well, I called them and they confirmed that Martha was in their employ but you see my dilemma.'

'When you married the lady, Crick & Son was a more respectable cover than a sleazy company that helped procure divorces,' Mickey said. 'With all the dirt that entails.'

'Well, quite.'

'Which does not explain why you lied to us,' Henry said coldly.

Dr Mason stared down at his hands. 'My wife is dead,' he said finally. 'If anything you have discovered comes out then her name and mine will be dragged through the mud. Every tabloid newspaper in the country will delight in this horror, this whole sordid enterprise. I may only be a country doctor, but you know how scandal feeds, gorges itself, when the person involved should be judged above all reproach. Doctors have the trust of their community and it is just the kind of story that the worst elements of the press would relish.

'My friends will abandon me, and Martha's name will be trampled beneath their feet. I will most likely be struck off. Truthfully, Inspector, I had lived with this fiction we created for so long that I'd almost forgotten that was what it was. And with the shock of all this . . . But you are right. I should have been more honest with you.'

'Is there anything else you've lied about?' Henry asked.

Mason shook his head. 'I've told the truth about everything that seemed important,' he said. 'I did love my wife. I would do anything to have her back here with me now. Even knowing that she had been unfaithful – I don't feel that I can fully blame her for that.'

'So, he lied about that . . . d'you think he *did* lie about anything else? That his grief was less believable?' Mickey asked.

Henry thought about it and then shook his head. 'Mickey, I know I'm not always as acute as you in reading raw emotion but there was a world of difference between his reaction to this and his reaction to my telling him that his wife was pregnant and also to the way he reacted on the day she was found, according to what the witnesses to that have told us. We'll have more information tomorrow, I hope, about the firm of M. Giles, Esq. And at least we know why she had the business card for that company in her possession. Considering the usual methods employed by such divorce agencies, I think we can guess how the card belonging to Mr Conway the private investigator came into her possession. The question on my mind now is was Martha Edgerton merely an office girl or was she more deeply embroiled in this sordid world?'

Over supper they discussed what Mickey had found when he returned to Benson's house.

'I lifted some clear prints,' he said, 'and I photographed

others on furniture that could not be removed. On brief examination they do not appear to match either Mr Benson's or the housekeeper's but that does not mean they could not be from another random visitor. Benson tells me that he entertains in that room from time to time and if the housekeeper's not allowed to dust, the prints could have been there for quite some time. He does not look to me to be a man who cares about his surroundings and indeed the dust got in the way of my print taking.'

'Do you think there is any significance in the missing three weapons?' Henry asked.

'I certainly hope not. I hope it is simply misdirection. And there is no absolute proof that the weapon taken, the halberd, was the weapon used to kill her. It could still be a rampaging butcher or it could have been an ice pick – that is something easy to lay hands on and easy to conceal. It occurs to me that a medieval weapon of the size suggested by the gap in the display case, would be hard to hide about your person. It would hardly fit in a suit pocket.'

Henry had been thinking the same thing and he found it an oddly reassuring piece of logic. 'If asked to speculate then, a heavy-duty ice pick would have been my first thought. Not the small ones to keep on a bar top, but the more robust kind kept in a butler's pantry to break the ice before it's brought to table.'

'In which case, what's happened to the weaponry stolen from the case? If it is random, is it unconnected? And when did it happen? Benson seems to have been totally unaware of the loss until you pointed it out to him. Had there been children around it would have occurred to me that it is the kind of theft a boy might indulge in. Something done in a moment of impulse, and then, however much repented, you have the difficulty of how to return such things.'

'Let us hope it is something as innocent,' Henry said.

It was not long after they had finished eating, and Henry had returned to his room, when a message was brought to him and a few minutes later he and Mickey were on their way to a small side street off The Westgate. It was not fully dark but there were a few people around on this quiet street and, conscious that they had been asked to be discreet, Mickey tapped softly upon the door. It was immediately opened and a rotund, short and grey-haired lady ushered them inside. The door opened straight on to the front room. A young girl had been sitting in the front parlour, but she stood up as soon as Henry and Mickey came inside. Henry recognized her immediately as the servant he had questioned briefly at Nora Phillips' house, an action which had caused her mistress a great deal of annoyance.

'I'm Nellie Richardson,' the older lady said. 'And before you ask, my sister-in-law is the Mrs Richardson who is housekeeper to Mr Benson, and who I understand you've already met.'

Henry acknowledged that they had.

'This is my daughter, Grace. You'll forgive this being a little cloak and dagger, but it won't do a girl's reputation any good to have the police around.'

'And will it do the mother's reputation any good?' Mickey could not resist.

'I'm a little beyond worrying about that, gentlemen. Anyone has anything to say, they can say to my face. But Grace has to mind her manners. She has a good place with the Phillipses and we neither of us want it threatened. And you did put her in a difficult position, sir. A young woman in service has no right to answer questions that her mistress does not approve of. You should know that.'

Henry apologized and Nellie Richardson nodded as though satisfied. 'Well, sit yourself down, the kettle is boiling and I will make some tea. And Grace will tell you what she wants to tell. This is her evening off, so she won't be missed, and you can talk to her a while, but I don't expect any harm to come from this. Am I making myself clear?'

'Crystal,' Mickey assured her.

Grace sat back down in the chair that she had occupied when they arrived. It looked slightly out of place in this little front room and Henry guessed this it been a discard, either from the Phillips' house or somewhere similar. It was upholstered in a deep blue and spoon-backed, with a low seat like a bedroom or nursing chair. The other two, a touch battered and the leather scuffed, were both wing chairs and he guessed they'd probably had a similar provenance. He took one and Mickey the other and when Nellie bustled in a few minutes later she fetched a dining chair and plonked herself down on that, folding her hands in her lap and looking inquiringly at the visitors. It was clear that she intended them to see to their business and then be gone, as quickly and as quietly as possible.

Grace busied herself with pouring tea and Mickey sensed she felt better keeping her hands occupied and her face turned away from them. 'I don't want to gossip,' she said softly, 'but that Mrs Mason, she was a lovely lady, really nice and always kind to me and Maudie. Maudie lives in at the Phillipses. So I don't want to speak ill of her, and I certainly don't want to speak ill of the dead.' She paused and handed Henry his tea. 'It's unlucky to speak ill of the dead,' she added.

'But the dead can't speak for themselves,' Mickey told her. 'So it's up to those still living to do it for them. And if you know something that had a bearing on Mrs Mason's death—'

Grace looked at her mother who nodded firmly. 'You've started now, my girl – you shouldn't start anything you can't finish.'

Grace picked up a cup and saucer with hands that were trembling slightly and handed this to Mickey. Her mother leaned forward and helped herself.

'Mr and Mrs Mason seemed like a lovely couple,' she said. 'But Mrs Mason was a very pretty lady, and sometimes men would not leave her alone. They would wait till her husband was out of the way and then make nuisances of themselves, say things that . . . that you really should not say to a respectable lady. Make suggestions.'

'With this at the Phillips' house?'

'Yes, but not just there. You see, sometimes Mrs Phillips took us, me and Maudie, to help out at functions. Charity events and the like, when they needed extra service. She used to tell us to keep at arm's length from the men because she said when men have had a drink inside them, they can be like octopuses. I'm sure I've never seen an octopus, but I now know what she means. Like they have limbs everywhere. And girls in service, they think we're fair game.'

'And I've always told Grace, an accidental heel in the instep will slow just about any of that down. The man catches you off balance and you happen to step back, well, it's his fault, isn't it?'

'It is indeed,' Mickey agreed. 'And how did Mrs Mason cope with their attention? Were there any particular men?'

'Mrs Mason always behaved like a lady and once when someone was really bothering me, she came over and she took them away, and she told them to leave me alone and most of the time . . . most of the time she managed to keep them at a respectable distance, if you know what I mean. But some men, they won't take no.'

Again, she glanced at her mother for reassurance. 'Get along girl, these gentlemen don't have all night.'

'And in particular?' Mickey asked. He drained his cup and set it down on the tray. 'Which men were in particular annoying?'

'Well, of course there was Mr Benson, but he was like that with all the ladies. Especially when he got a drink or two inside him. Not that I've ever seen him when he hasn't had a drink or two inside him. Even when he rides to hounds, I don't think he's sober then.' She bit her lip and added, 'I wouldn't talk out of turn like this, but you two are police, not people, if you get my meaning.'

Mickey told her that he did. 'And apart from Mr Benson.'

'Mum.' Grace looked really uncomfortable now.

Her mother sighed heavily. 'She don't like to say, seeing it's her employer she's talking about.'

'Mr Phillips?'

'The very one. Persistent, that's what you call it. Persistent. Especially when his poor lady was expecting her last one, heavy like she was expecting twins she was. And from very early on. We reckoned she be having twins but it just goes to show, you never can tell, little Noah was the sweetest, tiniest little imp of a thing, but Mr Phillips was a flaming nuisance all the way through. Thinks just because a girl is in his house that he has the right to put his hands anywhere.'

'Mum!' Grace was blushing.

'Well, he did. If it had carried on then, I would have made Grace find another position somewhere. As it was, I had a quiet word with Mrs Mason who had a quiet word with Mrs Phillips and it all stopped.'

'But I thought it would get me the sack,' Grace said.

'Better to get the sack than end up in it,' Nelly said sternly. 'You've got a nice young man sweet on you and when you've got money together between you, then you'll marry respectably. For now you have a secure position but that doesn't mean you should end up like that poor girl that worked for Mr Benson.'

Grace looked distinctly uncomfortable now.

'And did you get the impression that Mr Phillips got his way with Mrs Mason?'

'I wouldn't like to say.'

'Of course you wouldn't. I can understand that you don't like to gossip. You have to understand that this is a murder enquiry and you must not withhold anything that might be evidence.'

Grace swallowed nervously. 'I saw them once. She was in Mr Phillips' study and he had her pinned up against the desk. She had her hands on his shoulders like she was going to push him away but . . . but it was more playful, like. I thought she must be flirting with him and I thought to myself, Gracie, she's playing a dangerous game. But he was saying things to her like, you know we've always looked after you and Clive. You've got a lot to be grateful to us for, and I thought that was a really underhanded thing to say. I really, really did.'

'And him, playing like he's so respectable,' Nelly said.

'And did you get the impression that things went further?'

'I don't know, sir.' She looked even more uncomfortable now as though she was regretting this decision to say anything. 'You must think I'm a terrible gossip. I'm really not. It's just that Mr Clive, Mr Mason, he's been staying at the Phillipses and he's been so unhappy. He misses her so much and he's so full of praise for the Phillipses being kind to him and it just went against the grain, you know? Knowing what Mr Phillips really wanted in return for the kindness. Is it really kindness if it's got so many strings attached, that's what I want to know.'

Nellie Richardson stood up and began to collect the pots together, stacking cups and saucers back on to the tray and it was clear that she considered her daughter had done her duty and that was an end to it. 'I'm sure we can to rely on these gentlemen's discretion,' she said. 'Now you know about this, I'm sure we can rely on you for it *not* to have come from our Gracie. There will be other people will have seen and other people will gossip about it. And if you want evidence of more people gossiping about it, then you need to go and talk to old Miss Styles. She had words to Mr Phillips on more than one occasion for inappropriate behaviour.' She put great emphasis on the last two words and Mickey suspected that she had heard them from someone else and purloined them for her own use.

Henry stood and picked up his hat. 'Thank you for the information,' he said. 'If I might just ask one question. You talked about Mr Benson and that he has a reputation with the ladies and that he has—'

'Got more than one into trouble,' Nelly confirmed. 'One went away claiming she got a job somewhere else, but we all knew. You could see from her face when she came home again. And another, poor little thing, well, she disappeared altogether. Her mother was heartbroken. Rumour has it she went to see some woman, you know, some . . . woman who promised to help out. All I know is she never came back home and her mother was never the same again. Nor her father. They kept saying she'd just gone away, gone to stay with an aunt or something.'

'And she might have done.' Mickey felt the need to play devil's advocate.

'Seeing as both her mother and her father were only children, I very much doubt that.'

They left the Richardsons' home with the names of the girls that Benson was accused of getting in the family way, though what they were going to do with those names Mickey really had no idea. Tragic as the consequences might have been, unless the fate of the second young woman turned into a bone fide murder enquiry, it wasn't really in their purview.

'So, Dr Phillips was after his friend's wife,' Mickey commented.

'So it would seem. I wonder if he got his way.'

'We've not yet considered the blackmail angle.'

'Do you think it's worth considering? If she ended up having an affair with either of these men, and we certainly know that she had an affair with Benson, it's unlikely she would blackmail him to keep quiet about something that implicated her as well. Or do you mean that Phillips or Benson might have been involved with someone else? Someone who might cause trouble if their relationship with Martha came out? To do so would surely have laid herself open to accusations. Either Benson or Phillips might have sought to ruin her by letting her husband know or simply beginning some vitriolic talk about her. You know how fast gossip spreads, even gossip that has no foundation. And as a doctor's wife, she needed to be seen to be a pillar of the community, especially in a small town such as this where everybody appears to know everybody.'

'True enough, I just think we should keep all angles open. It will be interesting to see what further information arrives concerning M. Giles Esq. and Conway, the private enquiry agent.'

NINE

The following morning Mickey took himself off to the local chemist who had promised him space for the processing of his crime scene film, the wonderful timbered construction that was the Saracen's Head having no facility that even the usually ingenious Mickey could improvise as a darkroom. The Tudor building had small rooms and plumbing that was basic and somewhat scant, and Mickey could not justify inconveniencing a number of guests, just so that he could process his film in a bathroom. He had been told by the pharmacist that several gentlemen of the press had made similar arrangements and that he had charged each of them a small fee, just to cover the inconvenience.

Apart from the fingerprint camera, which was Metropolitan Police issue, most of the camera equipment that Mickey used belonged to Henry. Mickey travelled well-equipped but there was a limit to the gear that two men could transport. Mickey was therefore glad to make use of the kind offer from the pharmacist to make use of a back room – especially as he had said that he would waive his fee for the murder detectives.

Henry, meantime, had taken the advice of the redoubtable Nellie Richardson and had gone back to see Miss Styles.

'You were lucky to find me in,' Miss Styles told him. 'I usually reserve my morning for visiting, whether people wish to receive the visit or not,' she chuckled to herself. 'One of the few advantages of old age, Inspector, is that when you choose to do exactly what you wish, people put it down to venerable eccentricity and not just what might be termed bloody-mindedness.'

'It's probably fair to say that most people we visit do not wish to receive one,' he said.

'I imagine not. However, I am not most people and I am quite happy to receive you. But I don't imagine you have come here purely to be social, so what can I help you with?'

'It seems to me that Martha Mason confided in you perhaps more than was usual. You knew, for example that she was having this relationship—'

'Relationship is that what you call it. You are too kind or too sentimental, Inspector.'

'You told us you didn't know she was involved with Mr Harry Benson. In fact, you claimed not to know who she was having a relationship with. But I believe you had your suspicions regarding who that might be. Did you suspect that she was having an affair with Dr Phillips?'

Miss Styles tapped her fingers impatiently on the arm of her chair and considered the inspector thoughtfully. 'I thought it was possible. Yes. But I didn't know for certain, you understand. Martha did whatever she had to do to survive,' she said. 'As a young woman with few advantages apart from her own common sense and intelligence and a measure of attractiveness, she made shift where and how she could. My consideration is that she did so honestly.'

'Which does not answer my question. It has been drawn to my attention that Dr Phillips may have—'

'Oh, Dr Phillips certainly wanted to,' she said. 'Dr Phillips was . . . Well, he behaved very badly, that's all I can say. Clive Mason was meant to be his friend. His close friend. His confidant. Clive Mason helped every way he could to help Phillips set up in business. And yes, I've no doubt that the Phillipses helped the Masons. He put the odd patient Clive Mason's way, and he opened doors for them that would otherwise have been closed because of a lack of funds, such as places on the relevant hospital committees. And of course, that meant that Martha particularly was known to those in the social positions she might not otherwise have had access to. Believe me, Ephraim Phillips got his rewards, he demanded his own pound of flesh from Martha and had from Clive too, though the man probably doesn't realize it.'

'What do you mean?'

'Oh dear. Inspector, have you ever noticed the way that servants are ignored? That most people who should really know better will speak in front of servants as though they were invisible and deaf.'

Henry nodded.

'When one reaches a certain age one is completely treated as though one is a servant. Ignored, humoured, spoken to as though one needs a hearing trumpet even though my hearing is perfectly good. Placed in a position where it seems not to matter if conversations are overheard. After all I am a foolish old woman, what could I possibly know? What could I possibly do?'

'Then *they* are the fools,' Henry told her.

Georgia Styles reached over and patted his hand. 'A very correct answer,' she said. 'I'm sure your mother must be very proud of you.'

'I would hope she might be,' Henry said honestly. 'I would have liked her to have survived to be proud of me.'

'Well, that is something I am sorry for. But I won't waste platitudes on you. I have overheard conversations that unfortunately I can do little with, but which do beg questions. I know for example that Ephraim Phillips palmed off the dead and the dying on to Dr Mason, as long as they were not likely to leave a large bequest, of course. The elderly must be rich and polite to remain on Dr Phillips' list. My dear, I may be rich but I'm certainly not polite and will not be fobbed off with sugar pills and nerve tonics which, if I'm frank, is all Dr Phillips bothers to prescribe for his more senior patients. That of course and large doses of morphine for when he decides their time has come, whether *they* are particularly ready to shuffle off this mortal coil or not.'

Henry frowned. 'I'm not sure what you mean.'

'Oh, come on, man, you're not an idiot. Old folk like me, we can become a burden to the young who wish to get their hands on whatever it is we plan to leave them in our wills. I am fortunate. My mind is clear and my body usually does what I wish it to do, as long as I don't overtax it and I get my afternoon nap and my glass of sherry before dinner and a glass of port before sleep. But there are many of the elderly who have become an inconvenience, both to themselves and their families. Their minds are gone, their bodies frail and the sooner they remove themselves from this life the happier the heirs will be. It's no secret that Dr Phillips dispenses morphine with a very open hand. He would tell you it is for pain relief and of course some of it is, but he also administers it with, shall we say, a very *heavy* hand and does not discourage the relatives from giving a little extra, say in a glass of brandy, for comfort, you understand.'

'That is a considerable accusation to make.'

'It is, isn't it? But consider this, young man. I switched my allegiance from Ephraim Phillips to Dr Clive Mason something over a year ago when three of my *oldest* friends, who might not have been in the best of health but who still enjoyed life to the full, left this world in very, very quick succession. And guess what, our Dr Phillips was each time rewarded by the family for his kindness and consideration. That kindness and consideration, to my reckoning, added up to several thousand pounds. Now you tell me, Inspector, if that does not look suspicious. Martha certainly thought it did. Ah, that's perked you up. Yes, I did tell Martha of my suspicions and yes she did take notice.'

'When was this?'

'Earlier this year, I went to a funeral in January that particularly upset me. Martha was also in attendance and she came home with me after. I'm afraid I rather let the cat out of the bag at that point. I confess that I cried in front of her, which is not something I'm in the habit of doing, Inspector. I believe in keeping a tight rein on my emotions.'

'And did you think that Martha acted on your suspicions?'

Again the fingers tapped upon the chair, but then Georgia Styles nodded. 'She said she still had contact with a private enquiry agent and that she had some skill in this field herself. That before her marriage her life had been quite eventful. She said she would do what she could to look into this but without raising suspicion. She also said that Ephraim Phillips would not see it as strange if suddenly she took an interest in him. The same interest that he has tried to encourage previously. The man is arrogant enough to believe that she had simply changed her mind.

'But I spoke of conversations overheard, did I not? And one of these conversations was between Martha and Ephraim Phillips. I overheard him say to her that she must find her marriage a very barren one and that no woman could go for long without the attentions of a man. That it was unhealthy.'

'And how did she respond to that? Did she defend her marriage?'

'Oh yes. She said that she was in love with her husband, deeply in love – and if you had seen them together, Inspector, you would have no doubt of that.'

'But—'

'But, indeed. Dr Phillips seemed to imply that Martha's husband was either unable or unwilling to . . . to honour the requirements of the marriage bed.' She looked closely at him. 'But I can see in your face that this is not news for you.'

'I could not possibly say.'

'You have no need of saying. Dr Phillips made certain suggestions about his friend Clive Mason. Now I do not know if they are true, neither do I want to. If Dr Mason is a sodomite, then that is his affair. Though I do have to say that if it is true, perhaps he was unwise and unfair to marry a woman like Martha. You know she wanted children?'

'I didn't know her, so how could I know that?'

'Too true. She made do with Nora's, but I know it made her sad.'

'What did you know about her life before she came here?' Henry asked. 'About where she worked?'

Georgia Styles half closed her eyes and appeared to be thinking about this but then nodded. 'Probably a good deal more than anyone else around here. That nonsense about her being an office typist. Just so much humbug. She worked for a solicitor's company which also comprised a firm of private enquiry agents, under a different name but actually part of the same company. Some of these were based in Brighton, I believe, and also with offices in London, and they were employed in either obtaining evidence suitable for the divorce courts or in, how shall I put it, ensuring that appropriate evidence was . . . created. I don't need to tell you what sacrifices must be made at times in order for guilt to be proved in these cases. It seems a shame to me that reputations must be ruined in order for two people who made the mistake of becoming married to be freed from that state. How many unhappy marriages are there, Inspector? How many that should be walked away from, with no recriminations and no regrets.'

'A great many, I would think. You know as well as I do that the only grounds for divorce is adultery.'

'Not cruelty, not falling out of love, not a simple need to be free. It seems so unfair, Inspector, that nothing else counts and so adultery must be proved.'

'And Martha Mason, she worked for these solicitors, these enquiry agents. But you think not in the office.'

'I believe she began there, typing and filing and greeting clients and all the usual stuff that young women get up to in such companies, but Martha Mason was a very beautiful woman and also a very resourceful one and although she never told me directly I believe that from time to time she took the part of the other woman, the one who would sign the register with the man who sought to be divorced, or even at the request of the wife who knew that adultery must be proved but did not wish for the husband to actually be put through the difficulty of finding someone to commit the act with.

'I know that many marriages end acrimoniously, but there are many that just wish for release and I believe that these are the ones that Martha assisted with.'

For the first time in the conversation, she looked away from Henry and he knew that she was not really convincing herself, never mind him. But that she wished her friend to have been more innocent and principled than she probably was.

'Martha would sign the register, then go to the hotel room with the man in question, the private enquiry agent would come in and would photograph them and photograph the register. This evidence would then be given to the courts and adultery would be proved and the divorce could be finalised. I'm told it is a commonplace, so no doubt you have met this little scheme.'

Henry agreed that he was familiar with it.

'She told me all this in confidence, of course. And I would never have broken that confidence. But the fact is I have lost yet another friend, one that was kind and very dear to me and at my age, Inspector, you cannot afford to lose too many friends. Most are already gone ahead and my only hope is that when I finally cross the river they will be waiting there for me. But let me tell you, Inspector, I will be going in my own time and my own way and not because someone like Dr Ephraim Phillips decides that my death is appropriate and needful.'

'I take it he will not be remembered in your will,' Henry added with a smile.

Miss Georgia Styles laughed heartily. 'You can be very sure of that,' she said. 'My will is lodged with my solicitor, and my wishes are made very, very clear. I have little in terms of family, and they will be getting a small bequest, but I believe in rewarding loyalty and my housekeeper has been loyal to me these many, many years. Ellie has been more than my housekeeper – she has been my friend and support and it only seems right that the majority of my estate goes to her. I hope she still has some life left after I am gone, and I would not see her destitute. And I have it in my will, that should those few members of my family object, then they will lose the bequest that comes to them. They know this and my solicitor assures me that there can be no valid objection.'

Henry nodded. 'That seems somehow very appropriate,' he said. 'And is there anything else that you wish to tell me, while I'm here.'

She laughed again. 'You are very direct. I like that. I'm getting tired, Inspector, so I will be brief, but I think there is one more thing. Mr Henry Benson, for all his flash and outward display, is not as well set up as he would have the world think. I know for a fact that he has slowly been selling off the contents of that house for two or three years now. A painting here, a piece of silver there, the contents of his father's library. His father was a great student of the arts and the sciences. He and I were friends even after his marriage. His wife was a lovely woman so how between them they produced such a virulent progeny is beyond me. The man is an idiot and yet he had two intelligent parents. He's an ignorant oaf and yet his parents were both refined and generous by nature. But it occurs to me that a man in need of money, one who is used to having everything and faces the real possibility of destitution – at least in his terms – is a somewhat dangerous man. A wild beast is at its most vicious when backed into a corner.'

'And did someone back him into a corner?'

'I believe perhaps that Martha did. As I mentioned there were rumours about young women who had fallen foul of his attentions and there was one that there are worse rumours about. I know you heard this from Nellie Richardson because she came to see me this morning, very early, and told me what she and her daughter had informed you. She wanted me to know that she had urged you to speak to me again.'

'She believes this young woman to be murdered?'

'She believes that young woman to be *dead*. Now murder is perhaps too strong. The rumours say that she went to procure a termination of her condition and I'm sure I don't need to speak to you of how brutal such operations are even when they go well.'

Henry reflected that he was indeed familiar with the details, but he was quite surprised that an elderly maiden lady should know so much.

'It is possible that this killed her. It is also possible that she took her own life. But Martha counted Benson as being responsible either way and I believe she told him so.'

'Martha Mason was pregnant. Did she confide that to you?'

'No, but I had guessed as much. But don't look to Benson for that. I am certain, after talking to Mrs Richardson, that she broke things off with him last year, whatever he might be inclined to tell you. Her sister-in-law would have been aware had this affair continued. If she was carrying a child then the father was someone else.'

'Dr Phillips?'

'It's a possibility. I told you, she wished for children. I suspect that Clive would have come around to the idea eventually. After all, he would hardly want his state to be revealed, would he?'

'But would that not have made their marriage very unhappy?'

'People adapt when they love one another, Inspector. Martha had adapted to his requirements, and he knew this. It was deeply unfair, in my opinion, for him to expect she just settle back and ignore her own requirements, her own needs. I think perhaps she thought that he would come around.'

'I'm not sure that is likely.'

'Perhaps not, but desperate people can convince themselves of anything.'

'And was she desperate? Was this need for a baby so overwhelming?'

'No, it's not something I could understand either, Inspector. I think in that we're cut from the same cloth. I like children, I enjoy their company and I especially enjoy the fact that I can hand them back, but some women are meant to be mothers, and yes, I believe that need can become overwhelming. I don't imagine she planned any of this, but I do wonder if, had Clive rejected her, she would not simply have left him and found a way to raise her child elsewhere. I hope if that had happened, she would have come to me for help. She would have been given assistance, I can assure you of that.'

Henry nodded. Miss Georgia Styles had given him a lot to think about but he could see that she was desperately weary now and so he took his leave. 'I will come and see you again,' he said.

'I don't doubt it,' she said. 'I am, after all, the ageing spider that sits at the heart of the web.'

Otis arrived at the pharmacy just after Mickey left. Ordinarily he would have brought with him a Kodak self-development tank in which he could have processed his film and created his negatives even without the aid of a darkroom, but this trip had been a speedily organized and unexpected one. News of Martha Mason's death had caused a flurry of anxiety and hastily made arrangements that had Otis speeding north without time for proper preparation. Fortunately the pharmacist had a reasonable supply of materials to purchase and a tiny cubicle at the back of the shop that was often used by local amateur photographers.

Otis had waited until Mickey was a good distance from the chemist shop and had then gone in to stake his claim at his appointed time.

The pharmacist was absent. His daughter had charge of the

shop that morning. 'Oh, Mr Freeland, a little complication, I'm afraid. The police sergeant who just left, his film has been processed but the prints are not yet fully dry. I wonder, would you mind returning in an hour or so?'

'If I do that then my own prints will not have time to dry before I must send them down to London by the evening train. I need only to produce my contact sheets—'

'Oh dear. Oh, goodness. I don't want anyone put out, you understand, only this is such an awkward business.'

'And I promise I will not disturb the policeman's prints,' he told her.

He was sure she was on the verge of giving in, but unfortunately for Otis the pharmacist returned from his errand and was reluctant in the extreme to allow Otis to use the back room while the policeman's prints were still there. He was also reluctant in the extreme to lose the considerable sum Otis was prepared to pay, just to get his darkroom time.

Otis would have paid a good deal more to have access to Mickey's photographs but in the end a compromise was reached. A fresh sheet was laid out on a table in the pharmacy itself, not accessible from the shop. The photographs would be placed there and Otis could have access to the little room.

It would have to be enough, Otis thought.

A half hour later he was ensconced and a little after that he was examining the wounds to Martha Mason's skull with a hand lens.

One single wound, Otis said to himself. One wound and the woman was dead.

So who had killed her? With a slight shiver, Otis realized that recent experience suggested the names of at least two possible suspects – neither of which Otis would like to be in the same room with.

He wondered if Sergeant Hitchens or his chief inspector were currently aware of either.

TEN

In the early afternoon, Henry, Mickey and Sergeant Emory convened at the police station to discuss what they had so far. The evidence, such as it was, was laid out on the table in front of them.

'I have sent what fingerprints I managed to recover and photographs down to London,' Mickey told them. 'It will be late tomorrow probably before we get any kind of message come back. They will receive them today, but a fingerprint bureau works on comparisons in the morning and sends out its reports in the afternoon. They have their routine and we must wait on it.'

Henry nodded. He recounted what Miss Styles had told him that morning.

'So according to her,' Emory said slowly, 'either Mr Phillips is responsible for the child, or we should be looking for yet another man.' He shook his head 'I wouldn't reckon Mrs Mason for being a promiscuous type. Something about this does not ring true.'

'You would not have credited the doctor's wife with owning a gun,' Henry said, pointing to the weapon. 'And probably not with concealing money that her husband did not know about. Both of them took pains to cover up her past, not because she did anything illegal but because they considered it dubious. That to me speaks of someone who is deliberately trying to change their life, so if she had affairs, we must ask ourselves why. She's been married eight years, apparently happy. Did she leave her life behind, utterly and completely eight or so years ago, or has she always continued with a kind of secondary existence that her husband did not know about?'

'Well, all that is possible,' Mickey said. 'But it's hard to know when she'd find the time. She works beside her husband, she is on this committee, and organizing that fundraising event. I suppose you could argue that this brings her into contact with a great many people, and affords her opportunity at the very least. Perhaps that flirtation on one or two occasions has grown into something else. And then there is Dr Phillips; always on hand, always pushing. And perhaps her refusal actually added to her attractions.'

'But did he father her child?' Emory wanted to know. 'Or are we looking for a third person? And that's if we believe that her relationship with Mr Benson ended when Miss Styles thinks it did. Benson led you to believe something else.'

'He did,' Henry agreed. 'But do we believe him or does this simply play to the narrative of his, that women cannot resist his advances. Do we believe any of the people involved in this? So far honesty has not been in great supply. Though I'm inclined to accept what the housemaid Grace Richardson told us, and I'm also inclined to believe that Miss Styles at least believes she's telling the truth. But she can only tell us what she observed and what inference she drew from those observations and we all know people can be mistaken.'

'And so would you like me to go and fetch Dr Phillips here?' Emory asked. 'It seems to me that unless he is brought here, formally and forcefully, that he will be reluctant to say anything. We should challenge him on his relationship with Mrs Mason but we should also tax him on the accusations Miss Styles has made, regarding the misuse of morphine.'

'You may be right, but at the moment I prefer to tread more softly. We will question Dr Phillips, and we will tax him with what we know, but if all he was guilty of was overbearing flirtation, however reprehensible that might be, I do not want to risk reputations that could yet be salvaged. There are families here who would be impacted upon and a community that needs to trust those who serve them. If Dr Phillips proves unco-operative, however, then you may bring him through the town in handcuffs for all to see. And as to the morphine, that would be such an impossible thing to prove without a great deal more evidence. Evidence we don't have the resources to gather. My father was a general practitioner,' he added reluctantly. He hated speaking about his father, even obliquely. 'It is well known that doctors will sometimes oversubscribe, when the end is anticipated, to ensure that end is peaceful. It then becomes a moot point as to which finally takes the patient: the illness or the morphine. Where palliative care begins and ends is difficult to ascertain.'

'And Martha Mason was a doctor's wife,' Emory reminded him. 'It's likely she would have been aware of that. If her suspicions matched those of Miss Styles, then I'd be inclined to take notice.'

'Your point is taken,' Henry told him.

Mickey picked up the little key and examined it closely. 'There's nothing at the house or in the surgery that this fits and if you look at it, it's such a flimsy, ornamental bit of a thing. I could imagine it fitting a ladies' jewellery box, or even one of those strange little diaries you get with the lock on it. Like the one you bought for Melissa.'

Henry nodded. 'Melissa is my niece,' he explained to Emory. 'She is of an age where such things appeal to her. No, but you are right, it's not the key to a strong box, it is not the key even to a particularly large jewellery box. My mother had something like it that locked a tea caddy, but I could also imagine this hanging from a chain around someone's neck or on a fob. It looks more fanciful than useful.'

He took it from Mickey's hand and laid it on his own palm. The key was solid silver, which alone suggested decoration rather than use. It was small and ornate, with a little loop of flowers forming the head. He would have taken it for something falling from a charm bracelet had it not been just slightly too large for that and had it also not been so obviously cut as though to fit a very specific lock. But Mickey was right, it did look like something that would open a diary or a tiny box or even a large locket.

'Anything that fitted,' Emory said stoutly. 'I would think you could open by levering it with a table knife. It is a flimsy little thing. Isn't it likely it simply slid under the reinforcement in the lining by accident and we are reading far too much into this? That perhaps it fell off a bracelet or necklace and she put it in her bag for safekeeping and from there it simply wedged itself beneath the lining.'

'Entirely possible,' Henry agreed. 'But I remember the way it was found, folded in with the notes and that makes me doubt that explanation, and the husband did not recognize it as being from jewellery his wife owned. Mickey, Emory would you consider that this key is more symbolic than useful? An emblem of something, a token.'

Mickey patted his chest theatrically. 'I give you the key to my heart,' he pronounced solemnly.

Emory laughed. 'It is the kind of trifle a lover might give to his beloved, and if that was the case, he might want it back. But the gun interests me more. To conceal a gun with five rounds of ammunition, what does this tell us. Was she afraid? If so, why not take the weapon with her when she went out?'

'It was well concealed,' Henry observed. 'So perhaps the fear she had once experienced had passed? Perhaps she felt the threat had gone away. Perhaps she also felt that the crowds would protect her. She was with friends in a busy place if someone had threatened her. I would imagine there could be many other locations in which any threat could be carried out, much easier for any attacker than a busy race day.'

'So maybe there is an element of chance here, that she really did not expect to see this person or these persons in the crowd. That's if these unknown friends – if they were friends – have anything to do with her death at all. She was by all accounts a popular woman with many acquaintances and the two things may be totally unconnected. The timing is not so close as to make that impossible.'

Henry nodded at his sergeant. That was true. She had left Nora Phillips' side at about two fifteen and her body had been discovered a little before four o'clock. Allowing for perhaps fifteen minutes to get from where she had left Nora to where her body had been found . . . 'Her bag was found at three o'clock, which suggests that it was either dropped, abandoned, or taken from her not long after she left Nora Phillips. But I would also suggest that it could not have been lying around for long. The young couple who spotted it saw it poking up from beneath a bush. There was opportunity for many other people to have seen it and the longer it lay there, the more opportunity that afforded. So my guess, and it is at this stage only a guess, is that she still had her bag for quite some time between two fifteen and close to three o'clock. Unless, of course, her attacker took it from her, searched it, then dumped it because it didn't contain what he expected. Again, this must have been done before she was killed, and before three o'clock.

'Dr Phillips did not give a very accurate estimation of time of death, but then the body was still warm, the day was warm, and so the body had cooled very little, and he could say nothing apart from speculation that she had died in the previous hour and we know that to have been true. The body temperature had barely dropped.

'The travellers reported seeing the blue car still in place just before four o'clock,' Henry continued. 'The man on watch took himself off for a cup of tea at around that time, leaving young Charlie in charge. Charlie had not noticed the car had gone, but . . . we can probably assume that the car was still there a little before four. A little before the body was discovered. Martha Mason was concealed in the horsebox, but we are pretty sure not killed there. So if the owner of the car came to collect it, it's likely he either would have seen the killer, or that he is in fact involved. No one has yet come forward?' He looked at Emory who shook his head.

'Not the blue car, nor the little green van or the man in the blue suit without the hat.'

'So, how does this sound as a timeline of events?' Henry continued. 'She leaves her friend Nora Phillips at about two fifteen. She disappeared into the crowd, ostensibly to speak to a friend. She does not pass that same spot again because Nora Phillips was standing there for fifteen minutes. So she must have turned the other way, towards the stands or immediately towards the paddock where her body was found. Now we must assume, I think, that she had her bag until a little before three. Then either she or the killer cast it aside to be found beneath the bushes at around three o'clock.

'By four o'clock she's dead, the blue car is gone and the body discovered shortly after. The fact that her body was discovered quite quickly implies that people were passing through this area on a fairly frequent basis. A groom noticed the door was open, went to investigate. So again, I doubt her body could have lain there for long. The fairground folk saw nothing out of the ordinary. My betting is that the blue car is relevant to this crime and its position would have helped to shield the attacker from view, as Mickey's little sketch map demonstrates.'

'And so who has motive?' Emory ticked them off on his fingers. 'The father of the child, which may or may not be Mr Harry Benson or Dr Ephraim Phillips. It could be that either one of them wished for her to get rid of the baby and she refused. Their motive could be that she threatened to name them, or that she sought to blackmail. A dead mother and a dead child is an easy solution.'

'And so it is,' Mickey agreed. 'Don't forget there might be a third person in a similar position, as yet unknown to us.'

'Or it could have been someone from her previous life, someone she had evaded and feared enough to keep the gun in her home. Though it seems she no longer kept the gun in her bag – if indeed she ever did. Do we even know if she could fire such a weapon? Do we even know for certain that it was hers? Might it be something she picked up on her travels?'

'Then why conceal it,' Henry argued. 'If the gun happened to be some rather unusual souvenir, then surely her husband would have known about it. Such a curiosity might be something she would have shown off to friends. We've all remarked that it's an unusual weapon, so there might well have been a story behind it.'

'Unless of course that story is related to her work for the divorce lawyers or the private investigator. Though even then, her husband should have known, because he knew about her past.'

'He *claims* to have known about her past.' Henry seemed suddenly decided. 'But he's already disturbed at the thought that she worked *in* such company and *for* such a company. Surely he would be even more disturbed if she told him that sometimes she carried a gun, or that her profession required that she did because it could sometimes be dangerous. This casts a different light on things and is suggestive of something more than Martha Mason just being the occasional other woman, for legal purposes.'

Emory began to pack the evidence away in its box. 'So which of us is going to talk to Dr Phillips next?' he asked.

'I think that should be you,' Henry told him. 'You are local, knowledgeable of the local community and it would not be strange if you had heard rumours pertaining to the behaviour of Dr Phillips and wish to speak to him privately and confidentially – before the murder detectives from London stuck their claws into the matter.'

'A good thought,' Mickey approved. 'And then if he doesn't oblige you with what you need to know, you can bring him to us.'

Emory left Henry and Mickey Hitchens going through the witness statements that had started to filter in. Martha Mason's photograph and the basic facts about her murder had been bruited far and wide and witnesses had begun to come forward who claimed to have seen the woman at various stages of the day. There were a few reports regarding the green van and the blue car and one to do with the man in the blue suit without the hat. It would be time-consuming and probably wasteful of time, but the statements had to be gone through. Mickey split the pile arbitrarily and handed half to his boss.

Emory had left them and marched out of the police station looking important and heading for Dr Phillips' house.

On arriving he was told that the doctor had gone to his surgery and had not yet returned. He was told also that Clive Mason had packed his bags and returned home. When asked why, Nora Phillips had advised him that the doctor thought it was time he opened his surgery again. She was clearly not in full approval of this, but she told Emory that her husband had advised Clive that sympathy would lead to curiosity and curiosity might lead to a rise in numbers of those signing up for his list. In other words, it would be good for business.

'And what do you think of that, if you don't mind my asking?'

Nora shrugged and then fluttered her hands nervously. 'I'm sure the men know best,' she said, but Emory could hear that her words were empty. Nora was not at all happy about it, any fool could see that. 'I don't think Clive is ready. He's been so battered by events, I would hate to think that he might prescribe the wrong thing, or break down in front of someone.

He is a sensitive soul and a genuinely nice man.'

Emory couldn't resist. 'And is your husband a genuinely nice man?' he asked.

Nora put a hand to her cheek as though he'd struck her and stared in horror at Emory. He fully expected a sharp reprimand and knew he would have deserved it, but instead she just looked very upset. Eventually she shook her head. 'No, Sergeant Emory, not all of the time he isn't.' She stood then and Emory realized he was being dismissed. 'I must see to the children,' she said. 'I'm sure they will be wanting something.'

Emory made his way to Newark, making use of car and driver seeing as the London detectives had no need for it. He had the driver wait while he cut across the edge of the marketplace, where traders were already packing up for the day.

He caught Dr Phillips just as he was packing up and preparing to leave. Good timing, Emory thought. Phillips was quite surprised to see him.

'Developments?' he asked.

'I called at your home. I understand that Dr Mason has left you.'

'It seemed the best. One has to get back on the horse sometime. And he was getting restless.'

'I see. Dr Phillips, I have some questions to ask of you and they are of a very delicate nature so it's probably best I ask them here. I wanted to speak to you,' Emory bluffed, 'before I speak to Chief Inspector Johnstone, as I must do later when I make my report. I wanted to give you the chance to speak to me first, so I could clear the way, if it's necessary. Smooth the path, as it were.'

Phillips looked at him sharply, clearly puzzled. 'Well, out with it man, what's this about?'

'As you know, we're making enquiries all about the town. Speaking to all manner of people and all manner of classes, and as you can imagine some things are said that decent people might not choose to remark upon.'

Phillips was on his guard now. He looked narrowly at Emory. 'Such as?'

'Naming no names, there are those who wonder if your relationship with the late Mrs Mason was perhaps a little too close. That the two of you were perhaps a little too fond.'

Phillips' face was a picture, Emory thought, as he fought for an appropriate reaction. This, he thought, told him far more than Phillips was likely to with words. An innocent of these charges would be furious, would respond immediately, but Dr Phillips was having to think about his response and to consider who knew what and what was mere suspicion and what was common gossip.

'It's nonsense, of course. Martha was a friend, a good friend. Anyone will tell you that. She and Clive were both good friends. Nora was extremely fond of her, as was I, as were our children . . . To suggest that there was anything untoward . . . Frankly I am flabbergasted that you would even mention this. That you would come to me with such nonsense. That you would come all the way out to my practice and lay out such rubbish.'

He had been packing his bag when Emory arrived and he resumed this now, clearly agitated.

'Well, I thought it polite to come to you first. I could simply have gone to the detectives and told what I'd heard, and by rights that's exactly what I should have done. I should have spoken to the chief inspector or to his sergeant and made it clear that several individuals had made several similar observations.'

'I suppose the servants have been gossiping.'

'This was not told me from within your household,' Emory informed him, fudging the issue with half-truths. 'I wanted to tell you what was said first, give you a chance to reply before the inspector demanded to know the truth. It gives you motive, you see.'

'Motive? What the devil do you mean?'

'Motive because she might have decided to tell your wife you were having an affair, that the child was yours.'

'Damn it, man, that's libellous. Anybody dares say that in public and I'll have the lawyers on to them. Martha was nothing more than a friend. Whoever killed her wanted to rob her, nothing more. You're looking for motives where there are none, reasons where there are none. You go around accusing decent people of . . . of reprehensible acts. I tell you, Emory, pursue this and you are heading for trouble.'

Sergeant Emory shrugged mildly. 'It is my job to investigate, sir. I must report what has been said. If I do not then others will.'

Phillips was taken aback. 'Others have heard this nonsense?'

'Whatever constables are available have been making enquiries, house-to-house, you know that. And appealing for witnesses who know anything about Mrs Mason, who might have seen her on the day or indeed know anything that speaks to motive. Everyone seems to agree that she was a good woman, but someone wanted her dead, so you understand my position.'

'No, I don't. I don't understand it at all. I don't understand why you should listen to such rubbish and I don't understand why you should come in here and threaten me with it.'

Emory bristled. 'I've made no threat, sir. I'm simply doing my job. And I'm doing it to the best of my ability as I'm sure we all do. I simply came here to give you the opportunity to speak to me, in confidence, lay things out, like. Give you a chance to answer these rumours and accusations before the senior officers get involved and things get really unpleasant for you. But seeing as you don't want to hear this from me, it seems I have no choice but to—'

'All right.' Phillips sat down heavily in the captain's chair set behind the desk. 'I admit that I was fond. Martha was a bright, beautiful and intelligent woman. I am fond of my wife. Nora is a good mother and, within her own lights, an entertaining enough companion. She is loving and kind but, and you must forgive the way this sounds, she is not the brightest . . . not the most stimulating of companions. I suppose on occasion, I might – and I do say *might* – have shown a little more attention to Martha than perhaps was wise. But the fact that people comment on it, the fact that this was always done in company, shows the innocence of it. Surely you can see that.'

Emory looked sceptical but remained silent.

'And I mean what I say, that they are good friends. Well,

Clive continues to be a good friend and Martha will be very much missed by all of us. But to accuse me, to accuse me of having an affair with my friend's wife, of betraying friendship and marriage and, for that matter, of accusing Martha of doing the same. Why, man, this is beyond the pale.'

Emory continued to maintain the silence.

'I didn't even know that she was pregnant.'

'Apparently, neither did her husband.'

'Well then, that just goes to show.'

'Goes to show what, sir? I have to ask you outright: did you have relations with Mrs Mason?'

Phillips got to his feet and grabbed his bag. 'Get out of my surgery. Get out now. I won't hear any more of this.'

Emory nodded but refused to be rushed. 'I'm happy to go, sir. But Dr Phillips, it might be as well to bear in mind that I still have my report to make and you still have not definitively answered my question in any satisfactory manner. So it may well be that the inspector or the sergeant or both of them will come over to your house and ask questions again, where your wife and your servants might hear. I'm giving you the opportunity to answer me straight, and to do so in the privacy of your office, not at home or at the police station where there are other ears to hear and other eyes to witness. So I'm giving you one last chance, Dr Phillips, to answer me straight. Did you have extramarital relations with Mrs Mason? Is there a chance that you could be the father of her child?'

One look at Phillips' face told him that he wasn't going to get any kind of answer from the man. 'Out,' Phillips roared pointing at the door. 'Get out and get away from me and my family. You are not welcome. I am a respectable man with connections and you are a mere sergeant.'

Emory simply shrugged. 'That's as maybe, sir,' he said. 'But I'm working on an investigation with two detectives come all the way from London, all the way from the murder squad there, and frankly I don't think they give a damn about you being respectable or connected, begging your pardon, sir. So you may want rid of me, and you may even be rid of me, but I think those two are a very different kettle of fish.'

He opened the office door and stepped outside, pausing on

the landing. 'Still, I gave you a chance to talk to me private, like, I did all I can, so now I just have to go back and tell the inspector what you said, and what those we have been interviewing have said. No skin off my nose now.'

He left then, but loitered on the street corner, out of sight of the office door, curious to see what Dr Phillips would do next. In truth Emory was not quite as confident as he sounded. He knew the damage that someone with Phillips' influence could cause to him and to his career, but as he told Henry and Mickey earlier on, he was not a married man, had no ties and he had ridden out worse storms before. He had a feeling also that Henry Johnstone would protect him as best he might.

Dr Phillips came storming down the stairs from his office and out of the front door and Emory watched as he glanced left and right but did not actually seem to be seeing anything. He marched across the road and turned back towards the marketplace. Emory followed, slowly wondering where Phillips had parked his car and if he would go straight home. He was therefore a little surprised to find that Phillips paused outside of an ordinary terraced house, glanced nervously about him and then rapped on the door. A woman opened it and Phillips pushed his way inside.

Interesting, Emory thought as he took note of the address. He would have to make enquiries at the local constabulary and see who lived here.

'He stayed inside for about half an hour,' Emory told Inspector Johnstone later on that afternoon. 'I trailed him back to where he parked his car, which was close to his surgery, and then once he'd driven away I went to speak to our colleagues at the Newark constabulary and took a look at the register of voters. There are two people registered to vote at that address, being common owners of the property. A Mr Geoffrey Steiff, aged sixty years and a lady who claims to be his widowed sister, Mrs Regina Edwards, aged fifty-eight, a lady who was a midwife before her marriage and then returned to that work when her husband died. Neither has a criminal record, or has come to the official notice of the police before, but it is interesting that our man went straight there rather than coming home.'

'Interesting indeed,' Henry agreed. 'And very interesting that Dr Mason has chosen to return home and reopen his surgery. Mickey, I think we will cut along there before we have supper and we should ask both doctors about Mr Steiff and Mrs Edwards. Well done, Sergeant.'

'Anything interesting from the witness statements?' Emory enquired.

'A few sightings of Mrs Mason, or who might have been Mrs Mason. One or two look more certain because they describe her as being with another lady and several children. After she left Nora Phillips, there are two that might be worth following up. One describes her as chatting to a couple seeming on good terms and this is about two thirty by their reckoning. The second describes her as arguing with a man and is slightly later. But both are vague.'

Emory nodded. 'Will you be following them up, or will I?'

'I think I will decide that in the morning. In the meantime, Mickey and I will go and speak to Dr Mason. You get yourself off home.'

'I think I might get myself a pint,' Emory said. 'Drop in at the Last Whistle seeing as it's almost next door.'

It was six o'clock when they knocked on Dr Mason's door. He answered after a few minutes and stood back to let them come inside.

'So you decided to come back home?' Mickey asked.

'It seemed like the right thing to do. I can't keep on imposing. Besides I have a practice to run.'

'It's only been a few days. I'm sure nobody expects you—'

'It's not about what people expect. It's about what I need to do. I've never been one for hanging around doing nothing. I find it depresses me. And I felt that I was somehow in the way. Not that anyone said anything, of course, but people have their own lives to live and I have mine and I must make shift to manage without Martha. Do you know anything more?'

'Gossip and rumours, mostly,' Mickey said. 'But that's what we'd expect at this stage.'

Clive Mason opened his mouth as though to ask a question and then closed it again. Mickey guessed that he wanted to ask whether the gossip was about him, but then thought such a question might betray that there was something to gossip about. He was clearly not sure how much information Henry and his sergeant shared.

'A couple of possible sightings of your wife,' Henry said. 'She was seen talking to a couple and I have a description. Do you think you might recognize them? The woman had auburn hair and a lot of freckles and the man is described as dark and,' Henry paused, 'somewhat swarthy and foreign-looking.'

Dr Mason laughed, the sound seeming to burst from him so he could not control it. 'Oh my lord, I know who that is. Swarthy and foreign-looking, goodness that is priceless. Actually, if it's who I think it is, then he's part Italian. It sounds like Hazel and Gus Mancini. Hazel does indeed have a lot of freckles, and the most glorious auburn hair. I didn't think they were back in England yet. They went visiting Gus's grandparents; I believe they live somewhere just outside Rome. Their first baby is almost a year old and there have been complaints, loud and long, I believe, that the grandparents have not yet seen their great-grandchild. They are a sweet couple but it makes sense, when I think about it, that Gus should have been at the races. I believe he owns a part share of a racehorse. From what he says he doesn't own much more than the front leg but . . . but yes, that does make sense.'

'Does Mrs Phillips know this couple?'

Dr Mason thought about it and shook his head. 'I don't believe she does and frankly it's not the kind of friendship that her husband would approve of anyway. The Mancinis are scrap metal merchants, and so very much in trade, as he would put it. Ephraim seems not to have minded marrying into trade, but increasingly he sets his sights higher. The fact that his wife's parents have helped financially is, I think, something which grates on his nerves. Over the last few days it has become apparent that Ephraim sees life elsewhere as being more appealing and attractive, somewhere he can escape from his more humble past and cultivate his elderly ladies in peace, without being known as the grocer's son-in-law.'

Clive Mason sounded bitter which was not something Henry had noticed in his tone before.

'You had a quarrel?' Mickey asked.

Clive Mason dropped his face wearily into his hands and then shook his head. 'No, nothing like a quarrel. It's just . . . You can know someone for a long time but it's only when you live in close proximity to them that you begin to see all of the things you would ordinarily ignore or simply not be aware of. Nora and Ephraim have been kind enough, but I have been made very much aware of their kindness, if you understand what I mean. It made me uncomfortable and so I came home.'

Dr Mason gave them the address of the Mancinis but he had no idea who the man that his wife was later seen arguing with could possibly be.

They asked him about Mr Steiff and his sister, Mrs Edwards, but the names were not familiar to him. 'Newark is only a short few miles away,' he said, 'but that few miles can make a difference in terms of acquaintance. I don't recall Ephraim making mention of them either.'

'Well, that solves one mystery at least,' Mickey said as they left. 'So Martha Mason definitely did see a friend in the crowd, or rather a couple of friends, people she did not expect to be there. And if she knew that Dr Phillips would not approve of his wife's meeting with them, that explains why she took off on her own. So maybe the Mancinis can fill in something on our timeline, maybe they even noticed where she went after she left them. She can't have spent long in conversation with them.'

'I found it interesting, what Dr Mason had to say about his friend. So many people seek to bury their past as though they're ashamed of it.'

'Society is still largely closed to those from humble beginnings,' Mickey said. 'I remember your Cynthia complaining that there are some houses that still would not welcome her. Old money, old traditions. However successful her husband is in business, it is still nothing as far as they are concerned.'

Henry nodded, knowing this to be true. 'I think I'm hungry,' he said unexpectedly.

Mickey rubbed his hands together in great satisfaction. 'If *you* recognize that you are hungry, then you must be starving. And I most certainly am. We both think better on a full stomach and tomorrow we'll talk to the Mancinis and beard Dr Phillips at his lair again.'

ELEVEN

News arrived the following morning that threw their plans into something of disarray. A parcel arrived with the first train of the day containing information garnered about M. Giles Esq., solicitor, and also Mr Ernest Conway, private investigative agent. In addition to this was a record of the interviews that had been held with both men, and with some of the associates that worked with them, including a woman called Felicity Bennett, who had known Mrs Mason well before she had married.

'Though it appears that she wasn't called Martha at all. Her name was Mary Betteridge, and she was employed by the solicitors for three years, initially for general office duties and then also as an inquiry agent. She was then only twenty-one, so she met Dr Mason when she was only twenty-two at which point she left the company.'

'So she changed her name completely. This is definitely a woman who wants to leave her past behind. Interesting that she changed from being a Mary to Martha,' Mickey commented. 'Mary being the one interested in finding out about the world, and Martha confined to her kitchen.'

Henry frowned for a moment, not getting the reference, and then said, 'Oh, Bible stories.'

'So, will you be going down to speak with them?'

'I rather think I might. You and Emory can deal with things here. But I would like to know in detail just what young Mary Betteridge was involved with and feel I might be able to elicit a better response, face to face. There was a postcard in the desk from somebody called Felicity. I'm presuming it is the same young woman. Interesting that they kept in touch.'

And so it was that Henry went off on the next train, leaving Emory to visit the Mancinis and Mickey to pursue matters with Dr Phillips, and also to again challenge Dr Mason's knowledge about the lady who became his wife.

Henry did not notice that one of the press men followed him to the station and hopped on the train in the next carriage. Otis Freeland thought he could guess what was taking the detective back to the capital and wondered what he now hoped to learn from M. Giles Esq. and Ernest Conway.

Sergeant Emory, enjoying the privilege of car and driver that had been afforded to him by being part of the murder investigation, headed off for a day trip to Mansfield. Mansfield was a small market town only twelve or so miles distant, but Emory had never actually been there. He knew it to be a town with a large market square, several ancient public houses and that mining was a major source of employment. He had hoped to visit the White Lion, the establishment being recommended to him, but was disappointed to find that they would not need to go into the town itself. Instead, they followed the railway line two miles past the station (Emory decided not to report that he could have visited by train) and continued out into the countryside.

The Mancinis occupied a tall and somewhat sprawling stone-built house, next to the breaker's yard and scrap merchant which kept the family occupied. He was fascinated to discover everything from rusted locomotives to cars and trucks that had evidently been engaged in a game of chicken that didn't end well. He paused to study the front end of an Austin Seven that had lost an argument with a tree. He knew it was a tree because branches still protruded through the window. The front windscreen was smashed and the engine block shunted into the passenger compartment. Emory doubted anyone had walked away from that one.

Until this moment he'd not given much thought to what happened to vehicles written off in accidents, or for that matter where old locomotives came to die. Now he knew.

A tall man with his shirtsleeves rolled up, wearing a moleskin waistcoat, ambled across to where Emory stood.

'Do something for 'un?' he asked.

Emory introduced himself and explained that he wanted to speak with Mr Gus Mancini and his wife. The man turned and shouted over his shoulder 'Gus, polic'n for'un.'

A young man came out of what looked to Emory like a glorified shed. He was slightly more smartly dressed, but only slightly. It was clear that even for the members of the family this was a hands-on business.

Emory introduced himself again. And then told the young man, 'It's about Mrs Mason. I'm sure you'd have heard.'

His statement was greeted with obvious puzzlement. 'Martha? Heard what?'

'Ah . . .' Emory paused, wondering quite how to approach this. He went for the direct method. 'I believe you saw the lady in question at the races, back on bank holiday Monday. Unfortunately a little while after you'd spoken to her she was killed. Murdered. So as you can imagine when interviewing anyone who—'

'Murdered. Martha? You must be mistaken. We only spoke to her—'

'And unfortunately only a short while after that . . . She was found about four o'clock. Been bashed over the head.'

'By a bag snatcher? I'm not sure I understand.' The man gestured vaguely, waving both hands as though trying to grab hold of the truth. 'You'd better come to the house,' he said. 'I'm not sure I can believe this.'

The man in the waistcoat had been following the conversation with interest but now he wandered back to whatever he had been doing before Emory arrived and Gus Mancini led Emory into the house next door. It had been built, Emory noted, so that the wall facing the scrapyard was completely devoid of windows and the main aspect of the house was turned away, so that the actual front door did not face on to the road but rather round the side. It was reached through a pleasant garden full of bedding plants, along a brick-paved path and the front door itself was quite large, black with the big brass knocker. Gus led him past the door with an explanation: 'You mind if we go around the side, then I can take my boots off in the scullery.'

Emory followed him around the next corner and in through the side of the house. A small porch led into a scullery which in turn led into the kitchen. Gus removed his boots in the scullery, dropping them on to a rack and putting on a pair of carpet slippers. 'My mother always insisted. Said that it had taken her long enough to get carpets and now she had them she didn't want them ruined.'

It struck Emory as being a very sensible point of view but there was no suggestion that he follow suit. He followed Gus into the kitchen where three women were working, two at a table rolling pastry and one at the stove stirring a pot from which emanated a rather wonderful fragrance of beef stew. The woman stirring the pot had auburn hair and freckles and Emory remembered the description of Gus's wife.

All three women turned as Gus came in; he was clearly not expected at this time of the day. And certainly not in company with a policeman. The older woman at the table was introduced as his mother, the one slightly younger and slightly less grey as his aunt and the younger as Emory had guessed was his wife. Emory stood awkwardly in the doorway as Gus explained the situation in a mix of rapid Italian and less rapid English. To Emory's amusement he switched from one to the other mid-sentence and then back again. It seemed that all three women were familiar with both languages, but Gus in his slight shock and excitement found it hard to settle on one.

Gus's wife, Hazel, turned down the heat under the pot. Her mother-in-law hugged her, clearly concerned that the young woman might be upset and she glared at Emory as though it was all his fault. The young couple led him through the kitchen, along a short corridor and into a small sitting room. Emory had the sense that the house was actually larger than he'd first thought, and it seemed that it was home to an extended family. The corridor was dark, oak-panelled and with red, white and black tiles on the floor, but the small parlour was decorated in cheerful yellows and pale greens and light flooded in through the window. There were watercolours on the walls and a lot of books.

'This is our little sitting room,' Gus told him. 'Sit down and tell us what happened. Aunt Edie will bring some coffee and biscuits in a moment.'

Quickly Emory filled them in on what had taken place on the day they had seen Martha Mason. 'And you've not heard about this?'

'No, but then I don't think I've looked at the local paper. And it always takes me a few days to catch up with the national papers. As you may have gathered, this is a family business – if I'm not in the yard I'm in the office. We employ five people, but it's still all hands on deck.'

'I can't believe it,' Hazel said. 'We'd not seen Martha in an age, and it was so funny running into her at the races. We only decided to go at the last minute. We'd been travelling and went to visit family in Italy. It was so wonderful; I've never been so far in my entire life. We came back just over a week ago but when Mama offered to have Daisy, that's our little girl, so that we could go out for the day, I'm afraid I rather jumped at the chance. We don't get much time on our own and we actually got to see Gus's horse run.'

'Well, I think I might own the front leg, maybe even the hoof as well,' Gus said. 'But yes it was rather wonderful, not that we placed or anything – but this isn't about us, this is about Martha. What on earth could have happened? You really don't think it was a robbery?'

'Almost certainly not. Her bag was found, nothing had been taken.'

'What kind of sense does that make?'

They were interrupted by the aunt bringing in a tray with a pot of coffee, one of hot milk and a plate of what looked to Emory like plum bread.

Once she had gone, Emory said, 'I don't think there is any sense to it. But I want you to tell me about Mrs Mason. How did she seem? Did she seem concerned about anything?'

The young couple looked at one another and shook their heads. 'She said she didn't expect to see us there. That she was at the races with friends and she gestured back at somebody I couldn't see. The crowd was thick. But she said it was another doctor's wife and their children. She wanted to know how we were, what we'd been doing. It must have been six months since we last saw her. Gus's father made a donation to a charity and so we went along to the . . . Well, I suppose you'd call it a ball, if you're being kind. I suppose I'd call it a dinner and dance. Anyway, Martha was there and we happened to be on the same table, and that's how we met. I don't think we really know her – I mean not really know her. But she was lovely.'

'Was Dr Mason present?'

'Yes, yes, he was, and we liked him too. We talked, and we danced. There were two other couples on our table and we all got along like a house on fire. To be truthful I'd been dreading the whole thing, but in the end it turned out to be really enjoyable. So often you get stuck at these things with some vicar and his wife.' She put a hand to her mouth as though suddenly realizing she'd made a faux pas. 'What I meant to say is, a lot of the people that turn up at these things are very boring.'

'I know exactly what you mean,' Emory told her. 'Did Mrs Mason talk about her past, about where she had lived before she came to be married?'

'She said she lived in Brighton. I said I'd always wanted to visit. I'd like to see the Royal Pavilion. I have a book about it somewhere.'

'There aren't many things you don't have a book about,' Gus laughed. He gestured towards the bookshelves. 'But no, I don't think she talked much about that. We danced rather a lot, and I have to admit we drank rather a lot, and we chatted rather a lot, but none of it seemed very important.' He looked at his wife for confirmation.

'I think we were all a little giddy,' she confirmed. 'We talked about the work the charity did for all of about five minutes and we all asked each other what our husbands did for a living, and that sort of thing, and then it was all men talking politics and women talking about what we'd seen at the cinema and then at some point in the evening I think it switched and it was the other way around.' She shook her head, the pretty face growing suddenly serious and rather sombre. 'I can't believe it, she was such an alive sort of person.'

'And on the day you saw her at the races, what did you talk about?'

'We only talked for a few minutes. Gus wanted to see the next race because that was the one that their horse was running in. She wished us luck with that. We talked a little bit about Italy and about what she had been doing, but really it was only what, ten minutes or so. At most. We said that we must get together, and I checked that she had our telephone number. We have a telephone for the business, of course, and they had one for the practice. We said that we would see what could be arranged. I think it's rare for any of us to have had a day just for leisure, her husband's practice was getting busier and I know Martha helped him a lot. And with this being a family business it's often very hard to get away, but we were all eager to do so, to meet up again.'

'Did she seem ill at ease? Was she looking around her, for instance?'

Again they exchanged a glance and Gus frowned. 'Well, she was, but I didn't think anything of it at the time. I assumed she was looking for where her friend was with the children.'

'She said she must be heading back, that she'd promised she'd only be a tick.'

'She didn't seem ill at ease, I don't think. She seemed as relaxed as I remembered her.'

His wife nodded agreement. 'Then we went off in one direction and she went in the other.'

'Back the way she'd come?'

'I don't know, she came up behind us, calling our names. We turned around, and there was Martha. So I don't really know what direction she came from.'

'She went off towards the stands, towards the fairground,' Gus said. 'She said that her friend was going to take the children on the fairground rides, so I assumed that's where she was going to.'

Emory had a copy of Mickey's sketch map and he took it out now and asked the Mancinis if they could point out where they thought they had met Martha and the direction she taken when she left them.

'One more thing,' Emory asked them, a rather random thought just striking him. 'Was she carrying her handbag?'

'Well, I would imagine so.' Gus laughed. 'When do women go anywhere without their handbags?'

'No. She wasn't,' Hazel stated emphatically.

'Are you certain? Surely she would have it?'

'No, I know she wasn't. It was when we checked to see if she had our telephone number. She said she thought she did, you remember? But could I write it down for her just in case. And she apologized that she didn't have a pen because she had left her bag with her friend. I never thought anything about it at the time. She said they'd been picnicking, I assumed she'd left it wherever they were picnicking, not that I gave it much thought. Is it important?'

Emory nodded thoughtfully. 'I think it might be.' He pointed to the sketch map. 'This is where she left her friend Nora Phillips and the children. They waited for her for a quarter of an hour then went to the fairground. This is where the body of Mrs Martha Mason was found. As you can see, judging by the direction she took when she left you, she could have gone to the stands or to the fairground or across here towards the area where she died. But this is where her bag was found. As you see clearly, it is between where Mrs Phillips stood waiting for her and where she met you. I think that is a little strange.'

In fact, I think that is more than a little strange, Emory said to himself.

Detective Sergeant Mickey Hitchens was busy sticking his nose into places where it was clearly not wanted. He intended to visit the family of the young woman who Mrs Richardson had told them completely disappeared. He knew this was not really of immediate relevance to the murder of Martha Mason but neither was he totally convinced by the argument that either her affair with Mr Harry Benson had been over or that the child she carried was not his. So far another potential father had not emerged, apart from Dr Phillips of course, so until he did, Mickey was quite content to examine the circumstantial evidence against Mr Harry Benson – if only because he really didn't like the man.

He had first gone to Mr Benson's house and spoken to the other Mrs Richardson there, aunt to Grace, who worked for Dr and Mrs Phillips. Mr Benson was out, she didn't know where or when he'd be back and she wasn't very sure that she should welcome Sergeant Hitchens into the house with her employer not being present. But she did anyway.

'I looked in that room, and you've left that fingerprint powder everywhere,' she told him.

'I'm afraid I have,' Mickey agreed comfortably. 'It'll wipe off with a damp cloth. Though I'd rather you left it alone for a while. There might still be more to be learnt from that study of his.'

'I very much doubt that. All he does is sit in there and drink and smoke too much. And if he's in company then he sits and drinks and smokes even more.'

'If you disapprove of him so much, why do you remain?'

She shrugged. 'Because it's work,' she said. 'And because I had a great fondness for his mother and father and for him when he was small. I looked after him then. In those days, of course, this house had a full staff but the war ended all of that.' She smiled and the smile softened her features. 'Such parties they had. I used to help Madame dress, all silks and pearls and feathers in her hair. A beautiful woman she was and believe it or not he was a sweet boy.'

'And how long have you been in service here?'

'Twenty-seven years next May. Master Harry was a year old when I came. And a right handful he was then, but a darn sight easier than he is now, I can tell you. The trouble with young men his age is they've not seen the hardships their fathers went through. Judging by your age, you must have served. You and that inspector of yours, but the younger ones, all they want is to be irresponsible, to be mad and wild and gay.'

'I've been told that he has had to sell some of the family possessions. That he is not as comfortably off as he would like other people to think.'

She snorted. 'He was well enough off when his father died. Had he been as careful as his father, he could have run this place the way it is meant to be run and still be comfortably off, as you put it. He tries to keep pace with those who have more than he does, that's his problem. Gambling and drinking and womanizing, it would have broken his poor mother's heart. I'm glad she's not here to see it. Though if she had still been around I doubt if he'd have got away with it. After she died his father didn't seem to have the wherewithal to correct him. And I know I'm speaking out of turn, and frankly I don't care. I've been with this family a very long time and it cuts me to the quick the way he squandered everything.'

'From the way you spoke to him the other day, it seems he might be conversant with the way you feel. You'll forgive me for being blunt, but—'

'Why does he put up with me? Why doesn't he give me my notice? I'll tell you why, because no one else will work for him and he knows it. He has a reputation now and any young woman coming to work here would have hers ruined, whether she gave into his blandishments or not. I told him straight, I would have no more young women working here. So he told me that he would therefore hire no one else and that I must manage alone, as though that was a hardship. He rarely eats here, I send his laundry out to be done, and there are three rooms in this house that he won't let me enter to dust and clean, so my duties are not exactly onerous.'

'Three rooms?' Mickey asked.

Mrs Richardson looked shamefaced. 'I shouldn't have told you that. It's sheer foolishness. His study you know about, his bedroom, well he used to allow me in to change the sheets, though they are often in such a state that I told him he could do it himself. He occasionally remembers to put them in the laundry hamper and when he does I put fresh linen on the bed for him. But nothing more. I'm under instruction to touch nothing more in his bedroom. And the third room of course is his dressing room. Much of the rest of the house is covered down with dust sheets. You can't believe how much it saddens me to see the place like this. But what respectable young woman would allow him to court her, not with his reputation. What respectable father would allow his daughter to marry someone who would gamble her money away, who would never be faithful to her, and would leave her miserable and probably destitute?'

Mickey wondered how much of this was exaggeration and how much pure exasperation. Mrs Richardson had counted this place home for twenty-seven years – she clearly felt she had an investment in this great big, empty house and he wondered where she would go if her employer did dismiss her, or did in fact lose everything.

'Eliza Watkins,' he said.

'What about her?' she said sharply.

'Where do you think she went to? It's an open secret that Mr Benson was probably the father of her child, and an equally open secret that he probably paid for her to get rid of it.'

'You can't prove any of that.' She was defensive now. She might complain about her young master, but he was still *hers;* still in some part that little boy she had looked after from when he'd been only a year old.

'So what do you think became of her?'

'When a girl is shamed, she'll go away from those who know she's been shamed. I've no doubt she is in employment somewhere else where she isn't known, and I wish her well.'

'Did you provide her with references?'

'I would have done, had I been asked. I feel sorry for the girl, for all that she was foolish, I'd not see her unable to get a place. But she never sent to me for references.'

'It's hard to get a position without references,' Mickey observed. Unless they were fabricated, of course. If the girl had moved far enough away then it was possible that her references would not be checked. 'There are rumours that she died.'

'There are always rumours. People gossip, it is what people do. Especially about their betters.'

'And you count your employer as one of their betters.'

Mrs Richardson scowled at him. Then she seemed so reconsider. 'She was only seventeen. Flattered by the attention, I've no doubt. Her head was full of dreams and promises, she believed that he loved her, of course, but she was just another conquest. I can't deny that because it is common knowledge and because the fool of a boy never really made any secret of it. Eliza never told me when she fell pregnant, but I knew. Time was, in a household like this, girls were made to show the housekeeper evidence each month, that they were not in the family way. But I've never made my girls do that. There's a cook housekeeper we had when I first got here, she was a stickler for it. They had to show their rags, and there would be hell to pay if they were late, or they tried to get out of it. I often think now this was as much to scare the young men as it was to frighten the girls. Not that I should be speaking about such a thing to a man, but I'm assuming that you are a married man.'

Mickey admitted that he was. 'But we are moving away from the subject,' he said. 'You don't believe, any more than I do, that the girl is away working elsewhere.'

'Why should I not believe that? Why should *you* not believe that? No doubt she gave birth to the brat somewhere, put it up for adoption or left it at a workhouse or orphanage. I expect he gave her money. Of course, I'm not comfortable with this, but the girl was foolish and would take no telling. She would have it that she was special. That he loved her. That he wished to marry her. Have you ever heard anything as absurd? Men say these things and young wealthy men the more so, but do they ever mean it? Do they my eye. They say what a girl wants to hear until they get what they want, and that's that.'

'Perhaps so,' Mickey agreed. 'Did your husband also work for the Bensons?'

'No. I was widowed very early. Then this position became available, and I have been here ever since. My sister-in-law mentioned it to me, she knew the family, I came and had an interview and that was that.'

Mickey took his leave of her shortly after, wondering if he could manage to get a warrant to search the bedroom and dressing room of Mr Harry Benson. Out of curiosity, he wandered back around the house and into the garden. It must once have been a very smart affair, he thought, but it was now overgrown and heavily brambled. Evidently Harry Benson did not employ a gardener. He was aware that Mrs Richardson watched him from window as he stood on the terrace and then went down the steps into what had once been a formal garden. Low walls on either side of the path directed him down more steps and on to a lawn, surrounded by tall spreading trees. Beyond this he could see glasshouses and what he assumed had once been a kitchen garden. This had been a substantial and well-loved property, he could see that, and it seemed strange to him that the son could wish to undo everything his parents had built up here. Was this the result of hatred, resentment or just carelessness? Mickey would have given his right arm to own somewhere like this and it angered him that a young man, who'd been served everything on a plate, would squander it so completely.

And so it was that when he went to visit the parents of Eliza Watkins he was already predisposed to think the worst of young Harry Benson.

The parents and siblings of Eliza Watkins lived on the outskirts of Newark-on-Trent, in a tiny terraced house with a very tiny yard at the back of it. Mickey was familiar with such houses, he'd grown up in one, though his current home was a few steps up, having three bedrooms and inside plumbing.

But this was squalid. Mickey had been unable to get an answer by knocking on the front door and so had made his way round the alley at the back and found the wife. The husband was out, but Mickey didn't think he'd gone out to work and the woman was evasive when he asked her. A girl of about fourteen was helping her mother do the laundry, the girl using a posher to pummel sheets in a bathtub. The woman was putting sheets through a mangle.

'He ain't 'ere,' she told Mickey even before he asked. Mickey assumed she was referring to her husband.

'So don' think you're gonna get money out o' me. 'Cos there ain't no bloody money.'

Mickey assured her that he was not a bailiff or debt collector but was in fact a policeman. He was surprised to find that the woman actually seemed relieved, until he mentioned Eliza. The anxiety returned then, and she glanced meaningfully at the girl. Then telling the girl to get on with the job, she led Mickey inside.

'What now?' she demanded.

Mickey glanced around the house and decided that actually the sheets they were washing were probably not hers. The sheets had looked clean; nothing in this house, including the woman herself, looked clean. Downstairs there was a single room. He guessed that upstairs there might be one or two. The single room was used for living and cooking and there was no real comfort here. One old armchair that he guessed was the father's, some wooden stools and a pile of blankets and rag rugs in the corner, set on top of a folded paillasse on which somebody obviously slept at night and Mickey guessed by day made for extra seating. Mickey knew how difficult it was to keep the room soot free, especially when you used a coal-fired

range for cooking, but this room spoke of someone who had
given up even trying. Any surface that he accidentally brushed
against was greasy and grimy, and impregnated with coal dust.
Mickey guessed that anybody who brought their laundry here
did so because the woman was cheap and also because they
never got to look inside her house.

She was staring at him impatiently. If she was aware of the
judgements he was making, she gave no sign. It seemed to
Mickey that she simply wanted the business dealt with and
him gone.

'How many of you live here?'

'What you wanna know that for? There's me 'n the old
man, Becky you saw out back and four more little ones. Off
at school, ain't they. Though they'd be more use to me back
here. But I can do without the school inspector breathing down
me neck too.'

No wonder Eliza had been looking for an escape, Mickey
thought. 'Eliza,' he said. 'Have you heard from her? Do know
where your daughter is?'

'Like you care. He did what they all do. Got her in the
family way, kicked her out. I told her he was only after one
thing. Once he'd got that, he'd have no more time for 'er, but
listen to me? Did she 'ell as like.'

'And so what happen to her?'

'Went away, didn't she.'

'There were rumours she sought to terminate the pregnancy.
Who would she have gone to?' It was a question he did not
expect an answer to.

Mrs Watkins laughed at him. 'If you're done you can go.
Only two places Eliza can be, one is in some kitchen somewhere, and the other's in the ground. Either she found another
place, and don't want me to know where she is, or she's dead
in a ditch somewhere, poor little bitch.'

'Don't you care?'

'Where's the caring ever get me? She made her bed, let her
lie in it. What can I do to make a difference? You can't tell
young girls, foolish as ever, believed him, didn't she?'

'Do you think he paid for her to get rid of the child?'

'How the 'ell would I know. Girls like that, find themselves in the family way, who knows what they'll do. I seen enough what try and do it themselves, sure you 'ave too. Poor little bitches.'

He had, Mickey thought.

'But I don't suppose a murder detective will be called to the likes of that. I heard about that Mrs Mason what was killed. She were a nice woman and din't deserve that. But my Eliza were a nice girl too.'

Mrs Watkins left Mickey to absorb the implied complaint. Mickey had in fact investigated several deaths that had resulted from botched abortions, but he didn't think anything could be gained by telling Mrs Watkins that. She wouldn't believe for a minute that he was really interested. She had already turned away from him and headed back out into the yard where her daughter was trying to turn the mangle but she did not yet have her mother's strength. Mrs Watkins took back the mangling and pointed the child back to the battering of sheets. Their hands were reddened by coarse soap and, as it splashed on Mickey's foot, what he realized was freezing water. The doors to both outhouses stood open and he could see that one contained a few bags of coal and the other the wooden bench seat of an unplumbed toilet. The stink of it reached him even way across the yard. He wondered what night the dilly cart came round bringing the night soil men to collect the waste. He wondered if they called it the dilly cart round here.

He was going to tell Mrs Watkins that she should get in touch if her daughter should happen to contact her, but in the end he didn't bother. The chance of Eliza Watkins, if she was still alive, getting in touch with her mother seemed pretty remote to Mickey. He glanced back sympathetically at the girl. She had long brown hair, tied back with an old scarf and a blandly pretty face that had more to do with being young than being beautiful. What chance did she have, Mickey thought, or any of her siblings. Eliza Watkins must have felt that she'd fallen into paradise after growing up in a place like this. Of course she had believed Harry Benson, of course she had wanted, needed, to believe this man who had taken her to his bed. And of course she was dead, Mickey had no doubt of that.

*　　*　　*

Mickey's next visit was to Mr Steiff and Mrs Edwards, the brother and sister that Emory had observed Dr Phillips visiting. The house was only ten minutes' walk from the Watkins', and it was also a terraced house, but there the comparisons ended. Very clean white net curtains hung in the front room window, obscuring the view from outside. The front door was painted a glossy blue, the step was scrubbed and the door furniture polished. But there was no answer to be had when he knocked.

He had been aware as he walked down the street that several people had noticed him. It was, he thought, likely to be a place where women were home all day and where a stranger would be obvious. The next door opened and a stout middle-aged woman came out on to the street.

'They're not there. Gone away for a few days. A family emergency, so Mrs Edwards said.'

'When did they leave?'

The woman looked narrowly at Mickey. 'And why should I tell you?'

'Hopefully, because I'm a policeman.' He showed his identification.

'That says Metropolitan Police. You're not a local man. So why should I answer your questions about local people.'

'I'm up here investigating the murder of that doctor's wife at Southwell races on bank holiday Monday. We are speaking with anyone who might have known Mrs Mason, and Mrs Edward's name was suggested.'

The woman looked slightly mollified, but only slightly. 'Left last night. The cab came and took them to the station. And no, I don't know where they were going.'

'You spoke to Mrs Edwards before they left. She told you there was a family emergency.'

'She told me it was a family emergency – she didn't tell me what or where. I didn't ask. She left me a spare key, asked me to feed the cat for them. She's fond of that cat, she wouldn't let it starve. Not that it would starve, it has more sense than that. If it couldn't find Mrs Edwards it would come next door to me.'

'I don't suppose . . .?' Mickey began.

'The answer to that is no. I'm not letting strangers into that house. I don't care if you are a policeman from London.'

'I could get a warrant,' Mickey said.

'And why would you want to get a warrant? You said that Mrs Edwards' name came up because she might have known that dead lady. I expect a lot of people knew that dead lady, her being a doctor's wife. I don't suppose you'll be getting warrants for all of them. So what is it about Mrs Edwards, why do you want to get a warrant?'

Mickey realized that he'd overplayed his hand. He'd certainly met his match. 'How long have you known Mrs Edwards and Mr Steiff?' he asked.

'This is Mr Steiff's house. His wife died. Mrs Edwards lost her husband, so it made sense for her to move back here and keep house for him. Ten or twelve years ago probably, that happened. I've lived here nine. They're nice people.'

'I believe Mrs Edwards was a midwife. Perhaps that is how she met Mrs Mason.'

'Retired.'

'And how long has Mrs Edwards been retired?'

The conversation had attracted attention and the door on the other side opened. A young man popped his head out. 'Everything all right, Maev?' he asked. 'This bloke bothering you, is he?' He was, Mickey noted, dressed in a railway uniform so was probably getting ready for work, or had just returned from his shift.

'He's a policeman. Come asking about Mrs Edwards and Mr Steiff. I told him that they've gone away for a bit. But he seems to want their life history. And he's not even a local policeman. He's one of them from London.'

'Is he now? And why would you be coming asking about Mrs Edwards?'

Mickey repeated what he had told the other neighbour. 'So you see, this is a routine enquiry.'

'*Routine* nosiness, is it? Must be nice to be paid to snoop. Mrs Edwards is a good woman. Mr Steiff is a nice man. Retired, they both are. They help out at the church, teetotal they are, signed the pledge. Mrs Edwards works with unfortunate girls. She's a good woman.'

Mickey was interested to note that he had learnt more from this man informing an errant policeman that he should *not* be nosy, than he was ever likely to get from the first neighbour. 'And where did she do that then? Help out these unfortunate girls.'

'You're the copper, you can find out.'

As though in coordination, both neighbours stepped back inside and closed their doors, but Mickey was content. So Mrs Edwards helped out with unfortunate girls, Dr Phillips had been very angry at Sergeant Emory's line of questioning regarding Mrs Mason's pregnancy. He had taken the time, on his way home, to come and visit Mrs Edwards and her brother and then they had packed and gone off in a somewhat precipitous manner. So what did Dr Phillips not want them to tell Mickey and his inspector? Did it have anything to do with the poor unfortunate Eliza Watkins? And did it – Mickey felt he was pushing things in this particular line of speculation – have anything to do with the death of Mrs Martha Mason?

TWELVE

C hief Inspector Henry Johnstone had arrived in London and gone straight to the offices of M. Giles Esq., solicitor, Otis Freeland his constant shadow.

He had been told that the private investigating agent, Conway would also be present, as requested and the young woman, Felicity Bennett. Henry had been assured that all assistance would be extended to him which he interpreted as solicitor and private detective both seeking to cover their backsides in case of trouble.

Henry was aware of several private detective agencies in the area, including the famous Maud West based at Albion House, just around the corner.

The firm of Giles & Conway – Henry was somewhat surprised to find they were partners – was on the third floor of an office building that housed also a singing teacher, a seller of hair restorer, and various pamphleteers who had set up a small publishing house, which, from the flyers attached to their door, seemed to be religious tracts on the behaviour of young women, and the moral probity of abstinence. He was amused to find that the solicitor's office was on the same floor, and just along the corridor. He wondered if the proprietors of both organizations had interesting conversations should they accidentally meet on the stairs.

The offices of Giles & Conway were larger than they first appeared. A partly glazed door on which their names were blocked in gold led through into a spacious reception area. A young woman sat behind a rather imposing desk and a surprisingly comfortable range of chairs was arrayed opposite, where she could keep an eye on everybody. She asked Henry to take a seat and pressed an intercom on her desk, telling her boss that the inspector had arrived.

Henry was the only person in the waiting room. The wooden panelling had been painted white. Henry supposed that had been to brighten what might otherwise have been a very dull space, but as the paint had not been refreshed in quite a while, the effect was actually to heighten the sense that this was a gloomy room. There were pictures on the walls of racing cars and what looked, to Henry's eye, like the Le Mans circuit. A row of windows in the waiting area did nothing to lift the mood. The outside of the sash windows was grimy so that it was like looking out through fog. Not that there was much of a view, just a blank wall of the next building.

The door opened and a man emerged. He was wearing a blue pinstriped suit, very white shirt and a striped tie. School or regiment? Henry wondered. He crossed the room with his hand already extended to shake Henry's. 'Malcolm Giles,' he said. 'Chief Inspector Johnstone, please come through. May I say that your reputation precedes you and I'm very glad that we can at last meet. I'm only sorry that it is such a sad event that brings us together.'

Henry mumbled a vague reply and followed Malcolm Giles through into his office.

Malcolm Giles and his colleague Ernest Conway occupied adjoining offices behind the reception area. Both were large and were brighter than the room Henry had just left, the windows being cleaner and looking out on to Tottenham Court Road. Ernest Conway came through into his colleague's office, closely followed by a young woman with bleached blonde hair. She was fashionably dressed and carefully made up. Felicity Bennett, he assumed. Introductions were made and Henry invited to sit down. The receptionist, or secretary, or whatever she was, came through with refreshments. Malcolm Giles took a seat behind his desk, Conway perched on a corner and Felicity Bennett settled elegantly into a chair to Henry's left. She tucked her legs out of the way, crossing her feet at the ankles and folding her hands neatly into her lap.

Henry extracted papers and his notebook from the document case he had been carrying. He first showed the postcard found in Martha's desk to Felicity Bennet. It didn't say much apart from the fact that Felicity was enjoying a short holiday and that she missed her friend.

'And yet she kept it,' Henry commented. 'So your friendship

must have been important and yet I found no other correspondence between you?'

Whatever the trio had expected as Henry's opening gambit he suspected it had not been this. Felicity took the card and then nodded. 'I sent it earlier this year. It must have been Easter time. I visited an aunt for a few days. Mary . . . Martha and I spent some good times there, I thought about her and sent her a postcard.'

'But you didn't correspond regularly?'

'Is this relevant, Inspector?' Conway looked both puzzled and amused. Giles, the solicitor, mildly annoyed.

'I am trying to discover who killed Mrs Mason,' he said coldly. 'As yet, there are no obvious suspects; it might be that her death is the result of something from her past. So, I will decide what is relevant, Mr Conway.'

Conway frowned, shrugged and left his perch on the desk. He brought up another chair and settled himself into it. He had clearly wanted this interview to be brief, Henry thought, hence his consciously louche but not terribly comfortable position on the edge of his colleague's desk.

Felicity handed the card back. 'When she first moved north we wrote regularly. Once a week each way. But after a time her letters dried up and when I asked her about it she said she'd just been very busy. Well, I knew that – she was working all hours for that husband of hers and joining every board or committee going. She said in her letters that she wasn't that keen, but she thought the connections she made might be useful to Dr Mason.' Felicity frowned. 'It was funny. In her letters she always called him that. Dr Mason. Not Clive or even "my husband". It was like she was trying to tell me how important he was. That I was to be forever on formal terms with this man, even if my friend had married him.'

'Did you get the impression he disapproved of this continuing friendship?'

She laughed, 'Oh, he disapproved all right. She made no secret of the fact he wanted her to forget all about her old life and all about friends like me. She'd say things like, "Dr Mason is out so I thought I'd take the opportunity to write to you."'

'This seems very clear in your mind.'

Conway got up, took a small stack of letters from the desk and handed then to Henry.

'I can remember because I re-read them after I heard she'd been killed,' Felicity told him.

'We were concerned,' Giles said. 'Anything that might reflect badly on the reputation of our office, is of concern. When Miss Bennet said she still had letters . . .'

'You thought you should see if there was anything incriminating in them,' Henry finished for him.

'Not at all, Chief Inspector. We were merely concerned that there might be useful information. We want the killer found as much as you do.'

Henry tucked the letters into his document case.

'I'll want them back,' Felicity said quickly.

'And you should make out a receipt,' Giles added.

'And what exactly did Mary Betteridge do in your employ?'

The two men both looked ready to respond but it was Felicity who spoke first. 'She started as an office girl, same as me, but we'd been told there were opportunities for betterment and when they were offered we both jumped at the chance. Mary . . . Martha, was younger than me by a couple of years and I'd been an inquiry agent for six months when she came to work here. She was stepping into my shoes, I suppose, and she followed on after me.'

'And you are still employed in the same position?'

'Oh no. I'm a married woman now, so it wouldn't seem quite right.' She smiled at Conway. 'I'm Mrs Conway now. So I direct the girls instead. We employ three, don't we? As inquiry agents. Alongside five male detectives. Women are very useful; they can talk to people who wouldn't talk to men or they can get into places where men would just stick out like a sore thumb.'

'And of course it is a quite different situation for a man to be discovered in a hotel room with the young woman. To be discovered in a hotel room with the young man might lead to more than divorce proceedings.'

Felicity looked shocked. Conway laughed and Giles frowned in annoyance. This, Henry considered, seemed to be a general pattern among the three.

'If any of our girls produce evidence that does assist in a divorce, and we have of course never overstepped the mark of legality,' Giles said carefully, 'then at all times we make sure that one of their male colleagues is on hand. Our young ladies are never put at risk.'

'I'm sure that's the case,' Henry said. 'After all you need a detective on hand to take the relevant photographs, of the hotel register, and of the couple in question in their hotel room.'

'We fulfil a need, Inspector.'

'I'm sure you do. But not everybody approves of that; not everybody will be sanguine about it. I'm sure there have been instances where a divorce has been procured by a husband, the husband himself presenting the evidence of adultery, where the wife is not party to this and has not given her consent. I know of instances where the wife is then cut adrift, sometimes with children to care for and the husband goes on to marry his new inamorata, with little care for the families left behind. The enforcement of the laws pertaining to the payment of maintenance sadly often lags behind even the law pertaining to divorce.'

'We know of no cases like that,' Conway said quickly.

'And besides,' Giles, the more pragmatic one, added, 'we are employed to gain a particular end. What happens thereafter is none of our concern. Our detectives give evidence in the courts, a divorce is obtained, the rest is not our concern.'

Felicity looked somewhat uncomfortable and would not meet Henry's gaze.

'Mrs Conway, was your friend completely at ease with the role she played? Can you think of any incidents where this ended badly for her or that she was unhappy with an outcome?'

He was slightly surprised to see that Felicity looked relieved. 'No, nothing like that. We were always careful to make sure that the proprieties were maintained. We signed the register, not always with our own names of course, and then we would pose on the bed to have a photograph taken. We might take off our coat and hat, otherwise it would have looked somewhat strange, don't you think, but that was all. And then of course, we would disappear from the scene before the court case. The court will be told that the young woman could not be found, but that there was photographic evidence and that was enough.'

Henry nodded, he was very familiar with this ploy. It was not strictly illegal but it did occupy something of a grey area.

'And how many times did this happen. With Mary Betteridge?'

Again, Conway got up and crossed the desk, and came back with a sheaf of papers which he handed over to Henry. 'Obviously we cannot compromise client confidentiality,' he said. 'But these are summaries of the cases that Miss Betteridge was involved in. After all, the outcomes are items of public record, divorce having been obtained satisfactorily for all concerned.'

Henry flicked through the pages and then put these too in his document case. He doubted he'd get much more out of Conway & Giles but warned them that he may return.

He took the opportunity to return to New Scotland Yard, checking in with Central Office, catching up with proceedings on cases he was also obliquely involved with and also asking the fingerprint bureau if they had any matches on the prints that Mickey had sent down. Not yet, he was told.

He then went to his little flat and packed clean shirts and underwear to take back with him, having retrieved also the spare clothes that Mickey always kept in his desk. His train did not leave until the following morning and Henry had already decided that he would pay his sister a visit that evening, but in the meantime he sat down in his favourite chair, close to the window overlooking the river and began to sort through the notes that Conway & Giles had given him.

Shortly before seven, Henry arrived at Cynthia's house. Another few weeks, he thought, and the children would be coming down from school and the family would decamp to the south coast for the summer, Cynthia's husband owning another house in Bournemouth.

Cynthia had three children. The eldest, Cyril, was almost thirteen and had been away at boarding school for the last two years. His choice; he had informed his mother that he was missing out on fun and games and no longer wanted to be just a day boy. The youngest son, Georgie, was six and currently at prep school. He was already campaigning to board but Cynthia was well aware that her youngest boy was not capable of dealing with the demands as yet. He still occasionally wet the bed and Cynthia would not have him shamed.

The middle child, eleven-year-old Melissa, was undoubtedly Henry's favourite. He was not particularly good at talking to the boys about what interested them, sports and cars and aeroplanes. Here, Mickey came into his own and he was a frequent visitor at Cynthia's house. Melissa reminded Henry intensely of Cynthia as a girl and she had a love of books that they could both share and most recently a curiosity about science that had taken Henry a little by surprise but which he was doing his best to encourage. A little while ago he had brought her a microscope and in her last letter she had informed Henry that she'd been making slides of flies' wings and spiders' legs and that 'Nanny was quite squeamish about the whole thing'.

He had telephoned ahead and warned Cynthia that he might be joining them for supper and was very happy when Melissa had been allowed to join the adults, at least for a little while. Her father, Albert, had not yet returned from a business meeting and Cynthia said that it was unlikely he'd be back until late because they'd probably all end up at his club and so dinner was a very informal affair, just Henry and his sister and niece. They escaped from murders for a while and discussed the books Melissa had been reading. On a recent visit to Germany her mother had purchased a copy of *Emil and the Detectives* by Erich Kästner, and she and Mellissa were reading that together. Cynthia was a talented linguist and her daughter had a natural aptitude.

Melissa was yawning by the time Nanny came to take her to bed. She hugged Henry and kissed him on the cheek before going to say goodnight to her mother. Fondly, Henry watched as she left the room, the tumble of red hair so like his sister's. Cynthia now wore hers fashionably short, bobbed and shingled and very elegant, and she toned down her freckles with foundation.

'She's growing up so fast,' Henry said somewhat regretfully.

'She won't have to grow up as fast as we did, little brother.'

She poured them both more coffee and then asked, 'So what are you investigating this time? Is it that poor woman who was killed at the racetrack?'

'It is. Don't you think the Kästner book is a little . . . harsh for a girl Melissa's age?'

Cynthia laughed. 'I will admit that it is grittier and grimier than most books for the young – though do you remember some of those terrible, terrible volumes we had on the book-shelves? What was that dreadful thing about the boy being boiled alive?'

'I don't remember,' Henry admitted. 'I've a feeling that you hid that sort of thing from me.'

'Well, maybe I did. But Melissa loves to read and loves to question, as you know. Emil is a relatively gentle introduction to a very brutal world. I want my children well prepared. And what better way to learn a language than to read stories in that language?'

Henry could think of no appropriate response.

'You were telling me about the poor woman killed at the racetrack.'

'I was, but that poor woman is not all she seemed to be.' Briefly he told his sister what he had discovered and then said, 'Do you remember anything about the Kirkland divorce case a few years ago? I believe it got rather complicated with both the husband and wife suing for divorce on grounds of adultery. The husband, I believe, didn't want to have to make a settle-ment on the wife and so he'd tried to prove that she was the guilty party. But I can't remember the details.'

Cynthia raised an eyebrow. 'It's not like you to be interested in society gossip. I take it this has to do with the case.'

'Possibly. I'm not sure yet.'

'Well . . .' Cynthia inserted a cigarette into a silver and amber holder and offered one to Henry, who shook his head. He would drink his coffee first, but he lit his sister's and waited while she drew in a great lungful of smoke and then released it slowly. 'I will stop smoking,' she said. 'I began because I thought cigarette holders looked so elegant and it seemed a little foolish to wave the cigarette holder around with nothing in it. So you should be proud of me, Henry, I now restrict my cigarette

smoking to the end of the day. Unless I'm having a bad day.'
She smiled at him.

'So, what do I remember of the Kirkland divorce. It must
be what, nine years ago? Two very wealthy families, hers old
money, his new. Though I believe he is related to the Elliston
clan somewhere along the line. A cousin on his mother's side.'

'Elliston.' That name had cropped up. Henry put the thought
to one side for the moment to listen to Cynthia.

'I think it was a marriage of convenience as much as
anything, they were both in their mid-thirties, neither had
married before and I think there was pressure from their families just to get on with it. If I remember right, it brought land
and business together or something of the sort. You can bet
your last shilling that there was money at the back of it.
Anyway, it was only a year or two before each of them started
to play away. She picked up with all sorts, she was always a
good time girl though it has to be said she was getting a little
old to be one of the bright *young* things. *He* had a long-time
mistress, now what was her name, Maynard, I believe, Nancy
Maynard. Daughter of some tycoon or other. Needless to say,
not welcome in polite society, so I've never actually run across
the lady.' She grinned at her brother. 'And you know how
many doors are still closed to me, even though I am a member
of *nearly* polite society. There are still some places you cannot
buy your way into, no matter what you do.'

'And would you wish to?'

'Oh Lord no. I have enough of a time trying to be polite
to all the ones who do accept me. But anyway, Kirkland
continued this affair and tried to ignore his wife's antics. She
meanwhile is off in Monte Carlo and elsewhere, losing as
much of the family money as she possibly can. From what I
gather both her husband and her father had given her a generous
allowance, but she was always in debt. Kirkland paid off her
debts just to keep the family name out of it. There were
rumours that she'd become involved in something over here.
Gambling again, but with very unsavoury types you'll not find
in a regular casino. You know that Kirkland owns racehorses,
I suppose? I wondered with you investigating a murder that
happened on a racecourse.'

'No, I did not.' Elliston, Henry remembered. Emory had mentioned him. The man had been with a gaggle of friends at the races but had claimed to be too drunk to give a proper account of his day. Henry had discounted him as unimportant simply because his position meant that he was surrounded by other people and could hardly have wandered off, murdered a woman and returned to his entourage without being noticed. Plus he was an elderly man.

'Did two facts suddenly connect?' Cynthia asked. She was well used to the way her brother's mood changed and could recognize when his brain had suddenly worked something out.

'The connection with Lord Elliston. He was at the races that day. But that might be coincidence, of course.'

'Hmm . . . coincidences. You never did like those very much, did you.'

'So what happened?'

'Well, and this is from memory, you understand, he decided to sue for divorce, and goodness knows there was plenty of evidence of her infidelities. She gets wind of it and decides that she is going to sue him first. Of course, he's been having this long-term liaison. Everybody knows about his mistress, so that wouldn't be difficult to prove either.

'Anyway, I think she demanded a big settlement in order to let him divorce her. He said no and so she threatened to drag him through the divorce courts and ensure that the Maynard name as well as the Kirkland name was completely muddied instead of slightly dingy.'

'That didn't happen, though, did it?'

'No, can't have done, I'd have remembered that. I think she got her way in the end though, and she divorced him for adultery, but Nancy Maynard must have been named, musn't she?'

Henry thought back to the notes he had read before coming over here. The cases in which Martha Mason, or Mary Betteridge as she had been then, had been named as enquiry agent. Henry had no doubt that she, under an assumed name, had been the woman named in the Kirkland divorce. Somewhere, there would be a photograph of Martha and Kirkland together, probably in a little hotel room, the photograph taken by one of the male detectives that worked for Giles & Conway.

'I don't remember that she was. I believe they engaged a solicitor who provided a young woman to pose as the co-respondent. I'm pretty sure that woman was Martha Mason.'

'Your dead doctor's wife? My goodness, that's convoluted. Do you think this has anything to do with her death? The divorce was years ago and I think he's remarried at least once since then.'

'I don't know,' Henry admitted. 'Interesting though if he should happen to have been at the races on the day she died.'

He left Cynthia about an hour later and though he did notice the man who paused under a street lamp to light his cigarette, he thought nothing of it.

Otis went on his way. It was late, but his contact would still be up and he had a good deal to report.

He nodded briefly at the man walking back the other way. Otis wouldn't be following Henry home that night but Henry would be followed all the same.

THIRTEEN

Henry had not departed first thing the following morning, as originally planned. Instead he had taken himself to the office of the London *Times* and had requested information they might have regarding the Kirkland divorce. The facts were pretty much as Cynthia had remembered them.

There had been a photograph in the files, taken on the day that the detective from Giles & Conway had given evidence to the court. The court case was so high profile that a number of photographers had waited outside, hoping to get a decent picture of the injured party and the accused. Mrs Kirkland – soon-to-be ex-Mrs Kirkland – had posed for photographs, looking glamorous and assured. A man standing beside her was referred to as her solicitor and there was an unnamed man, just behind, with his face turned from the camera. He was so obviously trying to move aside, as though wanting to get out of the way of the picture, and Henry would have thought him unconnected, apart from the fact that Mrs Kirkland had a hand resting on his arm. But it was the action captured in the background that really caught Henry's eye; two men and a woman were getting into a taxi. One was Conway, the private investigator. The second he identified as Kirkland, there being other pictures in the article of the man himself. And the third was Martha. She had turned and was looking back at the little knot of people outside the court, at the very glamorous woman and her entourage. Henry had taken a hand lens and examined the photograph carefully and been surprised by the look of pure hatred on Martha's face.

So, he asked himself, was her association with Kirkland more than just a random act of professional deception?

On impulse he had telephoned the offices of Conway & Giles and asked to speak to Felicity Bennett, remembering belatedly that she was now Felicity Conway. She agreed to meet him and half an hour later they were drinking coffee.

'Mr John Kirkland,' he said.

'What about him?'

'You helped him obtain a divorce.'

'Technically, we helped his wife to obtain a divorce,' she corrected him. 'Mrs Kirkland won her case, he paid up, they got divorced.'

'And yet there was a photograph in the *Times* showing Mr Kirkland, with your husband and with Martha. All three were getting into a taxi and seemed on the best of terms. Could it be that your company assisted both parties?'

She frowned and sipped her coffee. Then shook her head. 'I wouldn't know anything about that,' she said.

Henry reached into his pocket. 'I was able to obtain a copy of this photograph from the newspaper offices.' He laid it on the table and pointed to the taxi in the background of the picture. 'I have a glass if you wish for magnification.'

She pushed the picture away. 'I told you, I know nothing about that. Look, Mary . . . Martha . . . whatever her name was, she was doing a job. That was all. So what if Mr Conway, if my husband, also helped out with the husband's needs. They both got what they wanted in the end and anyway, it makes sense they all knew one another, Martha was the one who helped create the evidence.'

That was true, Henry agreed. 'Do you know who this man might be?' He pointed to the discomforted figure, standing to the side and just behind the soon-to-be ex-Mrs Kirkland.

'No, no idea,' she said after only a very quick glance. 'Just a passer-by, from the look of him. Accidentally got caught in the picture.'

'Except Mrs Kirkland evidently knows him. She has her hand on his arm.'

Felicity shrugged. 'I told you, I don't know who he is. Look, I've got to be going.' Her carefully cultivated sophistication was slipping, Henry noted. She was genuinely rattled.

'I think you have every idea who this man is.'

'What's it matter now anyway? It was nine years or so ago, she's probably picked up with half a dozen men or more since then. So has he for that matter. He's already gone through another divorce.'

'Did he marry Miss Maynard?'

She laughed contemptuously. 'Marry Nancy Maynard. You've got to be kidding me. No, he married some heiress or other, some minor aristocrat, not even an English aristocrat. Hungarian? Polish maybe, I don't remember. It was in the papers and I remember looking at the picture and thinking it wouldn't last. She was all starry and he . . . well, he seemed only half there. Some men should never get married.'

A man at a table further back in the café got up and brushed past, the tables being set quite close. Henry glanced up, feeling that the face was somewhat familiar, but his attention was on Felicity.

'Were there ever times when a young woman became involved with the client? When perhaps that young woman overstepped the boundaries.'

'If you want to ask if Mary overstepped the boundaries, then say so. Yes she did, a couple of times. Truth is, Inspector, if she hadn't taken herself off to be married she'd have got the push anyway. Girls are hired to do a job. They do the job, it takes half an hour of their time, they get paid. End of story. The man never sees them again and doesn't even have their proper name. You do not get involved.'

'And did she get involved with this Kirkland?'

Felicity sighed and gathered her gloves back together. 'I really do have to go.'

'Then answer my question. Or I *will* have you arrested for interfering with a police officer in the commission of his duties.'

She laughed. 'You what? Is that even a legitimate offence?'

'Would you like to risk finding out?'

She stared at him for a moment or two and then gave up. 'All right. Yes, she had a thing with Kirkland. He took a fancy to her and found out who she was. I don't suppose it was that difficult for a man with his money. A bribe here and there. I think he actually liked her, she was an easy person to like, but I don't think she wanted to end up as another Nancy Maynard. And then her doctor came along and that was it.

She married him and off she went.' She looked puzzled for a moment and then said, 'Funny thing though, she was the "other woman" for a friend of his, a few months before. In fact, Kirkland actually requested her because of that. She got involved with him for a while too.'

'So she made a habit of it.'

'No, it wasn't a habit. But sometimes a man can show you a good time, give you a little extra cash, a gift or two. Of course I wouldn't do that now, but when I was young and free and single.'

'Sometimes the temptation is too much.'

'Exactly that.' She sounded triumphant as though so glad that he'd understood. 'That time went all wrong though.'

'Wrong? In what way?'

'Well, he'd come in asking about getting help with his divorce settlement, said he didn't mind being the guilty party, but that he didn't see what right his wife had to take money that had been in the family for . . . God, I don't know, generations. Martha soon found out he didn't mind spending it on her. He asked to meet some girls, to see which one looked like his type, so that his wife would believe what was being set up – seeing as the girl would disappear afterwards anyway.'

'And, Conway & Giles accommodated that?'

She shrugged. 'Not the strangest thing they've been asked. And besides, it made a kind of sense. Anyway, he chose Martha and when she was leaving work that day, he was waiting for her across the road. Well, they get into conversation and he asked if he could take her to dinner and she says yes. And they see each other a few more times, and then she finds out that he is violent. That he's been beating up his wife. The fact that he makes a habit of beating up women.'

'Did he hurt Martha?'

'Um, I don't think so. To be honest I don't know all the details, it was all a bit, well, sordid. Mr Giles sorted it all out but agreed that she would do her part for the photographs, but she didn't think it was right this poor woman would be left with nothing just because none of it was hers in the first place. I mean usually solicitors managed to get some kind of settlement, and I'm not quite sure what happened here, but there was some problem or complication. Martha reckoned the poor woman wouldn't say boo to a goose by the time the husband had finished with her. So she leaked information to one of the newspapers. She denied it, of course, but I was pretty sure it was her.'

'So she made an enemy. What was his name?'

'I'm not supposed to give names.'

'Mr Giles gave me information yesterday, about the cases in which Martha had been involved. I simply wish to know which one.'

She pouted, still obviously unsure. 'It was Mr Elliston, Mr Timothy Elliston. Lord Elliston's son.'

'Potentially a powerful enemy,' Henry said. And Elliston had been at the races. Had his son, had Kirkland?

'Yes, so you can imagine how surprised we all were when Mr Kirkland wanted her to be the woman in the photograph. Martha was not very happy about it, but she met with Mr Kirkland and he managed to persuade her. He said he was no longer friends with this other chap because he'd found out what he was like and that he never knew that he'd been violent to his wife. Anyway, he got his divorce and then Martha went off and got married, and that's all there is to tell.'

'And now Martha's dead.'

'Yes, well. I know nothing about that.'

'Was she already calling herself Martha before she left? You use the name very easily and casually, as though you're used to it.'

'Sometimes. We all used different names. Of course we did. You play a part, and you need a name to go with the part. It was just part of the job, but Martha suited her and sometimes we would forget and I would just call her Martha. Look, if you've done with me, I really must go. Some of us have to work for a living.'

'Take this photograph with you,' Henry told her. 'I have a second copy. It might be that you remember where you have seen this man before, because I know that you have. You are not good at lying, Mrs Conway.'

She snatched at the photograph and stuffed it into her bag. Henry waited for her to go, finishing his coffee and checking the time before picking up his travelling bag and heading towards the station. So, what had she told him? he wondered. He wished he had time to go back to Scotland Yard and look through the catalogues of booking photographs they held there. But his departure was already later than he had intended. Something at the back of his mind was telling him that he knew the face, but that it was not from recent history. Perhaps Mickey would know. Or perhaps he had just seen it in one of the society newspapers his sister read, and which he had skimmed on occasion. 'It is as well to keep up with the gossip, Henry,' she had told him when he had jibed her on this habit. 'You should always go into a conflict knowing your enemy.' Henry had the unsettling feeling that he was entering this particular conflict not knowing his enemy at all.

FOURTEEN

Henry arrived back in Southwell to find that once more events had overtaken them. Dr Mason's house had been broken into and Dr Mason had been attacked. On hearing the news, he made his way to the Mason house and found Mickey and Emory examining the French windows. The lock had not been fixed, and this was now the point of entry for a vicious attack.

'The neighbours heard noise, they came round and hammered on the door, this was about five o'clock this morning. Someone had thrown poisoned meat out for the dogs. The big one's dead, the little one might just pull through. Typical terrier.'

'We had constables doing extra patrols,' Emory said. 'But no one on the spot all the time, not since the doctor moved back. He said he didn't want that, and frankly we don't have the manpower for it. He said he'd lock his doors, but that back one, well we both know a child to get through it. But it was no child did this.'

The room that Mason had used as his dispensary had been completely ransacked. Medicines were strewn across the floor and books shredded.

'Has the whole house been attacked like this?'

'Mostly the downstairs. And much of the chaos in here has been caused because Dr Mason came down and confronted the housebreaker. It's possible they did not know the doctor had returned, the house was in darkness and it is well known that he'd been staying with Dr Phillips. Mason came down with the poker in his hand, but whoever was here disarmed him and turned his weapon against the unfortunate man.'

'Will he survive?'

'I doubt it,' Mickey said. 'We found him alive, only because the neighbour disturbed proceedings and set up a hue and cry. The neighbours came out and broke down the door and they found the poor doctor lying over there, half in and half out of the French doors.'

Henry walked over. A smear of blood seemed to indicate where a hand had grasped the frame. Blood cast off from a weapon, repeatedly raised and then falling on the unfortunate victim, had spattered across the walls and ceiling. A pool of blood stained the slabs outside the French doors. 'Did he say anything?'

'No, he was too far gone. Unconscious by the time the neighbours broke in. He is literally a bloody mess and I certainly doubt he will survive the day.'

'So what were they looking for?'

'The key?' Emory suggested. 'That makes no sense. Anything that key locked could be broken open with a teaspoon. So did he actually have what they sought? Was it here? It certainly doesn't look as if he knew he had it and surely if they thought he did, they'd have tried to extract the information first.'

'It's most likely they didn't realize he'd returned home,' Mickey agreed.

'Has anything been stolen from the dispensary? Those addicted to opiates, perhaps . . .?'

'No sign of anything being gone. Of course, it's hard to tell with all the mess, but Dr Phillips informed us that his colleague kept such medicines in that locked cabinet over there. The cabinet is still locked, it has simply been knocked to the floor.'

While Mickey examined the crime scene, Henry told them both what he had discovered in London and they exchanged information in return.

'Complications on complications,' Mickey said. 'But the connection to Lord Elliston is an interesting thing. I wonder if this Kirkland character was with him on the day. With this friend that Martha Mason made an enemy of.'

Henry left them to it and returned to the police station. It was mid-afternoon and he was hoping that any results from the fingerprint bureau would now have been forwarded to them. He was not disappointed. He read the communication and then turned on his heel and headed straight back to the Mason house.

Mickey Hitchens was kneeling on the dispensary floor, dislodging broken glass from beneath a cabinet.

'Mickey, we have a very interesting breakthrough. The photographs of the fingerprints you found on the door of the horsebox, well we have a match and it's a most unexpected one. The bureau has matched them to one Eric Columbus Davies.'

Mickey looked up in surprise. 'I thought he was still safely locked up inside.'

'It would seem not. He was released three months ago.'

'Well, well,' Mickey said.

Emory was studying them both with great interest. 'A known felon.'

'Indeed he is. And it's suspected. No, *more* than suspected, that he's killed before, though we have not been able to prove it. He's a known razor man, and I've seen the victims he's cut to ribbons. They won't name him, of course, but once you've seen a man's face cut in a particular way, you recognize the signature. He's an enforcer with the racing gangs, which probably explains what he was doing up here. And he was known to attack a man with an ice pick; the witnesses to the crime later retracted the statement and said only that they'd seen two men brawling and must have been mistaken about what they first reported. Though the other man's injuries were consistent with being smashed with an ice pick. His shoulder was almost severed at the joint.'

Belatedly, Henry remembered the photograph he had in his pocket. He took it out and showed it to Mickey, pointing to the man standing beside the ex-Mrs Kirkland. 'I feel I know that face, but I cannot place it.'

Mickey's eyes narrowed and he rummaged through his capacious memory. Finally he came up with the name. 'Johnny Sexton,' he said. 'Also affiliated with the racing gangs, but he's not been active for a while. He was a big man just after the war, but it went quiet in '22 or '23. I'd all but forgotten about him. Things begin to come together.'

'After a fashion,' Henry agreed. 'Now we must find *how* they come together and how Martha Mason fitted in with all of this. I think we will need to pay a visit to this Lord Elliston and see if he still has his houseguests after the races.'

*   *   *

Otis had observed Henry's meeting with Felicity Conway and seen him showing the young woman a photograph. He hadn't been able to sit close enough to catch the conversation; Henry spoke quietly, but the girl's voice travelled and he heard the name Kirkland. Kirkland; so what was the inspector on to?

What was it he was showing that girl? A photograph of what?

Otis had left his tea half drunk and pushed by their table, dropping his gaze and trying to make sense of the photograph. On the train he'd had time to think about it further and come to the conclusion that the photograph had something to do with the Kirkland divorce.

The contact with Martha Mason had been one strand; this was another. It seemed that he and the inspector were chasing the same clues.

And now Dr Mason was probably dead.

Otis left his position on watch and wandered back to where the press pack had gathered.

The household of Dr and Nora Phillips was in complete disarray. Walking there, Henry had glimpsed a swarm of reporters and photographers camped out on Burgage Green close by the police station. He had been careful to avoid them as he made his way down Church Street and on to Queen Street, thence to the Rope Walk.

The maid servant, Grace Richardson, let him into the house. She looked flustered and anxious. 'Madam is packing and will be taking the children away,' she said. 'Everybody's most terribly upset, sir.'

He was directed through to Dr Phillips' study. Ephraim Phillips did not look pleased to see him.

'What is going on?' Ephraim Phillips demand to know. 'Inspector, this is madness. I'm sending Nora and the children well away from here.'

'That is understandable. You will not be going with them?'

'How can I? I not only have my practice to run but now I will have to see to Clive's too. It may be possible that I can amalgamate them both, maybe take on someone else. It will have to be done.'

'Dr Mason may yet recover.'

'Have you seen him?' Henry had to admit that he had not as yet. 'If you had you would not be so stupid. Forgive me, Inspector. We are all deeply upset, as I am sure you can imagine.'

Dr Phillips closed his study door, shutting out the noise and confusion outside. Children running back and forth, excited to be going on a trip. Nora calling to Grace that she couldn't find something or other. Grace running up the stairs.

'I trust the ridiculous conversation I had with your sergeant will go no further.'

'If you mean my questions about your relationship with Martha Mason,' Henry said, 'then I still do not feel you gave him a satisfactory answer. I will do you the courtesy of waiting until your wife and children have departed, but we will speak again, Dr Phillips.'

Ephraim Phillips gestured impatiently. 'You're wasting your time. I didn't get Clive killed. I had nothing to do with Martha's death. You should be getting out there and finding the person that did.'

'Oh, make no mistake, I will,' Henry assured him. 'What is your connection with Mr Geoffrey Steiff and his sister, Mrs Regina Edwards? They live in Newark-on-Trent on—'

'I know full well where they live,' Dr Phillips said impatiently. 'Regina has a medical background; she sometimes helps out with young women who find themselves pregnant and are in need of care during that pregnancy. There is a hostel for unwed mothers close to here, she is reliable and knowledgeable and the girls learn to trust her very quickly. Adoptions are arranged and the young women go on their way.'

'And she does nothing else, for these young women?'

'I will not even deign to answer that. It is a foolish question. Girls who have fallen pregnant need antenatal care. Those who have fallen by the wayside and find themselves pregnant with bastards, still need antenatal care. The best thing that can be done for such girls is to find places for their babies.'

'I have one more small question. There are rumours that you are a little heavy-handed in your dispensation of morphia to the elderly and the infirm.'

Dr Phillips laughed bitterly. 'I don't have to ask where that must have come from. Miss Georgia Styles. Gossip extraordinaire. She could not accept that when three or four of her friends died this past year, it was because they were old and ill. If I gave morphine to ease the pain of their passing, then that is all I did. I do not like to see people in pain. It is needless.'

As long as they can pay, Henry thought. It crossed his mind briefly that his mother had died in great pain, despite the fact that his father was a doctor and had access to all the pain relief she might have required. But then, that was typical of his father.

'I wish to have a quick word with your wife.'

'Now look here, you just said—'

'The question I have to ask is nothing to do with you,' Henry told him coldly. '*We* will speak later. For now, I have a question to ask your wife about some of Mrs Mason's personal possessions. It seems to me that another woman might answer my questions far more aptly than you would, for example. Unless you have much more intimate knowledge of Mrs Mason's belongings then you have previously declared.'

Ephraim looked as though he would like to say more but didn't think he could control his temper. He pointed to the door. 'She's upstairs. You may go up.'

Henry inclined his head in mild acknowledgement and then left.

Grace was in the hall and she took Henry up to see Nora Phillips. The children were busy bouncing on the bed and their mother was making no attempt to stop them. She seemed utterly preoccupied with gathering things from the wardrobe and dumping them into a suitcase. Grace was taking them out again and packing properly. A large and fully packed trunk stood nearby; evidently her trip was not intended to be a brief one.

'Mrs Phillips? If I could have a moment or two.' He could see that she'd been crying.

'First Martha, and now this. Inspector, I do not feel safe in my own house any more. I do not feel safe anywhere.'

'It is probably wise to go away for a little while,' Henry

agreed. 'Not because I believe you are in any danger, but because this must play on your mind so much. Are you staying with relatives?'

She nodded. 'My aunt lives by the sea, the children will love it for the summer. And it is an age since I saw my sister and her family. We had planned to go, but these things kept being put off. I will put them off no longer. I simply want to be away from here, can you understand that?'

'Of course I can. Mrs Phillips, I have one little question to ask you. No, in fact I have two.'

She paused in the demolition of her wardrobe and sat down on the bed, finally noticing that the children were bouncing there. She told them to get off and to go out and play in the garden. Henry could hear them running down the stairs. She pointed to a bedroom chair and Henry sat down, even though it was too low for him. He stretched his long legs and tried not to look ridiculous.

'I have a photograph here . . . could you tell me if you recognize anyone?' He handed her the picture that had been taken outside the courthouse on the day of the Kirkland divorce.

Nora studied the photograph for a moment and then nodded. 'Well, Martha is in the background, isn't she? And the woman standing there on the step, I've seen her in the society magazine. Was she Mrs Kirkland? She's remarried, I believe, one of the magazines had pictures of her wedding about three years ago. I remember because Martha pointed it out to me. She said she met her once and I wondered how. I asked because they must have moved in very, very different circles and Martha said that once she came to the solicitor's office where she worked. I remember saying I didn't realize she had worked in a solicitor's office; I thought the business that she worked in was involved with imports, but she passed it off and said sometimes she worked in other places.

'I must admit, the idea of having a job really appealed to me. Having money of one's own and responsibilities that don't involve chasing children around the house.'

She laughed, slightly embarrassed. 'I must sound very ungrateful.'

'No,' Henry told her. 'I think most people want independence and money of their own. I think it is a natural thing.'

'Then you are an unusual man,' she said. 'Most men like their wives to be at home. Are you married, Inspector?'

'No. I know that many police officers are, but this job can make it difficult to maintain any kind of domesticity. I've never felt ready to inflict myself or my job on some poor woman.'

Nora Phillips laughed. Then looked guilty for finding something funny. 'There is something familiar about the man,' she said. 'But I can't think what.'

Henry took the photo from her and pointed to the figure of Johnny Sexton, standing beside the now ex-Mrs Kirkland. 'You mean this man?'

She nodded. 'I just have the feeling of having seen him somewhere, but I can't think where.'

'Do you have acquaintance with Lord Elliston?' he asked.

'Inspector, we most certainly do not move in *those* circles. I know him by sight, of course. He too has been in the society pages and I caught a glimpse of him at the racetrack last Monday. Can you believe that it is almost a week since Martha died? It just does not seem possible. None of this seems possible. Was that your second question?'

'No, my second question concerned this.' He took the key that had been in Martha's bag from the envelope in his pocket. 'I wanted to know if you'd seen this. If you had any idea what it was for. It was found in Mrs Mason's bag, it had either been concealed beneath the reinforcement of the bottom, or it had slid down in there. I wondered if you'd seen it before.'

'But of course I have. It fits this.'

Henry looked at her in astonishment as she went back to her wardrobe and from the top shelf took a small box that looked as though it had been made as a tea caddy. It looked old and some of the veneer was flaking. Nora brought it across to the bed and set it down and Henry slid the key into the lock. 'How long have you had this?'

'Oh, a year, no a little longer. Eighteen months perhaps. Martha asked me to look after it a year last Christmas, so yes eighteen months. She kept the key; I suppose she knew I would be tempted to look inside. But she also knew I wouldn't break it to get inside.' She looked a little shamefaced.

'It is human nature to be curious,' Henry told her. He opened the lid and peered inside, Nora looking over his shoulder.

'It's just papers and newspaper clippings,' she said, sounding terribly disappointed. 'I hoped it might be something really interesting.'

Henry had taken out some of the papers and was examining them. 'Oh, undoubtedly,' he said, 'Mrs Phillips, this is very interesting.'

'Well, well,' Emory said. 'It just goes to show that some questions have very simple answers.'

'It just occurred to me,' Henry said, 'that if the key was important enough to hide, but that it did not unlock anything in the Mason's house, or in the summerhouse, that it must unlock something that Mrs Mason still had access to. She seems to have had a lot of acquaintances but perhaps relatively few friends. I wondered about Miss Styles, and indeed she would have been my next stop, but as Martha Mason and Nora Phillips seem to have spent a lot of time together, I wondered if it was possible that she had whatever it was this key unlocked.'

'Had it been me,' Mickey said, 'I would have left this box with Miss Styles.'

'And Miss Styles would have found a way of opening it, a subtle way that did not involve a kitchen knife or a chisel or anything obvious,' Henry observed. 'That old lady is, as Emory told us, as sharp as a tack. Nora is just clever enough to hide this, and not to try and open it and also not to tell her husband.'

'It surprises me that she didn't tell him,' Mickey said.

'I imagine had he seen the box, and asked about it, then Nora would have revealed all. But I suspect that Dr Phillips is a little like Dr Mason and it would never occur to them to go rummaging around in their wives' wardrobes. It would also never occur to them that their wife would conceal anything from them, I think. In my experience men constantly under-estimate women and especially the women in their own lives. Emory, do we have those five-pound notes to hand? Would you lay them out on the desk for me?'

'All of them?'

'All of them. We'll need to make space. But keep separate the ones found in her handbag and the ones found in the evening bag. Mickey, if you can drag that other table over here.'

He had carried the little box back to the police station and then summoned Emory and Sergeant Hitchens back as well. The press pack had photographed him and called out questions, but they had not seen the box. It was a warm day and Henry had removed his jacket and slung it over his arm, managing to tuck the box out of sight beneath. He had taken little notice of the questions, only paused in the doorway to assure them that investigations were progressing and that a statement would be made the following morning. He wasn't at that point quite sure what that statement would be.

Now he began to empty the tea caddy, unfolding each of the clippings and the notes and placing them on the table while Sergeant Emory did the same with the large, white five-pound notes, a final one of which had lain at the bottom of the box. Henry placed that on the table beside the rest and then stood back and looked. He then took a note from his own wallet.

Mickey Hitchens whistled softly. 'Excellent work,' he commented.

Sergeant Emory looked puzzled for a moment and then said, 'Forgeries? Are these counterfeit?'

'Some of them certainly are. The printing is excellent, as Mickey says. The paper quality, now you see it in the light, is not perfect. I am not expert in these matters, Emory, but laying these out side-by-side you can begin to see.' He tapped the note he just taken from his own wallet. 'This I know to be genuine. I obtained it from the bank yesterday morning. One of those taken from Martha Mason's handbag also looks genuine. Hold it up and observe the watermark and then compare it to one of the others.'

Emory did so. 'Fuzzy,' he said. 'It's not as crisp. And the paper, now you mention it, feels a little different.'

'But not so different that anyone would notice, not unless they looked specifically. And how often do you lay notes side-by-side?'

'So how did she get so many? Was she part of the counter-
feiting gang? Did she not put Mrs Phillips in danger by trusting
that box to her?'

Mickey shook his head. 'Probably not. Taken alone, the
contents of the box would not be incriminating, just suggestive. It might be taken simply for a young woman's obsession
with a particular man, or should I say men. Many people keep
clippings, and the single note in the bottom might be just as
innocent. This however, I would think would be worth more
than all of these things together.'

He opened a small jewellery box that had been sitting in
amongst the papers.

'Pastes,' Emory said.

'I doubt it.' Henry took the box from Mickey and examined
the loose stones. 'Diamonds. This little box would have meant
danger to Nora Phillips had it been known about. This little box
is probably what they broke into the Masons' house to look for.'

He closed the box and set it down on the table, drew up a
chair and began to pay attention to the other contents of the
tea caddy. 'The names of these clippings tally with those men
that we know she helped obtain divorces for. It is perhaps
understandable that she kept those. The rest are more recent.
Emory, that looks like letters, see who they are from. Mickey,
these clippings are much more recent, and mostly relate to
Kirkland and some to Lord Elliston and also to his son Timothy
Elliston. Now that is a name I know. That is the name that
Felicity Conway gave me, as being the man with whom Nora
had a brief affair until she found out that he was beating his
wife. She gave evidence against him which resulted in his wife
receiving a proper settlement and also, it's likely, leaked
information to the press. We must look at the details of the
case, but that is it in brief.'

'The letters are from Kirkland,' Emory said. 'And they are a
little heated, if I may say so. Passionately heated,' he clarified.

'Indeed. And all of these people involved, we know are
likely to have been at the racecourse last week. Did Martha
know they would be there, did they know Martha would be
there or is it a chance coming together of the past and the
present?'

'When did Mrs Phillips say she obtained this box?' Emory asked.

'The Christmas before last,' Henry told him.

'Well, some of these letters are more recent than that. This one dates from October last year. And this one from March of this.'

'Does it indeed. So was Nora lying to us, or did Martha simply seize the opportunity to go into her friends' room and add this to the store of secrets she was keeping? Emory, will you go and enquire with Mrs Phillips and see if that is possible.'

Henry glanced at his watch.

'How long would it take us to drive across to Lord Elliston's estate?'

'It's around twenty-five miles away,' Emory told him. 'An hour and a little more.'

'It would be best if we put our knowledge into some kind of order tonight,' Mickey said. 'Be certain we all understand what it is we're dealing with, and then arrive with the morning milk. Men are less on their guard first thing.'

Henry nodded agreement. Because he had been delayed returning from London, it was already late in the day. Mickey was right, better to wait until morning and spend the evening collating the information they already had.

A soft tap on the door, and a constable entered. He had a note but seemed unsure who to give it to. Emory relieved him of it.

'It seems our Dr Mason gave up the ghost about an hour ago,' he said. 'The surgeon has arranged for a preliminary examination to be done this evening, should you gentlemen wish to be there. This being a murder.'

'This being a double murder now,' Mickey said sombrely.

FIFTEEN

Everything having been locked up in the police station strong room, Mickey and Henry had a quick bite to eat and then departed for the hospital. Mickey had seen the wounded man before he had been taken away, but now the corpse had been washed the injuries were even more evident.

'We don't have to guess at the weapon,' he told Henry. 'It was a poker from his own hearth. As I said we think he came downstairs and disturbed whoever it was. Came down, as he thought, armed, but his assailant took his weapon from him and used it against him.'

Henry had seen the weapon; it was currently wrapped in brown paper and locked away as evidence. It was long and heavy, and had a solid iron knop for a handle and it was this which had been used against Dr Mason's head and shoulders and arms. A mass of bruising covered his chest and shoulders and Henry could see that the right arm was broken, his left probably also. Deeply indented fractures of the skull had been the cause of death in all probability, and Henry was shocked that the man had even survived for the few hours he had.

'Did he manage to say anything?'

'He was unconscious when he reached us, he remained that way until eventually he succumbed to his injuries. Frankly I don't know why he wasn't dead before he arrived.' The surgeon turned the dead man's head so that Henry could see the worst of the injuries. 'Skull caved in, and there are at least two other fractures. There was no attempt to strike at the body, the arms as you can see are defensive wounds. His assailant simply swung for the head. This wasn't an attempt to stop the poor man, or even to wound. Whoever did this didn't care if he died. In fact I would go so far to say they wanted him dead.'

'There is no sense that his attacker might have questioned him, sought to gain information first?'

'No sign of torture, if that's what you mean. No, my reading is that the doctor came downstairs, armed with his poker. That there was likely more than one assailant, one took his weapon away from him, hitting him around the head and shoulders and left him lying on the floor.'

'It's possible the doctor sought to run first,' Mickey said. 'The body was found close to the French doors, that's the way we are certain they came in. My guess is they disarmed him, he ran, he was struck down.'

That all seemed very plausible, Henry thought. The doctor's clothes and possessions had been wrapped in another brown paper parcel and laid out on a side table. Henry undid the string and briefly examined what was inside. Blooded pyjamas and underwear, nothing else.

There seemed little to keep the surgeon for, a post-mortem would be carried out the following day but Henry doubted it would add anything to the current fund of knowledge. He and Mickey returned to the hotel and, Mickey as always still being hungry, asked for sandwiches and tea to be sent to Henry's room.

'To date,' Mickey said, 'what we have is likely to be a major counterfeit operation and the implication in that of a lord of the realm, his son and a cousin are involved. And a connection with the racing gangs, a razor-man and a bunch of other violent ne'er-do-wells. A right mixed stew we have here. So how does Mrs Mason fit in? She is known to Kirkland and to Elliston's son. She seems also to be known to Mrs Kirkland. Do we bring the ex-Mrs Kirkland into this mix as well?'

'For the moment, no. We have enough geese to chase.' He watched as Mickey bit into one of the thick cheese, mustard and ham sandwiches. 'How is it you are always ready to eat?'

'Brain food,' Mickey said. 'And your brain would function better if you'd eat more too.'

'My brain functions well enough.' But Henry poured himself some tea, topped up Mickey's cup and, reluctantly at first, helped himself to a sandwich. He bit into it and decided that Mickey might be right. His brain might need fuel after all. 'And how does Mr Harry Benson fit into all of this?'

'It's hard to see how. I've set him in a box to the side for now, he may prove relevant later,' Mickey said. 'If Mr Harry

Benson is involved, then my bet is he is being blackmailed or conned, rather than doing the blackmailing or the conning. I doubt Mr Harry Benson has the cunning for conning.'

'It seems from her letters that Martha Mason became very much involved with Kirkland again, and very recently. It's more than likely that the child is his. Why would you take such a risk? What is such an attractive proposition, that she became embroiled? Was she simply bored with being a doctor's wife? Was it money she wanted?'

'Any or all of that combination, I would think. She might have thought she was ready to settle for less than she actually wanted, that Dr Mason was a good proposition. He might even have got her out of a sticky situation if what your Felicity Conway says is correct, then she was about to lose her position because of unprofessional conduct. After all, she was merely the hired help, there to be photographed in an evidentiary capacity and then to quietly disappear into the background. Not a difficult job, but it seems she could not manage that. Did she want these men because they had money? Did she want them because it was adventure? I can't believe this woman was just simply foolish, and had her head turned by these individuals. She seems otherwise to present as intelligent, honourable even. A good woman as they say, at least on the surface of things.'

'Whatever her motivation, we can assume that she got into deep water.'

'Deep enough to drown,' Mickey agreed. 'And husband after her. One thing puzzles me, where did the gun come from?'

'Only one thing puzzles you? No, but you are right. The ownership of the gun seems an odd thing. She hid it away, didn't carry it with her, and didn't hide it in the box with the rest of the documents. And then there are the diamonds, how or where did she get them? And when? She cannot have had them with her when she first married. No, my guess is that Kirkland gave her those too. Possibly the weapon as well. He must have known the kind of men he was involved with, maybe he wished her to defend herself. Maybe he believed that no one would ever suspect a doctor's wife could be involved in anything underhand, especially not one with such a reputation.'

'But he knew her past, others could have found out too. Once you factor that in to the equation, then she looks like a much more suspicious proposition.'

'Well she is certainly that now,' Henry said. 'Her husband too, so whatever she may have done or may not have done they are now our responsibility.'

Mickey nodded. He took his leave, taking the rest of the sandwiches with him. 'I will see you at dawn,' he said.

SIXTEEN

I t was only seven o'clock in the morning when they arrived at Cropwell Bishop, and at Campsey Hall, country seat of Lord Elliston. Turning in through the open gates, and down through a long, tree-fringed drive, Henry saw horses, thoroughbreds. Then past a stable yard, and a manège.

'Well, the workers are already hard at it,' Mickey said. 'Beautiful beasts,' he added, nodding at the horses. 'Though I've never felt the urge to ride one.'

The driver brought them to the front of the house and parked the car at the foot of twelve steps leading up to a neoclassical building. 'Posh,' Mickey observed. 'Moneyed.'

Henry led the way up the steps and rang the bell. The door was opened by a butler who informed them the family was not yet fully risen, though his master was at breakfast and he would see if they could be received.

'See if we can be received,' Mickey said. He sounded more amused than annoyed. 'There are a lot of people about, for this early in the morning. And I don't think most are stable hands.'

Henry was still standing on the steps and he glanced back over his shoulder. He could see into the stable yard from where he stood on the steps, the master of the house must delight in the observation of his horses, he thought. Those looking after them were easily identifiable by their clothes, and general disposition. Beside the stable block was what must have been a carriage house, with accommodation over it for the coachman. This was now used for the garaging of cars and Henry could see that there were several men inside, eating breakfast and playing cards. They wore cheap suits and were looking over suspiciously at the car and driver and Mickey and Henry.

The butler returned and led them through to a dining room. A sideboard was set with chafing dishes and three men sat at a long table. Henry recognized Lord Elliston from photographs he had seen and also Kirkland. The third man he assumed was Elliston's son; this was confirmed a few moments later. 'Sit down, gentlemen. Breakfast with us, or at least have some of this really very good coffee.'

Henry accepted the coffee and took a seat at the table. Mickey said thank you to the coffee and then went to look out of the windows, the view on to parkland and more horses seemed to delight him. 'Fine beasts,' he said. 'I was saying to my chief inspector as we came along the drive, wonderful animals, but they would look slightly big to me, I've never felt the need to ride one.'

Elliston laughed, and the slight look of apprehension left his face. 'Indeed, they are fine beasts. And I have ridden since I was a boy. I recommend it, there is no finer exercise. A *chief* inspector, now I am impressed. But what can I do for you?'

'It is actually Mr Kirkland we came to see,' Henry said quietly. 'And the matter is a little delicate.'

'We are all family,' Elliston said. 'And I'm sure John has no secrets. Anything you wish to say . . .'

John Kirkland looked somewhat doubtful, but he did not contradict his relative. Instead he poured himself more coffee. 'Of course. But I can't imagine what you want with me.'

'Mrs Martha Mason,' Henry said. 'I believe she was known to you.'

'No, I don't believe so.'

'You wrote her letters. A number of letters. The contents were rather . . . passionate. And lead us to believe that your relationship was of long-standing.'

'No doubt forgeries,' Kirkland said flatly.

'No doubt,' Lord Elliston agreed. 'A man in John's position, well . . . women sometimes try to force their attentions. To take advantage. No doubt this woman—'

'Helped you to obtain your divorce, some nine years ago,' Henry said. 'She worked then for Giles & Conway.'

Kirkland laughed. 'Ancient history,' he said. 'But yes, then I do know Martha Mason, if the lady in question was then Mary Betteridge and yes, I will agree, I saw her a few times after the deed was done. But nothing came of it, nothing ever would.'

'It seems you met with her again, you wrote her letters. It seems you had an affair, much more recently. The last of the letters was dated in March and suggested that you met at the races which you all attended just over a week ago, on the bank holiday.'

'If it was at the bank holiday meet, you're out of luck there, Inspector. We were together all that day, no one met anyone apart from our own party. And we were a very merry party, were we not. Now gentleman, now that we've cleared that up, enjoy your coffee, have breakfast. John and I have business to attend to, my son will show you around the estate if you so wish,' Elliston said with an air of finality in his words.

'You seem to have a lot of employees that don't have much to do,' Mickey said, finally coming over from the window and pulling out a chair. He poured himself more coffee and sipped. Then added cream and sugar. 'Nice,' he said. 'I couldn't help but notice as we came up the steps, in the old coach house, you seem to have a half-dozen loafers camped out there, playing cards. Do you employ people to play cards, Lord Elliston?'

Elliston's eyes narrowed. 'What I do or do not employ my people to do is none of your business, Sergeant. Now gentlemen, finish your coffee and then I suggest you depart, or I will be complaining to your superiors.'

'Hmm.' Mickey topped up his coffee again. 'This *is* good. If you're quick, you can still complain to Mr Fred Wensley, he's our chief superintendent. But he is due to retire so you will need to be quick. But my guess is, Lord Elliston, that he would simply say that we are doing our duty. And after all double murder is a serious business.'

'Double murder?' Mickey had Kirkland's attention now.

'Unfortunately, yes.' Henry took up the story. 'Dr Mason, Mrs Martha Mason's husband, was attacked and killed in his own home yesterday. The house was ransacked, it seems whoever attacked him was looking for something they believed either Mrs Mason or Dr Mason possessed. No opiates were taken, no money, despite there being some in his desk drawer.'

'Perhaps the housebreakers were disturbed. Perhaps they did not have time to take anything,' Elliston objected.

'They took time to systematically beat the poor man to death.'

Kirkland turned pale. Elliston just looked annoyed. So far, his son had not really reacted to any of this.

'Shameful,' Elliston said at last. 'I wish you well with your investigations. But now we do have business to attend to.'

He dropped his napkin on the table and stalked out of the dining room and Kirkland followed. The son, Timothy, leaned back in his chair and lit a cigarette. 'I remember her,' he said. 'The bitch almost ruined me. I for one won't be grieving over her.'

'So, what do you make of all that?' Mickey asked as they drove away.

'That there are indeed a lot of loafers around on the estate, that are not employed by him. So who are they? I don't think that's too difficult a question to answer. There were no faces I immediately recognized but I do wonder if Eric Columbus Davies or Johnny Sexton are among their number.'

'Do you think we could get a warrant to search?'

'I think Lord Elliston is a man with a great deal of influence. I doubt we'd find a judge in the county would grant us a warrant, not without more evidence. But he's in it up to his neck, I guarantee that.'

'Kirkland looked shocked when we told him about the doctor. I would see him as the weak link. And I would give a great deal to hear the conversation that is going on now. I doubt Elliston or the son knew that Kirkland was seeing Martha Mason. Hopefully we have put many cats among pigeons.'

Mr Otis Freeland had shadowed Henry and Mickey from the hotel that morning. He'd overheard Emory giving instructions to the driver for the very early start and had followed cautiously behind. When it became obvious that they had gone into Lord Elliston's estate, he parked his own car and approached through woodland behind the stables. From there he had observed Chief Inspector Henry Johnstone and Sergeant Mickey Hitchens on the steps outside the big front door. He'd seen them looking around and had followed Henry's gaze. When they went inside, he crept around the side of the stable block to try and get a better view of whatever it was that Henry had been looking at. He had just raised his camera to take some pictures, not sure if they would be useful but at least give context to his investigation, when he sensed someone behind him. He began to turn so the first blow hit his shoulder, rather than his head. The second made contact with his hand and the camera dropped to the ground. The third blow glanced off his temple as he struggled to get away, but it felled him and he sank down into blackness. He was aware of being lifted but then even that perception went. Mr Otis Freeland was carried back to the woods and dumped unceremoniously into a hollow where he was covered with leaves and left for the animals to find.

To say Lord Elliston was furious with his younger cousin was an understatement. Kirkland did little to defend himself but stood with his head down and shoulders hunched against the barrage of words and arguments that he knew were well deserved.

'Of all the stupid bloody idiots in the world,' Elliston said finally. 'And did you arrange to meet her?'

Kirkland nodded. 'I wanted to get my letters back. She promised to bring them.'

'And you told *him*. You told him about the letters.'

'No, not exactly. I mean, he found out somehow that I was seeing her. I didn't tell anyone. Only Timothy.'

'That's the same as telling him, isn't it? You damn well know he's got Tim in his pocket. For God's sake, man, you know what we're up against here. Much as I hate to say it, Tim's a bad'un and no mistake. But we had a chance to get out of this, free and clear. I've long since given up on trying to save that boy of mine.' He paused and looked with something like compassion at Kirkland. 'Did you care about her?'

Kirkland frowned. 'I'm not sure I can have real feelings for anyone. But yes, I suppose I cared for her. Then things come to an end. I wanted her out of the way, and I know it was foolish of me to write letters. I wanted them back. I didn't trust the woman with them.'

'Well, she is out of the way now,' Elliston said.

*   *   *

Otis's attacker was feeling pleased with himself having dealt with the problem. But then Frankie Beans was not the sharpest knife in the drawer. Eric Davies was far from impressed when he was told that there had been a 'snooper' and that Frankie had taken care of it. He brought the ruined camera to Eric as proof.

'So, dead, is he?'

Frankie nodded.

'And you checked he was dead.'

'I hit him. He fell down. I dumped him in the woods. I covered him with leaves,' he added hopefully.

'You hit him. He fell down.' Eric shook his head. 'You better show me,' he said. 'See who this snooper is.'

'I bringed 'is camera,' Frankie said.

'I can see that. Lead the way.'

Frankie led Eric behind the stable block and showed him the blood on the ground where he had hit Otis as hard as he could. He then led him into the woods, got confused, and led him back out again. After a couple of attempts, he led Eric to where he thought he had buried the body, in the little dip. Eric looked down at the leaves and branches, now scattered. There was blood on the ground here too, and a trail of it leading away. 'Not dead then,' Eric observed.

Frankie was puzzled and upset. 'I hitted 'im,' he insisted.

'Just not hard enough,' Eric said. He returned to the stable yard for reinforcements and they spread out through the woods, walking back towards the main road, as though beating for game. There was no sign.

SEVENTEEN

Henry and Mickey arrived back at the police station to find that someone had come looking for them. A very shamefaced Mr Harry Benson and another man of about the same age, who was introduced as Bertie Adams, were sitting in the reception area on hard wooden chairs and trying desperately to stay out of sight of the press pack, assembled on the green outside of the police station, and to which they were visible every time the doors opened.

Harry Benson jumped up as soon as Henry came into the reception. 'At last,' he almost shouted. 'We've been waiting above an hour for you, Chief Inspector. That fool at the desk wouldn't let us through into another office, he said we must sit here and be watched.'

Henry glanced across at the desk sergeant and nodded his head in agreement. 'That is procedure,' he said. 'You cannot blame a man for doing his job.'

The desk sergeant twitched an involuntary smile. Moments later they all trooped through, Benson, Bertie Adams, Sergeant Emory, Mickey and Henry into an empty office. It was, Henry thought, a little crowded, but he was liking the look of anticipation and anxiety on Benson's face and on that of his companion, so did not feel inclined to send anyone away.

'And so what brings you here?' Henry asked.

'The things from the display cabinet that were stolen. But it seems they were not stolen. It seems I have been very foolish. Bertie here will tell you how foolish. But we were playing cards, and we were very drunk, and I simply did not remember until Bertie reminded me. So here they are.'

Adams cuddled a large brown paper parcel. He came forward and set it down on the table where it landed with a loud, metallic clunk. 'We ran out of things to bet on,' he said a little shamefacedly. 'So Harry had a look around his room, and I said I'd always fancied the halberd and the funny knife and anyway we played cards and I won and I won them. I came home and I shoved them under my bed, and there they've been ever since. I'd almost forgotten. And Benson here, he'd completely forgot. You've never seen anyone so falling down drunk as he was that night. I could have bet his house on the turn of a card and he would have lost it. I didn't though. We just gambled on stupid things.'

Emory undid the parcel and displayed three weapons, those missing from the display cabinet.

'Can anyone verify your story?'

'Sophie, the housemaid, she came in the morning after, to empty the gazunder. She pulled it out from under the bed and got the shock of her life when she saw these things there. First off, I couldn't remember where they came from. Mother gave me a right dressing down for frightening the servants and then I remembered where I'd been the night before. I then forgot all about it. And it was only when Harry came over and he said you'd been searching for the stuff, taking fingerprints in his room and all that, well . . . He wasn't best pleased when he realized I'd had this rubbish all the time.'

Henry regarded the two young men with great solemnity and then said, 'You will go with Sergeant Emory and you will have your fingerprints taken. My sergeant will examine these, we will question your mother and your housemaid and if your story is verified, then we will say no more about it. I hear this area is famous for its temperance movement. Perhaps you should join the society and take the pledge.'

Mickey waited until they had left with Emory, and their footsteps had receded down the corridor, before bursting out laughing. 'Under the bed with the gazunder,' he said. 'Oh, that is priceless.'

'Well, provided their story can be verified, at least that answers one question. It is one less thing we need to be concerned about.' He paused and studied the weapons on the table more closely and then, indicating a knife with a sickle-shaped blade, said, 'This is the closest, I suppose. But I think the profile is wrong anyway. When the surgeon inserted his finger into Mrs Mason's skull and brain, he said there was no

curve to the blade that had made the injury. This blade is flattened and has a definite curve.'

He wrapped the paper back around the weaponry and set
it aside. 'So now, we need to put our evidence together so
that we may obtain a warrant to search Lord Elliston's property, and search it thoroughly. Mickey, my instinct is that this
is not simply about two murders. All of these strands tie
together, there are at least two deaths, and a major counter-
feiting operation. The diamonds may or may not be part of
that, they may be a separate issue entirely. Those involved in
this business range in status from street gangs to lords of the
realm, so this investigation is going to have ramifications and
impact far beyond what has happened in this sleepy little
town.'

It had become obvious that whoever owned the camera,
whoever Frankie Bean believed he had killed, had escaped
them. Eric Columbus Davies was not a happy man. Frankie
knew that he was annoyed, knew that he was angry but could
not quite understand why. Frankie had done his best, hadn't
he, he'd dealt with the snoopy man, but Eric Davies was not
content with anyone doing their best if that didn't reach his
standards and expectations.

He led the way back to the stable yard. The men around
him were silent, anxious, knowing that for all Eric was quiet
and calm seeming now, the storm was about to break, and
Frankie would get the worst of it.

'He's a dim lad, he meant no harm. He did his best. No
doubt he thought he got the bugger.'

'He didn't, though, did he? So whoever it was, he is now
walking around scot-free. Free to run his mouth. Becks, Will,
take the cars, get out on the road, find him.'

They went, not bothering to ask who or what they might
be looking for. Neither man wanted to hang around for what
would happen next.

'Frankie, boy. Here. Come over here.'

Frankie Bean knew that he was in trouble but he had no
idea how much. Eric swung a fist and Frankie was down. The
knuckle duster he wore caught the light, brass sparking gold

and then he hit Frankie again. Frankie hadn't even had time to scream but by the time Eric had begun to slow down, and the other men had pulled him away, less than a minute had passed and Frankie had been dead for most of it.

Kirkland watched from the dining room, sickened and scared. Eric had killed Martha, Kirkland knew that. He'd heard say that it had just been one blow to the back of the head and having watched Frankie Beans die, he sure as hell hoped that was the case.

EIGHTEEN

It was mid-afternoon. Phone calls had been made to Scotland Yard and to the local constabularies. Magistrates had been spoken to. Evidence collated and now all Henry could do was wait. His wait was interrupted by the desk sergeant coming to find him and telling him that there was a message left for him. That a boy had brought it in. A boy called Charlie who reckoned the inspector would remember him.

Charlie, Henry thought. One of the fairground boys, the one who'd been on watch when the blue car had been driven away.

He unfolded the piece of paper he'd been given. The hand was not expert, but the letters were clear enough and the message said that Henry should come to where he had met Charlie before, and there he would hear something of use to him.

Henry and Mickey Hitchens slipped out the back door and, careful not to be seen by the reporters, made their way to the racecourse and the paddock where they had met Charlie and his people. Charlie was there and another man with him, and they had a van.

Henry recognized the man as being Reece's second-in-command, his brother-in-law Gavin Cafferty. 'You need to come with us,' Cafferty said. 'Boss needs to see you. It's about that woman what was killed.'

He would say no more. A place was made for Henry and Mickey to sit in the front, and Charlie settled in the back on a pile of blankets. Henry was surprised when he eventually realized the route they were taking was out towards Lord Elliston's home. He wasn't afraid, he did not feel threatened. But he was eminently curious.

Mickey had noticed the route as well and did comment on it.

Cafferty would not be drawn. He said simply, 'We have one of our stopping places out this way. After the races, some folk go another way, some others join our party before we move on. A friend came to us asking for help and said he needed to speak with you. You'll find out when you get there.'

With that they had to be content. They turned in through a farm gate, and beyond a section of woodland was a derelict house and beyond that the encampment. It could not be seen from the road; you'd have to know it was here, Henry thought.

'Man who owns the land is distant kin. Farmers here have given us our rights for generations. Tradition, tradition is important.'

Henry got out and glanced around. He had been in travellers' encampments before, and this was similar. Cooking fires were burning, children running and playing. There were no horses here, the showmen travelled by motorised vehicle and a couple of the rides were parked up on the far side of the site, ready to be moved on. Everything looked clean and neat. The screen of the toilet pit was over on the further side and the paintwork and brass on the vans washed and polished.

Reece had seen them arrive and walked over. He beckoned to Henry and Henry followed him to a van parked beneath trees. A woman sat on the steps but she moved as they approached and Reece led them inside. A man lay on a bunk, his head bandaged and his arm strapped across his chest. He opened his eyes as they entered and Reece helped him sit up.

'This is Otis,' he said. 'Otis has a lot to tell you.'

Then Reece left them to it.

Otis leaned back against the wall of the wagon. His face was very pale apart from the bruising which seemed to be developing even as Henry watched. He'd clearly been badly beaten.

'I managed to drive away,' he said. 'But I couldn't make it far. I just hoped I had remembered right about the stopping places and that they would definitely be here. I suppose my luck was in.'

Mickey was carefully examining the man's face. 'You have a curious idea about what constitutes luck,' he said.

'Luck, in this case, means the man who hit me was not very good at his trade. It could have been a lot worse. I could have met with Eric Davies or Johnny Sexton. Had either of those been responsible, I'd have been telling all I know, should I have had the chance, but also be dead as a doornail by now.'

Henry took a seat on the other bunk and Mickey settled beside him. 'Reece said you have a lot to tell,' Henry said. 'So you'd better begin. Incidentally I have seen you before. You paused beneath the streetlamp to light a cigarette on the night I visited my sister. You were also in the cafe when I was speaking to Felicity Conway. You bumped against our table as you left. At the time I was uncertain you were the same man, and besides I needed to speak to Felicity Conway. So it seems you have been following me.'

Otis nodded and then winced and wished he hadn't. 'Our paths were destined to cross long before Martha died,' he said.

'Then you'd best begin at the beginning and carry on to the end,' Mickey told him. 'But don't take all afternoon, we're hoping to get a warrant to raid a house.'

'Elliston's place,' Otis said. 'In that case I had better get on because what I tell you will probably help. But maybe we can save a bit of time by you telling me how far you've got. What you think or suspect is going on here. Time is one thing we are very short of.'

'Well,' Mickey said, 'there are counterfeit five-pound notes, and we suspect that Lord Elliston is involved with that, willingly or not, and that his cousin, John Kirkland, might have a finger in the same pie. We suspect that Mrs Martha Mason knew at least part of this, maybe Kirkland told her. She certainly had some notes in her possession and was taking a keen interest in both Kirkland and Elliston. She had previously told a friend that she was once an enquiry agent, something her husband wished to keep very quiet. And that she was still in contact with some of her old colleagues. But the friend was concerned about something completely different, that a local doctor might be treating his patients a little too liberally with the morphia. That he might even be procuring abortions for young girls in trouble.'

'We suspect that Martha arranged to meet someone at Southwell races. Was that you?' Henry said.

'Not me, no. She told me she was going to arrange to meet Kirkland. That she believed that Kirkland was the weak link in all of this because he was frightened. She had letters of his that she knew he wanted back, so she promised to bring them along to the racetrack and that she would find a way of getting them to him. But something went wrong. Kirkland didn't see her but Davies followed her. It's likely she tried to get away, but he killed her. I'm sure it was him. I know he was there and I know he knew all about Martha.'

'And are you the enquiry agent that she was still in contact with?'

'Not directly, no. She did get in touch with Giles & Conway, but they took very little notice of her. They saw Martha as unreliable, I believe. It was when she contacted John Kirkland that she came to my notice, or rather to the notice of the organisation I work for. I can't be more specific, I'm afraid. She seems to have contacted Kirkland when Giles & Conway knocked her back. She knew Kirkland had been divorced for a second time and I think she wanted to know who he'd used to facilitate that. Anyway they met up, and one thing led to another and Martha became involved with John Kirkland once more. Of course, that brought her to the attention of Timothy Elliston. A man who certainly held a grudge. Anyway, over time, Martha being Martha and keeping her eyes open she realized that Kirkland was not only ill at ease but that he seemed to be surrounding himself – or rather Timothy Elliston seemed to be surrounding himself – with very dubious types.

'When she worked for Conway, the jobs she did were not always salubrious. True, it was mostly just assistance with divorce cases, but occasionally she was involved with would-be blackmailers; she was certainly aware of the underbelly of our society. And she had very much been aware that the first Mrs Kirkland divorced her husband at the behest of Johnny Sexton. They had been seeing each other for quite some time, Kirkland didn't like it but what could he do? You may know that the first Mrs Kirkland ran up some very severe gambling debts. This threw her in the way of the criminal types, of whom Johnny Sexton is one of the worst.'

'And is that association still relevant?'

'Fortunately for her, no. Her father threatened to cut her off without a penny unless she mended her ways. He paid for her to go to America, put her in a very expensive clinic in California, with orders that they would not let her out until she had come round to his way of thinking. She finally married a film star that she'd met during her rehabilitation. I'm not entirely sure this is what her father intended but it is probably better than Johnny Sexton.'

'And so you made contact with Martha Mason.'

'Our investigations were then underway, Martha seemed like a useful person to cultivate, she was almost on the inside of the organization but on the other hand she was above suspicion in her everyday life.'

'You used her to obtain information.'

'We hoped to use her to turn Kirkland. If Kirkland gave evidence . . . Martha had been told that she must distance herself, that it was becoming too dangerous. And we believed that she had. But then Kirkland wanted his letters back, Martha contacted me and said she felt she ought to give them to him. Kirkland had also given her counterfeit notes. He'd said they were a gift, but she became suspicious and asked me to check one of them. I realized this was the beginning of the evidence we needed because they matched others that we had previously obtained. We came to suspect that the operation was being run from Lord Elliston's country estate. But he's a powerful man with powerful connections. We required more evidence. The Kirkland link was excellent, but . . .'

'But it never occurred to you that Martha might be putting herself in the firing line by agreeing to meet Kirkland at the races.'

'We had told her not to. She informed me that she was going to be there anyway, with friends. That it would look strange if she suddenly refused what would normally be a treat, a day out away from everything. We told her that she must remain with her friends, that she must remain in busy places, that she was to ensure that she was not intercepted. We told her to forget Kirkland, that she should simply post his letters back to him.'

'That would have been eminently sensible,' Mickey agreed.

'Martha was an eminently sensible woman, most of the time. But there was something about her that loved this sort of adventure, that pushed boundaries. She believed that if she spoke to Kirkland one more time, she could perhaps entice him away from the path he had taken. Persuade him that he could be protected if he spoke out against his associates. I told her that this was foolhardy in the extreme and that she must not do it, but how was I to stop her?'

'You were at the races that day?'

'With several of my colleagues. We kept Elliston under surveillance. Kirkland too, but it is almost an impossibility to carry out surveillance on a race day, I'm sure I don't need to tell you that. We lost Kirkland. We assumed that he'd gone to meet with Martha Mason. One of my colleagues saw her drop her bag and kick it beneath some bushes shortly after she left Nora Phillips. He took the opportunity to search it but found nothing. He then put it back, not knowing what Martha intended. He'd seen her talking to the Mancinis, and satisfied himself later that this was a perfectly innocent conversation, so he seized the opportunity to search the bag at that point, thinking she would spend some time talking to this couple that were obviously friends but when he returned, the Mancinis had already gone to the owners' enclosure and Martha to her death.

'He went to where she told us she was going to meet Kirkland. There is a gate at the end of where the fairground had set up, through that there is a paddock where the larger transports had been parked. Through that again was the one where she was killed. He spotted Kirkland, but not Martha, so probably at some point she had been intercepted. I'm sorry there is a great deal I don't know. I returned to make my report that evening, then the news arrived that Martha had been killed, I literally turned myself round again and came back up here.'

'You should be in the hospital,' Henry said.

'No, too many questions will be asked. I'm safe enough here. Now' – he held out a scrap of paper – 'I have written here a name and a telephone number. Contact this man and tell him that Otis Freeland judges that there is enough evidence to move on our targets and that to wait will give them time to disperse. In fact, we are already against the clock, Inspector. My being there would have warned them that something is wrong.'

'Did you give Martha a gun?'

'I did, yes. And I still have mine. You'd better make use of it.' He pointed to his jacket. 'In the right-hand pocket. Much good it did me,' he laughed weakly.

Henry went in search of Edgar Reece. 'When did he arrive here?'

'An hour before I sent the boy to you. We patched him up, waited until he was able to talk. He wanted to get a message to you and so we did.'

Henry calculated quickly. Could he take men from the encampment, would Reece be willing for him to do that? As though reading his mind, the showman told him, 'I got men posted at various points, instructions to report back should there be movement at the Elliston house. The nearest police station is five miles that way, Otis's car is there, you'd better get yourself in it, and summon the cavalry.'

Minutes later, he and Mickey were on their way.

'So what department do you reckon he works for?' Mickey asked.

'It probably has some obscure number attached to it,' Henry suggested. 'And I doubt we'll ever get the full picture. But I'd be content with an arrest and a hanging.'

NINETEEN

It was dusk by the time everyone was assembled. The name and telephone number that Otis had given them had opened doors in a remarkable fashion, but Henry was still worried that time was against them. Reece's men had reported that there were signs of packing and movement and one car had already left, with a driver and a passenger. Both male. They'd noted the make and the registration number for Henry, and promised that one of their number would also be following. Henry worried that Reece's men were treating this far too lightly, that they were seeing this almost as fun. But there wasn't a great deal he could do about that and he was grateful for the intelligence.

Now there were twenty officers, all armed and set up around the perimeter. Mickey and Henry had taken the path through the woods that Otis had earlier followed and now had sight of the stable block and the main house. What appeared to be a man's body lay on the gravel. No one seemed to be taking much notice of it. Men moved purposefully, loading boxes into the backs of trucks and vans.

'I see no sign of the stable hands,' Mickey said. 'It's to be hoped they've come to no harm.'

'I'm more concerned they may become hostages,' Henry said. He spoke briefly to an officer who was with them, who nodded and began to move around to Mickey's right. Henry beckoned and he and Mickey moved forward. Both were armed now, Henry with Otis's weapon and Mickey with an ageing Luger, though its mechanism was smooth and had been kept well-oiled and Mickey had announced himself satisfied.

There seemed to be no one on guard at the back of the stable block – all were occupied with packing and loading, and Henry was able to peer through one of the windows. Four men sat inside, they were not bound but they looked uncomfortable and anxious and Henry realized he was probably correct in his assumption; the men had been detained to be used as hostages should the gang be surprised. As Otis had predicted, his discovery and escape had sent the whole wasps' nest to flight.

The window was small, too small for a man to climb through so they would have to find another way to get them out. Henry retreated and Mickey followed. 'We have no chance of getting through the door,' he said. 'The only entrances are at the front of the building and we will be spotted instantly. But I wonder if it is possible to arm those inside, so at least they can come out fighting, should the need arise. Two of them at least look old enough to have served in the war, and they are all countrymen – they will know how to handle a weapon.'

They withdrew to the main police line and a few minutes later had managed to rustle up a couple of spare pistols and a shotgun with two cartridges. Mickey wondered if the local officers had gone out raiding all the local farms, assembled an armoury from weapons kept at the back of drawers, kept there since the Great War had ended. Cautiously they moved forward again, aware that the rest of the team would now have circled the house.

'Twenty men, against armed and dangerous thugs probably numbering at least that.' Mickey looked worried. 'There will be casualties on both sides.'

'And if we can get these through that window, there will be twenty and four,' Henry said.

The oldest of the four men heard them first, turning sharply at the gentle tap on the window. Henry put his finger to his lips; he had his warrant card in his hand so the man could see it. He signed that they should open the window and cautiously this was done.

'They locked us in here.'

'Are there more of you?'

'Two more young 'uns. In the coach house. They beat a man to death, God, it was a dreadful thing to witness. Then they rounded us up, locked us away.'

'This might even the odds for you,' Mickey said as he began to pass the weapons through the window. 'I'm hoping you can all shoot straight. When we attack, they will come for you, seek to use you as shields. You won't survive it unless you fight back. Even if these men take you with them, they will kill you.'

The man nodded to show he understood. 'What about the two boys in the coach house?'

Henry was already pulling Mickey away. 'We must go.'

'We will do what we can,' Mickey promised.

Henry pulled him back into cover as a figure appeared around the side of the stable block. The man looked suspiciously around. He went to peer through the window where Mickey and Henry had just been speaking to the incarcerated men and Henry held his breath. He breathed out again as the man turned on his heel and disappeared. Those inside had had the sense to close the window again and must have concealed the weaponry. Hopefully they would keep their nerve.

Nothing more to be done, he thought. He heard the whistles blowing to signal the attack, and for an instant he was taken back more than ten years, whistles blowing as the men advanced from the trenches. Mickey grabbed his sleeve, pulled him forward and he was back in the here and now. From inside the stable block they heard gunfire and shouting. They ran, keeping low, around the side of the stable block and joined the fray.

Inside the house, Elliston heard the gunfire. Kirkland came running in from the hallway. 'What the hell is going on?'

'It would seem we are under attack. I suggest we sit down and wait to see who is victorious before we do anything rash. If the police officers win, then we will be arrested. But we can plead coercion, that we were afraid for our lives and the lives of our families. Men like us do not go to prison, Kirkland.'

'Where is Timothy?'

'He left some time ago, along with Mr Sexton. Rats always leave the ships when they are sinking.'

'And yet we remained here?'

'Believe me, Kirkland. This was the better option. Tim can only run so far. His so-called friends will squeal on him. He is too deeply entrenched. However, there may be some chance for us if we keep our nerve and keep calm.'

'Calm,' Kirkland almost screamed. 'How can you keep calm?'

He moved towards the window, trying to see what was going on.

'Get away from there. Do you want to get yourself killed? Have you not realized there are people out there shooting at one another?'

Horrified, Kirkland came and sat down at Lord Elliston's side.

'Where are the servants? Where are the stable boys?'

'If the servants have any sense, then they are in the basement well out of the way. As to the stable boys, I have no idea. But we can't expect help from them. No, we must sit here and wait this out. See which side is victorious. Then we act accordingly.'

Kirkland looked at him in disbelief. 'You're mad,' he said.

'If necessary,' Lord Elliston said. 'If necessary, then that is exactly what I will be.'

Two men fell as Mickey advanced and fired, he saw another go down out of the corner of his eye. They were moving towards the coach house, determined that they would do what they could for the two boys inside.

He was aware of somebody storming out of the stable block and he wheeled, and then realized that it was one of the men they had armed. He had seen Henry take cover in the turn of the wall and knew that his boss had spotted him.

'Come,' he said to the older man who now held one of the pistols. 'My inspector will give us covering fire. Show me where these boys are held.'

They kept low and ran together, Henry providing the covering fire as Mickey knew he would. He had little ammunition, but what he had he made count. Turning back when they reached the coach house door, Mickey could see seven bodies lying on the ground, four of them wearing civilian clothes, two uniformed. One was the man they had seen slumped on the ground before, that they'd been told had been beaten to death. It looked as though some of the gang had run towards the trees, and there were men in pursuit. Henry joined them and they entered the coach house together.

Above them they could hear footsteps. 'There are three rooms,' Mickey was told. 'I do not know which one they put the boys in.'

'Go back outside, take cover in the trees. Gather your people together if you can, and keep them safe,' Henry told him.

He nodded, peered cautiously through the door and then took off.

'So,' Mickey whispered. 'How many rounds do you have left?'

'For Otis's weapon, three. But I also have this. And this has five rounds.' He drew from his pocket the little Beretta that Martha Mason had concealed among her scarves and gloves. 'I borrowed it from the evidence room,' Henry said. 'I suspected we might have need of it. We will deal with the consequences later, I think.'

'Well, in total you have eight, and I have three, so I suggest that you take the lead,' Mickey said. Outside the gunfire seemed more distant now. Mickey wondered how many were holed up in the coach house. They had the advantage, the high ground, as it were. Good sense told Mickey that they really should wait for reinforcements to arrive, and then hope that the hostages would be given up. Reality told him that they would not. The two boys were innocents in this, and Mickey had seen enough innocents killed.

The upper story of the coach house was reached by a flight of narrow stairs at one end. There seemed to be no other way up and Henry and Mickey knew that they would make ready targets for whoever was above them. 'We must be silent and we must be swift,' Henry said. 'I will lead the way – at the top of the stairs I'll fire into the ceiling. Hopefully that will give us an element of surprise as we enter the room. We must just buy ourselves seconds and then act decisively.'

Mickey nodded. 'Best be on with it then.'

Henry moved. Mickey let him get on to the fourth step and then began to follow, aware that if someone shot Henry and Henry fell back, there was nowhere for him to go but to crash into Mickey and take them both down. Henry hugged one wall, and Mickey the other as they climbed upwards. The stairs doglegged and Henry paused before turning sharply. He then took the final stairs at a run, firing shots ahead of him, aiming high. Shots were returned. One hit the wall an inch from Mickey's head. Another shot was fired, and he heard Henry swear. Mickey was on his heels now and entered the room a split second behind his boss. There had been three men in the room, and the two boys. Mickey recognized one of the men immediately as Davies. He had hold of one of the boys, his fingers twisted in the child's hair and a gun pointed at his temple. Across the room the other boy stood between two members of the gang. He looked terrified, but the men were more concerned with Mickey and Henry and did not have hold of the child.

Even as Mickey took this in Henry had fired and one man fell. The child ducked down and Mickey prayed that he would stay there. He wheeled around to face Davies. A second shot, and a shot returned but Mickey couldn't look round to see what had happened. He heard a body slump and hoped it wasn't Henry. The fact that no one shot him in the back implied to Mickey that Inspector Johnstone was safe, though he was swearing like a trooper and a moment later Mickey heard him ordering the child to stay down, to stay where he was. So that just left Davies.

Davies looked as though he was enjoying himself. He had pulled the boy's head back, exposing the throat and almost taking the poor mite off his feet. He couldn't be more than twelve or thirteen, Mickey thought.

'Now come on, Davies. Let the brat go. I never heard that you were one for killing kids.'

'And what have I got to lose, copper? I kill this one, it's just one more. They can only hang me the once, whatever the tally. So how about you stand aside and let me go down those stairs.'

'And you'll be walking into a whole posse of police officers,' Mickey told him.

'None of which will want to be responsible for me shooting a kid,' Davies retorted. 'So you just get out of my way, copper. Now I'll walk out of here with this boy, and then I might think about letting him go.'

Mickey wondered if he could take the shot. The boy's body was held close to Davies and although the man's head was visible, Mickey was uncertain whether he could get a shot off before Davies took his. Dimly he was aware of Henry shifting position and Mickey moved too, as though undecided about letting Davies head for the stairs and go down. He drew back across the room, still talking. 'I suppose you did for that poor woman. The one at the racecourse.'

Davies just laughed. 'Not exactly a challenge, was she? One blow and down she went,' he gestured, as though miming what he'd done and just for a split second his weapon moved away from the boy's head. A split second of hubris, but it was enough. Mickey fired, but so did Henry. Davies fell.

EPILOGUE

Otis Freeland was walking by the time the funeral happened, Martha Mason and her husband placed side-by-side in the churchyard. He attended the church service but did not make himself known to anyone. Henry acknowledged his presence but waited until after the internment to come over and speak to him.

'Two dead here,' he said. 'Two police officers, and three more wounded in the line of duty. It is a mess, Mr Freeland.'

'And you were injured too,' he indicated the left arm, supported by a sling. 'Indeed, it is a mess. A major currency fraud has been prevented,' he said. 'But I agree that sounds like little compensation. The diamonds, incidentally, were taken from a piece of jewellery that belonged to Lord Elliston's wife. You know that he was widowed. It seemed Mr Kirkland removed the jewels and gave them into Martha's safe keeping. He told her that they would run away together, but then . . . Well, it seems he did not think she believed him. She promised to return his letters, but what he really wanted was the diamonds. He eventually confided all of this to Timothy Elliston and he of course told Davies. Once that was done, Martha's fate was sealed and that of her husband. She knew too much and besides, she had the diamonds. It is pure good fortune that Nora Phillips is safe. I've no doubt they would have come to the same conclusion that you did.'

'And so what now for you?'

'Well, I will give evidence, of course, as an enquiry agent brought in by the government to look into forgery and fraud. This being my area of expertise.' He smiled at that. 'After that, who knows?'

'And is your name really Otis Freeland?'

Otis grinned. 'I do rather like it,' he admitted. 'We may meet again, Chief Inspector. And when we do, you may call me Otis.'